HOPE IGNITES

Hope Ignites

This book is set in the typeface *Athelas* designed by Veronika Burian and Jose Scaglione.

Paperback ISBN: 9798394939211

A Publication of *Tall Pine Books*
119 E Center Street, Suite B4A | Warsaw, Indiana 46580
www.tallpinebooks.com

| 1 23 23 20 16 02 |

Published in the United States of America

HOPE IGNITES

PATRICIA E. SIMMONS

DEDICATION

• **Heavenly Father:** I adore you! Your creativity ignites me! You are the most incredible Artist, Scientist, and loving Father. You have created imaginations in us that have endless possibilities. Thank you for inspiring me to write this novel. May it honor you!
In addition: I extend my gratefulness to the following:

• **Husband Gregory Allen Simmons:** Thank you for being my biggest fan and loving me unconditionally. When you first got eyes on my work, you did nothing less but encourage me to complete it.

• **Chloe Simmons and Emmily Morando:** Thank you for graciously reading this book and providing input during our vacation together. You inspired me to continue.

• **Editors:** The Holy Spirit, Ms. Casie Duchak, Dr. Robbi Henson, Google Drive Grammarly, my sister Linda Stockstill. Your input has brought my book to a new level.

- **To Family and Friends:** Kathy McGraw, my life friend who has been there for me through good and bad times, Women's Bible Group, Sons Joshua and Brian, extended family, and friends; Your prayers and support are an unmeasurable value that has been more precious than Silver or Gold!

Lastly, I want to recognize a sister in Christ, Kathleen Summers. She has been struggling with a health issue and still shines despite of it. Kathleen, you are my inspiration for the Corinne character. Continue to soar, my sweet friend!

Thank you All!

Sincerely,
Patty Simmons

CONTENTS

Dedication .... *v*
Prologue .... *ix*

1. Crossing Paths 1
2. Wren Reflects 33
3. Drake Dreams 43
4. Drake's Journey 53
5. The Development 63
6. Influence 79
7. On the Mend 99
8. Spiritual Roots 107
9. The Dance 115
10. Making Amends 141
11. Liberty 171
12. Getting Acquainted 187
13. The Festival 203
14. Coming Together 215
15. A New Day is Dawning 231
16. Adapting 241
17. Truth or Fiction 255
18. Acting out 265
19. Wren's Return 269
20. Jesse's Hope 279

The End Letter from the Author 291
About the Author 293

PROLOGUE

A Space dome secretly hovers above the earth, hidden from the chaos found below on Earth. It is 2033, and Earth's cyclic systems are revolting against the keepers of the planet.

The people have taken the gift of procuring the earth for granted. They have not protected and guarded its virtue. Earth's natural cyclic system can no longer support the expanse of pollution dealt out in significant proportions. Its overburdened system, which all living things require, is desperately beseeching restitution for its failed maintenance. Two groups from Earth's population views emerge in response to this cry. Group one creates laws of do's and don'ts campaigns to clean up things and restore balance to the cycles of earth's systems. The other group's view moves, believing it is too late to fix the natural cyclic system. It promotes finding other solutions like relocating to living habitations outside the earth's realm and pushing for evolution to extend life using self-healing properties.

The second group calls themselves, **Procure Earth Society.**

The **P.E.S.** group campaigns for a seemingly solid solution to the planet's cry for help. The general population is initially open to their ideas; however, that season is short-lived. The P.E.S. incorporate technology in conjunction with self-healing properties developed from specimens found in nature. The general public does not agree on moral grounds. They feel the Procure Earth Society has gone too far and are unethical, going against the grain of the general public's acceptable avenues of finding a solution to Earth's distress call.

The emotional upheaval provokes violent protests, which turn into vigilante groups. They begin hunting for active society people to eradicate their movement. They do not like that the **P.E.S.** encourages technology to enhance the human state. They feel that these scientists and their plan to address their inevitable demise are an intrusion against God and man. They feel incorporating technology that mutates the original design of the human makeup should be considered criminal.

Now that Society members recognize they are in danger, their mode of operation for the **P.E.S** group quickly changes. They must take drastic measures to ensure their cause continues and are driven into hiding. It is a great sacrifice for anyone to commit to the secret group and what they must do, so it is not for the faint of heart.

An abandoned space station positioned above the earth named the **Dome** becomes a sanctuary. P.E.S. scientists secretly inhabit the station, and their families, accompanied by any lab equipment and technology needed to continue their cause. They move where no vigilante group can interfere with their progress.

This space station, formally sent up by Global powers in the past, has been vacant for many years since the withdrawal of government funding and irreconcilable global differences. Though it appears inoperable to the public, it has to operate minimally to not fall from space and bring material falling out of the sky down to earth. The people that oppose P.E.S. believe they have successfully halted the operations of the P.E.S. But they have not.

What happens is that a government officials' task force called the Global Elite comes to Procure Earth Society with a solution. The Elite officials let P.E.S. know that they know the truth about the Earth's ecological condition and that it is imminent to take drastic measures to save humanity. Since they are responsible for the upkeep of the abandoned space station, they feel it necessary to support the Secret Procure Earth Society's objectives by suggesting they take occupation of the Space Dome without the public being informed.

They propose to offer P.E.S. the space station as a sanctuary. The elite officials keep a low profile in the public eye. The Procure Earth Society agrees to take the excellent opportunity to escape their radical opponents. They gather accumulated funds needed to operate in space. They inhabit the Space Dome. A few members remain behind and blend in among the general population. Remote locations are selected across the globe to provide safe passage for those allocated permission to travel between Earth and the Space Dome. Drake is one of the scientists that have traveling privileges. He also has clearance to visit other nearby planets.

Drake is seen on Earth as a renowned Technological Engineer who designs mobile module homes. On the side, he installs elite security systems. His identity among the Procure Earth Society is the highly esteemed Scientist known as Doctor Silverman. He merges his innovations from his deceased Scientist Mother's work, which are associated with finding solutions for humanity to live a long, productive life.

Drake returns to earth to help set up security for a newly acquired property of the P.E.S. The Science Dome community found this property among a less populated, peaceful community that accommodates new landowners. Leaving his son Jesse and daughter Abigail behind on the dome is difficult, but his leaving at the same time the children attend a Summer survival training camp is a perfect time for his departure. Scientists have a lot of pressure from the Procure Earth Society to find more solutions to their projections for the future. Thus this getaway has a twofold purpose. It's to balance his work with applicable downtime to relax and refresh.

CHAPTER ONE

CROSSING PATHS

Now on assignment back on earth, Drake takes one last scan across the clearing of the foothills, looking for any wild herbs or greens he may have missed before returning to his module. He finds pleasure in the hunt for new specimens, and his research requires natural ingredients that promote health and contain healing properties. The variety collected thus far is coming together quite well. He likes this location; it is suitable for both work and play.

A cool breeze swirls around him, bringing a mist that filters rapidly through the woodlands of the canyon. Its haze consumes the area he is gathering specimens, and a sense of mystery encompasses him as he watches uninhibited waves of spiraling smoke maneuver effortlessly through the terrain. Drake cannot see anything through the mist but the hand in front of his face. It halts his activities, and he decides to find a place to squat down at the foot of a nearby tree and consider what his senses tell him. Drake knows, at this point, that he is vulnerable and needs assistance, so he pulls out his location device and activates its services. Drake wants to get help finding his way back to his dwelling, yet despite his desire to return to his post, he most likely will wait until the mist clears out. Drake is also very in tune that the longer he is visually handicapped, the more likely he might encounter something or someone, and that encounter he does not want. Dome's protocol for visiting Earth and other worlds is to avoid contact with native people as much as possible. He must not jeopardize the safety of the Dome and Earth members of the Procure Earth Society. If outsiders suspected him of being a significant part, he could be in danger and be forcibly coerced to reveal secret information disclosing the locations of those that went into hiding.

Leaning against a tree, Drake pulls up a weather report on his device, confirming the weather condition that brought forth the mysterious haze. He decides activating his robotic sentinels to check the area is a good idea. These sentinels use heat-finding sensors to detect nearby life forms. A perimeter check is now in the process, and all he has to do now is sit against the tree and wait for their report before he heads back to his campsite. While waiting, Drake reflects on how he came to this specific location. The Dome officials suggested this place because it had a two-fold purpose. Drake would set up security for a new property purchased by the P.E.S. and incorporate downtime to look for new or undiscovered plants with healing properties.

The Waters are assigned to manage the property. It is

a good location for Dome travelers to come and go without detection. This trip, he hopes to prove to be less taxing and more relaxing. The community surrounding this location is less affected by the conflict of interest the world is having against Domes's scientific objectives. These escapes usually provide him time to partake in hobbies he and his mother used to do together. He finds having that reconnect time doing what she loved relaxes him. He has fond memories of working alongside his mother. Though her primary job was perfecting robotics for the Military Base, she loves her hobby over robotics. She is passionate about finding and reproducing natural resources gathered from unfrequented places known to generate self-healing properties. Whichever location provides an area with woodlands, mountains, prairie hiking, spelunking, or pond diving supporting the research, they found both exciting and relaxing.

Unbeknownst to Drake, a young woman named Wren is stranded and feeling vulnerable within the mysterious mist. Sensing danger, she slowly reaches for the reigns of her horse Ginger and walks her as close as possible to her. She guides them both to a rocky cove to take cover and pulls out her gun. Wren keeps as still as possible, listening for any indication that something is closing in on them. Wren hears a whirring noise that seems to originate from below. The noise is operating erratically and becoming louder and louder, which means it is nearing her location. She cringes as she hears it coming closer and closer, yet as quickly as it seems to draw near, it abruptly disappears as fast as it came. The rock conceals her and her horse, and she is relieved. Wren decides to remain in her hiding spot until she senses it is safe to come out. She ponders where the source of the whirring noise may have been generated from. It does not fall under the guise of nature, so she assumes something is amuck. Goosebumps appear on her arm. The fog lifts, and she gathers her belongings, thinking it a good idea to cut things shorter than she planned and return to the Ranch. She loads her belongings on Ginger and prepares to head down the path. She looks forward to returning to her family's safety; however, she pauses from actually mounting her horse because she must follow through with one more thing before heading down. It's a ritual she does before she leaves. Her boldness overrides her fear of whatever made that noise and the chance they might return to discover her. She pulls out her instrument from the odd-shaped box and lets it rip.

Drake notices the haze dissipating just as he starts to feel anxiety coming over him. When it is deemed acceptable measures to move forward, he is alerted to an additional disturbance near the clearing. He puts on his glasses, touches the sides, and zeros in on a young buck and a rabbit romping about in a playful transaction. He smiles, amused at the oddity of the woodland community's acceptance of one another. Stepping out from behind the tree, he notices a slew of edible berries ripe for the picking. He places the last batch of picked berries into his pouch when a thorn snags his finger, causing it to drip blood. He scorns the thorny attacker and instinctively puts his finger to his mouth to suck out the dirt to prevent germs from dispersing back into his blood. He locates his medical device from his tool belt and runs it over his injured finger. The puncture instantly closes, leaving a red mark as the only evidence of any mishap.

Drake pulls out his handkerchief from his pocket to wipe the new sweat on his brow while catching a glimpse of one of his sentinels heading back to the module. He is startled upon hearing a sound resonating above him. He transfixes his ears to listen to the melodic notes. He marvels at how lovely they are and finds amusement in how the waves of musical sounds bring peace to his soul. It accentuates that he is not alone and must investigate the source. Maintaining his elusive position, he takes cover in the camouflage nature provides and edges upward among the tundra bordering the path. Moving nearer and nearer to the source, he becomes more interested in "who" is behind the captivating sounds. How could anyone producing something so hypnotizing be dangerous? His curiosity sets him up for not only a challenge but an adventure. He is being lured onward as if by magic, similar to the pied piper his mother had read in a storybook.

Drake nears the point of disclosure, and the sound suddenly ceases. He instinctively squats down and plunges deeper into the woods. Contemplating what he should do next, he feels comfortable moving onward again. He hears pounding hooves advancing down the path. Drake ducks back down behind a tree and, in haste, gets his foot caught in a root that causes him to hit the ground rolling in a tumble. He stops short of rolling smack into a bolder. He is lying on the ground, breathing rapidly. He composes himself and dusts himself off. He looks around for a reason for his fall and narrows his search to a small group of perfectly woven vines. The culprit likely caught his foot in a nature-made snare of intertwining roots exposed above the ground. Drake inspects his foot, and at the crime scene, he realizes he lost his glasses during the tumble. Debris covers him head to toe, and he commences to smack the dust and debris from his pants. He notices a tear in his pant leg and is exasperated. Drake shakes his head in disbelief at a day he encounters many blunders. He picks up a rock, throws it at a tree near him, and takes a deep breath becoming more determined to find the source that brought him to experience his unfortunate mishaps.

Drake tries to imagine who the intruder might be. As far as the Waters knew, there should not be any reason he would encounter anyone on their property. Yet they made it clear that there are no guarantees. Drake is reminded that if he did come across someone, he is to avoid contact if possible, and report the incident to the Waters, and let them deal with the intruder. With that pre-informed notice, he predicts that this intruder he is searching for is heading towards him on horseback. He cautiously returns to cover behind a tree. While waiting, he glances down at the bottom of the tree and spots his glasses. He whisks them up. After straightening up the bent frame and wiping off the dirt on the glass, he places them on his nose. He touches the side earpiece to enhance his focus. He peers past the tree and catches the intruder on a horse descending the mountain path.

Adrenaline courses through him, and it feels like his heart will jump out of his chest. He places one hand over his heart and, with the other hand, touches the side of his glasses to observe with increased visual magnification. The steed and person before him are both magnificent and radiating beauty deserving of praise. The horse dawns a glossy coat and braided tail, and its physique is well-formed and suited for royalty. The woman rides the horse like a goddess, and her hair bounces as it flows over her tan shoulders.

While pulling at his attire and demanding order, he notices a spider scurrying up his shirt and squeamishly flicks it away. He knows he must put off foolish fears and gather the courage to do what he must do. He stands in a military stance, takes a deep breath, and exhales. He grounds his thoughts, withdraws a hanky from his pant pocket, and wipes the beads of sweat trailing down his forehead. Stuffing the damp cloth back into his pocket, he scolds himself for not listening to the "no fraternizing" with any trespasser directive. His curiosity gets the best of him, and he devises a plan of introduction suitable to meet her. He has to present himself in a way that gives him the advantage.

The sun spotlights her. Light rays stream through the treetops shining on her long, dark, auburn hair, flowing fluidly over her female frame. Her locks seem to dance with each movement the horse makes. He looks at her fondly, and his stomach begins to flutter as he musters the courage to walk out of the shadows and into the light. Now placing himself in a vulnerable position, Drake removes his hat, rubs his three-day-old scruff on his chin, and moves to a spot where she can see him.

Drake's hope ignites when he deduces a "Dance" brewing, and even if it is but for a brief time, he will hopefully have some fun. He touches the side of his invention and zooms in on her. He studies her like a piece of art.

With further magnification, he sees her eyes. They twinkle like the stars. Her countenance radiates joy as she rides her horse. He quickly sketches the details of her sleek shoulders and womanly curves in his journal. He notices a cowboy hat dangling on her back, held on by a thin strap, and pouches attached to her saddle. He is alerted to seeing a possible firearm and another odd-shaped case he can't identify, hanging from the opposite side of her saddle.

He notes how much he loves his unique spectacles. They enable him to free up his hands for something else. Because of that advantage, he can use his hands to scribble notes about his plant discoveries or pull out a gun to protect himself. The opportunity for him approaches. His comfort zone is bridged, and he will soon engage with the unknown. He is trying to decide whether or not to open himself to what lies ahead with this pending encounter.

As Wren descends the mountain and is about to enter the clearing, she senses something is off. She pulls back on the reins and comes to a halt. Her gut tells her there is a threat, even though the specifics are unknown. She knows some predators move in these parts, so she must be cautious. Wren carefully places her hand on her rifle, removing it from its sleeve. She ever so discreetly releases the lock and slides it onto her lap. Carefully Wren scopes her surroundings and listens for any noise or movement indicating evidence of potential danger. Seeing her gun on her lap puts a new flavor to the table. Drake crouches back out of sight in the brush after calculating how she may react to him. He chooses not to make any introductions just yet.

Wren pats her horse's neck and whispers to Ginger.

"Keep your guard up, Ginger; something is not right."

Her horse snorts the air and lifts her head up and down while raising her legs. It instinctively mars the path beneath, warning the intruders by pounding the earth with its hoofs. Seeing this magnificent animal restlessly interpreting a scent it is uncomfortable with smelling, raises the stakes of the two being in protective mode against Drake. After a brief moment, the fawn he saw earlier romping with a rabbit jumps out of nature's camouflage, running towards its mother into the clearing. Wren sees the romping and lets down her guard. She concludes they are the reason for her senses sending alerts. Wren puts her rifle back into its sleeve and continues towards the clearing. She does not suspect anyone other than the playful woodland duo watching them.

Drake follows at a safe distance. He backtracks as she moves down the trail to where he once was earlier in the day. Who in their right mind would want to spook a gun-toting person? He takes note of the route she chooses to take. She could take a safer path back from which she most likely came, but she prefers a course that provides more challenging terrain instead. Taking a tighter grip on the reins, Wren bends close to the horse's neck and, with a squeeze from her legs, glides the horse over the fallen log with poised ease. They both flow together, landing with success. She looks so delighted.

"She has spunk," he says to himself.

Watching them jump once is entertaining, yet he witnesses her return for yet another jump at the fallen tree. Drake can't wait any longer and does not want to lose out on the encounter. He courageously steps out of the wooded camouflage and walks up the path toward her. Aware of her gun, he lifts his hands, not appearing to be of any threat.

"Hello! Nice riding!"

Surprised, Wren sucks in a big breath and abruptly swings the horse around to face him. Her horse lets out a whinny that represents an uneasy response to the presence of a stranger nearby. Wren maintains control and firmly brings her horse to a posture of war. Her gun is out of its protective sleeve again, pointing in his direction. He wastes no time, having no desire to be a bullseye for riveting bullets. Drake shouts out.

"I am camping here! I am no threat!"

He approaches slowly, holding his hands in the air. Wren is unsettled with her thoughts sounding off like banging pipes. Inundated with questions, such as: (Where did he come from?), (Why would there be any person out here in this particular location?), (Is he alone?), (Is he a free spirit living off the land?) Wren bends down and whispers to her horse,

"Let's investigate."

Trotting over to his position, she stops within a safe distance, demonstrating a determined demeanor. She is not a woman of frailty as one might assume to come from a beautiful woman of her stature, and she exudes an aura of someone that should not be taken lightly.

Both the horse and rider seem very comfortable with each other. The horse dawns a beautiful bronze coat and dark black mane with highlights of lighter brown. Its tight arched tail and beautifully toned body give the horse empowerment. It carries itself as if it has a sense of belonging to horse nobility. He concludes they complement each other well.

She is close enough now to make further deductions regarding his presence. Resting her rifle across her lap with one hand, keeping it within easy access, she guides her horse with the other hand to get a better fix on this stranger. She must gain the upper hand and make the most of that small window of opportunity while they approach the stranger, and she must be the first to ask questions. She could not help but notice his rugged handsomeness, dark, mysterious eyes, and thick, chestnut brown hair. He is causing a stir within her. She talks to herself, trying to obtain some ground of possible reasons he could be there. He must be camping nearby.

He is aware that both she and her horse are unsteady. Cautiously both Wren and Drake ascertain how much of a threat they are to one another. Drake notices she is whispering something to her horse, as if she were giving it instructions. He figures she has a plan.

Closing the gap of proximity between them, Wren shouts out to him.

"Hello."

She responds without hesitation and quickly starts an interrogation. She attempts to shoot questions, not leaving room for this stranger to ask her questions. During the conversation, she will observe his silent body language and listen to his verbal responses.

"How long have you been observing us?"

Drake recognizes her mode of alertness. He knows she is preparing to defend herself if need be. He can see her hand remains on her gun. He responds.

"Just as long as needed."

Ignoring his invalid comment, Wren moves in closer. Wren spouts off another question.

"Are you visiting someone?"

Drake decides to play along with her inquiry but will only submit concrete answers and replies.

"You could say that."

Wren draws closer and comes to a stop. He becomes uneasy and is concerned she will pick up on his sudden insecurity. Instead of coming across as strong as he intended, he gets lost in his thoughts. Her voice absorbs him, and he checks out from their present interrogation and gets caught up with the softness of her voice. He sees her spunk, and he likes that. Chuckling to himself, he thinks the odds of finding someone like her out in the clearing are not probable.

Wren needs clarification on what is occurring with Drake. He seems in a daze, maybe caught up in his thoughts, and she decides to get him out of it.

"Hey, did you hear me? Hello?" She waves at him as if flagging down a cab.

She is perplexed by his silence and the amused smile poised on his face. Shrugging her shoulders and cocking her head in wonderment at the portrayal of his thoughts, Wren notices that he is gnawing on an earpiece of his glasses. She finds something about him odd, even child-like, and finds the situation possibly dangerous but stimulating. Her red flags are waving, and her uncle Spence who trained her to defend herself, would be busting at the seams if he saw her predicament. She knows she has to be careful and decides it is a good idea to take the posture of a warrior. She whips her hair back with a jerk and raises herself erect. She focuses on the seriousness of their meeting, and with each step she moves towards him, narrowing the gap, she notices her stomach doing flip-flops. She thinks of a million things she wants to know about who he is and that she must be crazy taking a chance to meet a stranger alone in this area. She gains the grit to confront him, guides her horse to a halt, and pulls out a transmitter to call her family. Wren discloses her location and the situation she is presently in with a stranger.

Drake finally returns from his thoughts to the present reality and tries to make light of the embarrassing moment he placed himself in. He does it quite a bit, and he suspects she feels uncomfortable and must have concerns that put her on alert mode. Drake tries to recoup lost ground with her. He places his hat in one hand and waves the other. Grinning, he yells out to her.

"You ride well."

All that comes to mind for Wren to say is,

"Thank you."

Wren wants to maintain a position of having the upper hand but finds herself relaxing instead. She stands down from her warrior position and smiles. She spouts off her response with a flamboyant aire.

"I love the feeling of freedom I get while riding. Ginger is my right hand, you might say."

Drake is relieved she appears to have let down her guard and is less inclined to shoot at him. She is now communicating in friendly banter.

"Yes, I get that. You two complement each other beautifully in a horse and woman way."

Wren narrows the distance between them. She decides to have fun with her explanation. She slowly removes her right foot from its stirrup and juts it before him. She is extending her leg in a flirtatious way, trying to make a point that her legs maneuver her horse.

"The best way to guide any horse is by applying pressure with your legs."

Wren smiles at his squirming discomfort. He is caught off guard by her leg in front of him, and she sees the smirk on his face. She carries on with her enlightenment. Tenderly patting her horse's neck, Wren explains.

"Ginger is trained to react to a squeeze of the legs, and she also listens to my voice."

Drake figures she has to know what she is doing. He speculates she is intentionally putting her nicely formed leg right into his proximity to the "no safe zone." A primitive technique in which she is using a woman's distraction technique to invade his space. She most likely is observing his reactions next to see what he would do. He reminds himself to remain in a no-threat mode to her, but he cannot resist tormenting her a bit.

"Nice legs!"

She notices that he is smiling with clear-cut admiration and gets his humor. She quickly pulls back her extremity to its original position against the horse and is now agitated for putting herself in a vulnerable place. To end the awkwardness of his quirky admiration, Wren yells out to him.

"So Mr. ...?" Indicating she was looking for a name.

Amused, Drake projects his hand toward her.

"My name is Drake Silverman, and you are?"

Nodding her head in recognition of him and not taking his hand, she keeps her hands on the saddle's horn and remains on guard. She is determined to stay large and in charge of the added height of her horse. Introductions are going to be on her terms.

"My name is Wren McCarthy."

After Drake straightens out his hat and puts it on his head, he places his hands under his armpits while rocking back and forth on his khaki camouflage boots. Wren holds on to the reins and proceeds with her questioning.

"So, Mr. Silverman, besides camping, why are you here?"

Drake hesitantly responds while repositioning his feet. He uses that moment to remind himself he must choose his words carefully. He takes a deep breath and calmly presents his guarded position so as not to disclose vital information.

"I'm here to help the Waters with their security setup and take time to refresh and gather my thoughts." He stops with a grin and awaits her response.

Chuckling to herself, Wren vicariously thinks of how anyone might gather one's thoughts. To her, it would be like lassoing a calf in a rodeo or calming the "gerbil in her wheel." It is quite a task, yet playing her instrument in "The High Place" provides an outlet for her inner voice. The song releases her heart's melody to her heavenly Father as her unique offering. However, her privacy and freedom are compromised now that Drake is invading her place of retreat and solitude. Nevertheless, she must be reasonable because she gathers he must have a reason to be there.

He is interested in how she processes his presence. He figures she must know how to defend herself among the wild acreage, and he likes that! However, he has to be cautious to ensure he conceals his true identity and who he represents while being there. Wren continues with her questioning.

"Are you staying at the bed and breakfast with the Waters?"

"Yes, in a way." Drake swallows hard before continuing with his response.

"They have a nice bed and breakfast."

Wren squints her eyes because she is unsatisfied with that response and prods again for a more thorough explanation. Drake slowly responds.

"Well, the Bed and Breakfast is pleasant. However, I requested to camp on their property.

I obtained permission to gather resources if found appropriate for my science research."

"Oh, you are some kind of a scientist?" Drake gasps with a surprised look that she came to that conclusion so fast. He attempts to make light of it and change the conversation's trajectory.

"I like to think of it as a hobby, to gather experiences living among nature to influence my module designs and discover plant specimens that might be another resource to promote healing. Wren was curious and relieved that he seemed to be an educated person that sought to improve things in the world.

"Well, that sounds interesting. You will have to share more if we get a chance before you leave."

"I have a mobile unit I designed in the woods pointing

the other direction behind him. I prefer my privacy." Wren still has questions unanswered.

"Well, that explains why you are here."

Wren turns her attention to the direction of the Inn. She continues her inquiry while shielding her eyes with her arm to block the sun's glare from hurting her eyes.

"How do you read the Waters?"

Drake hopes to satisfy Wren's curiosity, but nothing that would reveal the personal details of how he got there and where he would be going after. He continues to note in his mind of little traits Wren would unknowingly display while conversing. Did she blink, hesitate, have uncontrolled twitches, or fiddle with her hair or fingers? He already deducts she is full of spunk. Wren, unaware of Drake's reading, continues her concerns to Drake about her new neighbors.

"They have been new neighbors. Hard to get to know." Trying to navigate the release of information, Drake replies.

"I feel the Waters are good people just wanting their privacy, and they have displayed nothing but genuine kindness and hospitality towards me," Wren responds.

"I'm delighted to hear that! I wouldn't know anything other than what our family is experiencing thus far with them. They are peculiar and estranged neighbors, and our family has received no experience of them being neighborly. They make it clear by posting signs that they want their privacy. They do not even have the courtesy to invite us in when we stop to welcome them." Wren removes her hat, pointing it at him while scratching her head. She pauses and then continues.

"The fact that our neighbors welcome strangers like you, making odd requests, I find to be breaking news and perhaps a positive thing to hear! It remains questionable, and the verdict is still out on that conclusion." She lets out a chuckle and displays feelings of puzzlement and amusement. Realizing it is crucial at that point to move past the pleasantries and get serious for a moment, Wren asks him.

"Do you have any paperwork proving that the Waters have permitted you to stay on this particular section of land and not the Inn?" Before answering her, Drake notices that she has no ring on her left finger. With that intimate revelation, Drake boldly uses the Miss title to address her.

"Why yes, Miss McCarthy, I have the permit right here." He takes it out of his pocket and slowly offers it to her.

Wren thinks to herself; he must have noticed she was not wearing a ring that would typically indicate her being married or of single status. She is impressed yet remains high on her horse. He still stands before her humbly on the ground at her steed's feet. Drake backs away so she can read it without feeling vulnerable in his proximity. Looking over the paperwork, Wren replies.

"It looks legit." She pulls out her radio and again provides her family with information for them to check out Drake.

Wren folds the paperwork back into the neat square as it was when he had presented it to her. Handing it back to him, she responds.

"It appears as if all is in order."

She looks directly into Drake's eyes.

"Thank you for showing me. These questions I asked are much milder than my family would have asked you if they were here. Don't doubt they will still check out your story."

"I understand." Drake counters." If I had a beautiful daughter wandering the land property alone, I would want to check out those imposing on their stomping ground."

Wren is feeling caught off guard that he interjected she was beautiful.

"Well, yes indeed." Wren wrinkles her nose and continues to poke for the fun of it. She delivers a witty comeback.

"Any loving parent would do that, yes?"

They both laugh, and Wren changes the direction of their conversation. She realizes she has pressing problems to remedy. He is witnessing her being on the Water's land, and he could expose her failure to comply with the Water's directions and reflect poorly on her family's integrity. She is "in a pickle." She has been so in the moment of finding out about this stranger that she failed to note an important aspect to consider. He notices the "mode of alarm" she transitions to. She sheepishly requests.

"With all seriousness, addressing the where and how we have encountered each other, would you mind not letting the Waters know exactly where you met me?"

Drake finds it delightful that he has the upper hand now. Kicking the dirt in accord with smacking his hat on his leg, he responds.

"My lips are sealed."

His quick-witted response takes her aback. Wren ignores his obvious amusement regarding her situation with the Waters and explains further.

"This is not the first time I have crossed the boundary lines, and I have crossed more times than you could count, despite the new neighbor's warning signs, which they immediately posted upon purchasing the property. Thank you for agreeing not to squeal; I do not want to start any quarrel with the neighbor."

Drake is amused. But it will be something he will have to contend with them on how he met Wren.

"Well, Miss. Wren, I am glad you crossed the line today."

Drake extends his hand again, hoping she will feel comfortable dismounting, but she does not concede.

"I do not mean to offend you, Mr. Silverman. I would like to get off my horse and chat some more. However, right now, I truly need to get back. I have some chores I need to get done. If we don't get the opportunity to chat again, I hope you have a pleasant stay and succeed in finding inspiration and relaxation."

Wren prepares to leave and turns again towards him, and shares.

"Oh, I almost forgot to ask, how long do you and your family plan to be here if they are here?"

Drake was quick to pick up on her tactic of gathering more information.

"Miss McCarthy, if I told you everything now, you would not need to have a conversation with me again, would you?" Wren decides to have some fun and toys with him.

"Ok, are you saying you want to see me again?" She

now displays body language with an eyebrow raised and a sheepish grin.

"Well, Mr. Silverman, perhaps we will get a chance to chat again."

She taps Ginger on the thigh and trots off, eventually into a cantor, looking back and shouting,

"Nice meeting you!"

His response disturbs her. He grins. Wren speaks to herself.

"I would like to see you again, Drake Silverman. You have my interest for sure. Dang, he's so handsome, and I bet he has many gals on the side drooling after him."

Her radio goes off again. Wren abruptly halts her horse to pick up the call.

"Sis, You there?" Cassidy shouts.

"Are you a safe distance from Drake?" Wren responds.

"Yes, I am good, Cassidy! I am just leaving the clearing." Both Cassidy and grandfather shout in unison.

"He's all clear!" She is hoping he cannot hear her obnoxious home groupies.

She smiles and waves a salute in respect to him, signifying his clearance. She turns her attention back to the radio.

"How can you already know that? I just met with the guy that our estranged neighbors allow camp on their land?"

Cassidy tells her about the neighbors stopping by to discuss their vacationer, Drake, who is camping on their land, and Wren becomes more suspicious of him.

"How timely and odd that the Waters responded so quickly."

Wren ends her radio chat and considers inviting him to the ranch. She looks back to see if she can still see Mr. Silverman. Is he still standing in the exact location he was when she and her steed took off? She decides to turn around and take another whack at Drake. It looks like she will get to know him after all. She plans to approach him with a warm greeting and let him know he is welcome to visit their ranch if he is available. She sees him and tells Ginger.

"Good! He has not left yet!" She trots back to him. When within range to talk, she opens up a conversation.

"Mr. Silverman, my family cleared you. Is the offer still good for me to join you for a friendly conversation?" Drake smiles and points to a large boulder nearby where they can sit and continue their talk. He hopes she will be more at ease this time. She dismounts behind tall grass near the rock he refers to and waits for him to walk there. Her firearm is strapped across her shoulder; thus, Drake assumes she is still suspicious of him. He asks her about her adventures on the land.

"Is it common practice that you take adventures out here alone?"

Wren still finds herself a little on edge and scans the nearby wood line for evidence of other people. When she feels comfortable, she turns her attention back to Drake and responds to his question.

"Personal Adventures out here, you ask? I like being on my own in certain instances."

She lets loose the reins, giving her horse free mobility. Wren taps Ginger on the rump, signaling to her that it is ok to feed on the grasses nearby. Drake is impressed that her horse gladly complies yet remains close as if guarding Wren. Drake continues to drill Wren.

"So what is it you like so much about roaming around?"

Wren continues answering his questions. She feels it fair to let him inquire about her.

"I enjoy a specific secluded area above that I do not wish to disclose." Drake smiles and replies.

"Well, we all need those places. I like time to myself as well."

Wren stands by the boulder with one foot on it. She still has her gun strapped across her shoulder and one hand on the shoulder strap for quick access. He gets up from the rock to stand eye-to-eye. He does not like the scenario presently occurring.

"I'm sorry, Mr. Silverman, I prefer that you sit and I stand, if you don't mind, for I do not know much about you yet."

He feels agitated now. She has the upper hand, and she knows it. She continues talking as if trying to maintain control. For now, he will play along. Wren continues to scope the perimeter while talking.

"It is my favorite place to come. I've never seen anyone else out here before I met you today, so I guess you rate it up there as a new adventure."

They both laugh at that. Her stomach growls. Wren glances at her stomach and then at him. She pats it as if it would soothe the rumbling. Drake counters.

"That must mean it is time for your lunch?"

Both giggle. The conversation stops with the sound of the radio dispatch blurting out the correctness of Drake's presence again, but now it is only generated by her sister.

"Sis, Mom, and Dad would like me to tell you to be careful, and if you are considering inviting Drake to visit, get back to the ranch as soon as possible." Wren quickly responds with a moment of embarrassment.

"Got it, sis." She turns to Drake.

"As you might have overheard, you have an invite from my family to visit. Suppose it would not be too presumptuous to ask. A window of opportunity has presented itself, and you are welcome to come for brunch on the ranch?"

He evaluates his hunger pains and the excellent offer. Still, Wren had already bounded off to find her horse before he could reply. She mounts Ginger behind the tall grasses and trots back to him. Drake finds it amusing. He knows where the boulder is that she is most likely using to mount her horse. She returns to where he is standing and maneuvers her horse beside him. She halts the horse, extends her hand, hoping he will accept the offer, and hop on the back of the horse with her. She expects a positive response due to the vibes he sends during their banter. He seems interested in her.

She does not detect any mode of transportation he might have. She concludes she should offer it again.

"Brunch?"

Drake stares at her hand and tries to gather a response. She threw him off guard due to her directness, and he now feels uneasy.

"Well, I am not sure. You mean right now, this very minute?" Displaying an ornery grin. Wren comes back with a response.

"It is the time frame between a late breakfast and early lunch, you know?"

Standing with one arm on his hip, holding his hat, he gets up and shifts his feet before he responds.

"I know what brunch means, and I find it odd. I mean, you threw me off a bit."

He is Looking at her with a perplexed expression. Drake continues to talk.

"Do you feel comfortable asking a total stranger? You want your family to meet a guy you just met?"

Now Wren is feeling a little humiliated. She is the one that put herself in this moment of embarrassment and rejection. She quickly tries to recover her dignity and blurts out in her defense mode,

"Well, you are welcome to pass if you prefer. Your predicament is understandably off-putting. I apologize, for we are just kind folk and stupidly open-minded. I am confident my family's motives operate from their inquiring minds, and they most likely want to determine if you are a decent person roaming near our property. The invitation from the family still stands if you are free for a few hours. After a light lunch, I can give you a short tour of the ranch."

Drake takes a moment to contemplate the pros and cons.

"Well, I am close to taking you up on that offer. However, I think I will pass this time. There are things I already planned needing to get done. However, I do want to thank you and your family for the hospitality and kindness you have extended to me." Wren responds to his rejection.

"Ok then, it is what it is." Wren is feeling foolish again.

The heat from embarrassment is starting to flash up her neck and onto her cheeks. She needs to get moving before he sees it extending to her ears. She doesn't need to be any more embarrassed than she already is experiencing. She hates that her body reveals her emotions so quickly. Leaving no time for him to respond, Wren gives Ginger a vocal command and squeeze of the legs and quickly turns and gallops off, leaving dust behind her. She did not want to hear his response, and her expression of so-be-it emphasized her exit. He watches until he can see her no more. Quietly he responds, knowing she could not hear him speak aloud.

"It is good to meet you, Miss McCarthy. You are feisty! If our paths cross again, I may consider your proposition of visiting your ranch and getting to know you better."

Since the courting of his deceased wife, Drake never met anyone he wanted to pursue more earnestly until now. There was a time he considered a relationship with his wife's best friend, Javelin, because it was easy. They were already acquainted, and she was already present in their life. She is the one that cares for his children while he works. Not considering love of any kind, it would be easy for him to slip into an intimate place of commitment and play house because he knew how to do that due to being married to Corinne. He and his wife had an excellent relationship, and he knows it's his singleness he truly has difficulty walking out.

The Domes health team helped him maintain a healthy mentality towards Javelin. They helped him to navigate the grieving process and remain best friends with Javelin. He could not break up her engagement with her true love because it was easier for him. How selfish that would be. Content with where he landed, he decided to focus solely on raising his children and working with the Dome team to find solutions to help humanity thrive. His children and work bring him purpose and a sense of accomplishment.

Drake thought he might not need another relationship, but now he waivers with that thought. He tries to reason it out. It is more likely a brief detour that will take him off the trail for a short while, and then he suspects he will eventually grow weary of the chase and return to his routine. However, he must not negate the possibility of her intrusion, which could risk exposure to his mission. However true it may be, he finds the scenario with this woman presents a welcomed and unexpected twist to his otherwise mundane day. The anticipation of this chase is exhilarating.

Wren is feeling deflated. It's as if someone has stuck a pin in her, allowing all the air to escape. Courageously she smiles and stops to look back, and he has already disappeared into the tundra. Well, that is a disappointment, she thinks to herself. Wren starts talking aloud.

"How frustrating and humiliating it is to leave him behind that way. Why must the burden of the act of flushing be upon me? Now I must figure out how to orchestrate this encounter with the family. What should I tell them?"

Wren gently pulls Ginger to a halt and dismounts a short distance from the ranch. She frequents this location often to sit and read from time to time.

In this particular place, a hammock hangs between two trees. It beckons her. Wren walks ahead of Ginger, guiding her by the reigns amongst trees. She releases Ginger to snack on the tundra while she plops on the hammock and replays the recorded version in her mind of what had happened with Drake. Wren swings back and forth, moving her fingers over the tall grasses that have taken over her little space of open refuge. Unbeknownst to her, her uncle is observing her from the front porch. She breaks off a piece of the grass and begins switching her leg. Thinking about how she will relay her encounter with Drake to her family, Wren knows she must leave out some things to spare her from her family's scolding. She did not need anyone else to tell her how foolish she is. She is angry at herself for allowing herself to be part of a potentially dangerous situation. She let Drake get "under her skin."

The heat started radiating up her neck to her face again. How stupid of her to assume he would abruptly accept an invitation to the ranch to meet her family. Though it is a neighborly thing to do, he knows they were flirting, or is it in her imagination? Maybe he assumes she is just a nutcase desperately seeking a man. If he is not interested in her, he probably is envisioning her family grabbing hold of him and forcing him to be a part of a shotgun wedding! She moans.

"Good gracious!" Sitting up on the hammock, she flips her legs over the side. She rolls her eyes and throws her head back, releasing a noise of exasperation.

"aaaahhhhhh!"

The more she rehearses the words she had spoken to Drake and how he responded, the more mortified she becomes. He was just toying with her, she concluded. Yet what would she have done if he said he would have gone with her? That is something she will torture herself with later.

Before Wren could put her presentation together for her pending family inquiry, her uncle Spence rode up to join her on Rodney, one of the Ranches' fastest horses. He did not display a happy expression, and he jumped off his horse and joined Wren leaning on the tree to which her hammock was attached.

"Hello, uncle."

"Wren, what were you thinking? That man could have been your end!"

"I know, uncle. Showing him her gun, she counters.

"I took precautions. Besides, he abruptly appeared, and I was caught off guard."

"Yes, her uncle responds with understanding. That is when it is most dangerous! We need to discuss this person."

Wren's uncle gathers the reigns, ready to jump back on his horse while looking towards the direction of the scenario she had just left. He looks at Wren with a serious look.

"Perhaps I should take a ride out to investigate this fella myself."

Wren shutters at the thought and quickly responds.

"No! There is no need for that. He wants his privacy, and I was intruding in his space, Uncle. He is kind, cleared by gramps, and stays in our new neighbor's land. Please, uncle, I was jumping a log with Ginger on their property; I know I am not supposed to."

She took off her hat and smacked her leg with it.

"It is my fault we crossed paths. If you investigate in haste, it could throw us even more odds with our neighbors." Her Uncle responds.

"Well, how do you not know he won't tell them?"

Wren stops and reflects on her and Drake's conversation. She processes it. She says.

"Well, he said he would not, and I believe him."

Her Uncle relays a startling possibility.

"Well, niece, I am not sure about that." Wren is put off guard.

"What do you mean?

"The Waters are at the farm talking to your parents right now. Wren is instantly enraged.

"Well, that snake of a man! How could he get to them so fast? Perhaps by radio like she did."

Wren jumps back on her horse and canters back to the Ranch. Spence finds it amusing that Wren is so agitated with the man, and he jumps on his horse and follows behind. As they near the barn, Spence jumps off before she dismounts and helps her down from her horse. He talks to her as they take the horses to their stalls. They are silent while removing the saddles, and Uncle Spence breaks the silence.

"Listen, you need to calm down. We do not know why the Waters are here for the second time today. Let's keep our wits about us and discuss how you got into this mess later. I suggest we approach our neighbors with no presumptions and gather information. That is if the Waters will freely give it up. Doing this will help to know how to approach him if any other future encounters occur."

"You go on ahead, Uncle. I will take care of the horses. I am afraid I cannot control what comes out of my mouth now." Her Uncle ruffles the hair on her head and pats her shoulder. He continues with playful banter to bring a smile back to her face.

"This fellow has gotten under your skin?" Chuckling, he lifts her chin.

"Listen, Wren. I see you are interested in this guy. In all seriousness, it is a humbling experience, but perhaps this could be a person you are destined to meet and should consider being open to that. Maybe it is not just a coincidence you crossed paths, and God does work in mysterious ways. Just be patient and wait to see what this fellow reveals about himself."

Wren silently watches her Uncle walk towards the ranch. She respects her Uncle's advice and ponders on God's ways in this. She considers the possibility of Drake being someone God may have brought into her life. She asks herself not to rule it out but cannot go without being cautious. It is time to review what she would say if there were another encounter with Drake. How should she react?

CHAPTER 2

WREN REFLECTS

In her bed, Wren tosses and turns. Sleep escapes Wren, so she throws aside her blankets and gets up. She grabs her robe from the chair, slips on her favorite pink socks and cushioned slippers, and heads downstairs to the kitchen. It is common for her to head to the kitchen when she has bouts of restlessness. She makes herself a cup of camellia tea, cups her hands around the warm mug, and heads back upstairs. She ventures out on her balcony and grabs her beanie hat and scarf from the back of the door. She opens her doors and embraces the coolness of the night air. With her mug cradled in her hands, she leans over the railing to look over the land momentarily. Wren decides to retrieve her throw off the end of the bed and wrap herself up tight and cozy before sitting on her one-person wicker swing. She sits with one leg underneath her, allowing the other to hang down to touch the deck below to propel her swing. Wren feels an inner twisting of possibilities arising. She thinks about Drake and weighs what it might look like to date him but gets interrupted. Her stomach is growling. This occurrence usually happens when she stays up too long. Wren peels off the blanket and throws it back on the bed. She closes the balcony doors and heads downstairs to gather food and another cup of tea.

"Dang, it! Why do I get so hungry at night?"

She considers her options. She opens the refrigerator and sees the leftover chicken and noodles. She closes the door and opens the freezer.

"Hum."

She may have loaded baked potato skins or a few prepared oatmeal raisin cookies she can pop in the oven. Instead of returning to her room this time, she ventures to the front porch with her selection. She grabs a quilt off the couch, tosses it over her shoulders, and heads to the patio. The screen door lets out its screech. Wren hopes it will not wake anyone, but Grandmother is already stirring. She hears movement downstairs and assumes there is another restless sleeper beside herself. She figures whoever it may be must be gaining comfort on the front porch. She slips quietly out of bed, grabs her robe and slippers, and goes downstairs to connect with them.

"Perhaps they need company."

Pulling up her robe collar to cover her bare neck Wren takes occupancy on the porch swing. She takes a moment to inspect the quilt and feels the weight. Her Grams inserts thermal sheets inside her quilts. It works well against the crisp night air. Wren loves them. It is great to have an outside area where family members can gather. They have a swing, rocking chairs, a play table with chairs, and eight stairs leading down from the porch for seating. As she gazes into the open starry night, an owl hoots in a near-by tree. She loves the sound of them. She recalls being sad when she first realized that her night at college in the city meant having to sacrifice not hearing the owls like she was accustomed to hearing on the Ranch. The metropolis living has difficulty experiencing the true magnificence of the open skies and wooded night sounds. The glow from the city lights produces a type of light pollution. It hinders the ability to see the stars with clarity. However, clear night skies on the ranch display spectacular brilliance.

Wren went to a neighboring college to acquire a master's in Education. She chose to teach Special needs students. It felt very empowering to her to represent those less equipped to function independently. These special few were a segment of society that the public tended to forget. They are typically overlooked and seen as more of a burden to society. Wren has a passion for being one of those that stand in the gap to represent those that have difficulty speaking for themselves. Wren offers her students an educational environment incorporating music. Students diagnosed with severe learning disabilities have shown benefits from music therapy.

Wren retains the same special needs students until Junior High level. She likes having permission to take them on field trips to her family ranch. It is an incentive to encourage her students to try their best academically. The students look forward to it. They love the freedom they experience feeding the horses and farm life. They love the hayride that goes on a route that takes them around the perimeter of several fields. The first stop delivers them to a pumpkin patch, where helpers and family members accompany the children to help them select the perfect pumpkin to take home. The second stop is at a group of picnic tables where they receive a cup of apple cider and a doughnut. The third stop is at the big red barn, where they enjoy feeding and petting farm animals and taking group pictures.

Wren treasures her close-knit family. Her parents, sister, grandparents, uncle, aunt, and cousins live on the ranch. The privilege of ranch living means they reside there and contribute to its work and play. Everyone has a part or chore they are responsible for, and they find it gratifying to see how well they make it happen together.

Dad arranges tours of the ranch once every fall season. His words usually are as follows.

"The ranch's history starts with my parents, Theodore and Lola McCarthy. The expanse of the property stretches over 800 acres. The acreage allows for raising cattle, horses, beehives, farm wheat, soybean, corn, gardens, and apple trees. Additionally, there is land dedicated to protecting plants and wildlife. Windmills pump out water, and solar panels supply the ranch with electrical power. The ranch is off-grid due to natural resources. Natural springs, wells, and rainwater collection provide all their water needs. Plowed gardens and hydroponic greenhouses grow and provide fruit trees, herbs, vegetables, and flowers. The resources collectively generate all the income required to support the families. The jobs needed to maintain the ranch are divided between family members and a few hired hands to work with the cattle. Jobs align as best as possible, considering individual likes and abilities. They all help to maintain the success of the ranch. Lastly, The success of the farm lies in how the family takes pride in doing well jointly with anything put before them on the farm and in life."

Wren's and Liddy's chores are feeding, grooming the horses, and maintaining the stalls. A veterinarian stops on regular health checks, teaching them how to tend to minor injuries the horses may need in his absence. They know how to apply salve to minor cuts or scrapes, as the horses may require. Both women can do all aspects of the job individually if necessary. It is essential to trade off with each other in case someone has something else they need to do. Some chores must be performed daily, while others can wait until another day. It is good because it gives them individual liberty to do other things occasionally. If sickness occurs, causing one to miss a lot of time, other ranch hands will pick up the slack.

One of Wren's favorite chores is riding the fence line, checking the perimeter for any breaches cattle might escape through. After she checks for breaches in the fence and finds all good, she takes the opportunity to seek solitude. Unlike the livestock not allowed to go past their set boundaries, Wren permits herself to cross to find alone time on her favorite spot on the mountaintop. You can only get there by using the neighbor's access. In her mind, crossing boundaries is justified in two parts.

First, prior owners and neighbors gave Wren a free pass to cross so she could gather strays and access her sacred location. It is "Grandfathered" in her mind. It is standard neighborly protocol in those parts to allow adjoining properties to access each other's property to retrieve AWOL livestock who occasionally escape using their innate rationality, thinking the grass is better on the other side.

The second reason she allowed herself to cross over the adjacent neighbor's line is that she has a private location where she finds solitude. It is like finding paradise for her. There is tranquility there that she is not able to find anywhere else. She did not want to let it go. She expects no different treatment from the new neighbors. She truly feels they will come around after they become accustomed to how the folk does things in those parts.

This day after completing her fence duty, Wren takes the liberty and rides her horse to The High Place she calls her "secret place." There she would spend alone time communing with her Heavenly Father. Today, Wren is delighted as she watches a beautiful dance given by a skinny waterfall trickling down the rock wall with grace and elegance. Listening to the rhythm of the drops hitting the water at the bottom is soothing. Cascading mosses and ferns fill the deep crevices between the stones like tufts of fluff. Earthy aromas fill the air. Wild berries dot the landscape nearby, which she loves to snack on. The effect of all the sights, smells, and sounds promotes a mystery of intrigue. She celebrates God's Creation.

Walking over to the terrace, Wren calls "God's Ear," she looks out at the beauty of the Canyon, embraces the solitude, and offers her melodic sounds to the Father. The violin is how she presents her worship, taking advantage of the natural acoustics that catapult her notes to Heaven's Ears.

Her parent's influence has broadened her scope of what a girl can do or be. Her father invites his daughters to step out of society's "gender hat." Not having boys to pass on his father's man-favored hobby of hunting live game opportunity is extended to his girls. Wren jumps at her dad's invitation at age ten. She cherishes those times she spends with him. Her mom is a strong independent Artist. She is both creative and spiritual. She encourages her daughters to find their "Special Fragrance." She found this poem written by Patricia Simmons, a local artist, and had it framed. She hung it in the girl's room.

In His Presence

Climb onto God's lap and sit for a while.
Embrace His heart with the innocence of a child.
Envision Him gathering your very essence,
receiving your gift, for you are His present!
Anticipate Him reaching out to capture
your unique fragrance with joy and with laughter.
Always remember that you are in His sight.
You are perfectly loved and God's great delight.

Her mother raises them to be thinkers and learners and imparts the truth of what she learned about the Heavenly Father's heart. Because of their mother, Wren and Cassidy know there is more to a good woman than her physical allure. They are to embrace the benefits of being God's child through His son Jesus and proudly display the banner over them that God stands behind. Their mother hopes they have a close relationship with their Heavenly Father above all else. They are encouraged to stay aligned, no matter how old they get. They must remember that they are always the Heavenly Daddy's little girl that can always crawl up in his lap and be his daughter. Wren looks up to see her Grams coming through the front screen door. She joins Wren, sitting in the rocking chair, and her Grams starts the conversation.

"It is inspiring, isn't it?"

She starts to get up in honor of her, but her Grams motions her to stay put. Wren notes what her Grandmother is wearing: Rose-colored pajamas, a multicolored wool knitted sweater matching hat, and fluffy slippers. Her cheeks are rosy, and her face is full of light.

"Doesn't it look like tiny night lights? Grandma adds.

Wren chuckles at Grams thinking of the stars being night lights in that way. Wren replies.

"Yes, I can see that!" Grams continues.

"God carefully named and placed each star in its place."

Wren thinks about the lights in the heavens. She knows the natural eye cannot behold the expansive mystery beyond the normal sight range. Heaven's visible attributes are but a small piece of God's artwork. With but the testimony of the stars, how can anyone ignore God's existence? Creation is a gift. No man or coincidence could have made so many extraordinary anomalies in creation that work. Grandma and Wren quietly observe without a word spoken for a spell. You can hear the rhythm of grandma's rocker moving back and forth and the sound of Wren's quilt dragging across the floorboards with each swing sway. Grandma rises after a while, moves over to Wren, and tenderly kisses her on the top of her head. She senses Wren is in a good place and leaves her to the wonder of solitude. She returns to her bed beside her husband and pats him on the arm, signifying all is well.

Wren loves the ranch life because it offers her a home that helps guard her against making bad decisions as a single woman. She prefers the protective qualities it affords her in many ways. Yes, she must adhere to the family hierarchy, but she is willing to conform to her family's rules since they help her live in a way that pleases God.

Returning her thoughts to the present, she finishes her tea and last potato skin. She places her cup in the kitchen sink and returns upstairs to the comfort of her bed. She tucks two pillows behind her head and one between her knees. She pulls the quilt to her chin and commences the "snug as a bug" routine she has applied since childhood. All extremities are in except for one dangling foot she leaves out to regulate getting overheated. She soon falls asleep, thinking about the heavens and the encounter with Drake.

CHAPTER 3

DRAKE DREAMS

Drake thinks back on his first interaction with Wren. He has concerns. The after-thoughts of his actions taken towards Wren bring emotions of remorse. He asks himself why he stepped out of hiding. By revealing himself, he jeopardizes the safety of the Procure Earth Society. He has taken a significant risk of exposing his connection to the secret P.E.S. group and the newly opened secret Location at the Waters. In addition, she poses a considerable threat to the balanced emotional state he worked so hard to obtain after the loss of Corinne. He cannot deny that he is fascinated with her. His mind is wrestling. He turns his thoughts to the kids to distract him from further debating his erratic actions encountering Wren.

Finally, he gets to connect with his children, Jesse and Abigail. They are at a Summer survival camp. Here, they will be introduced to docile and hostile life forms and learn how to approach them. They must learn how to respond to both kinds of life forms and expand the boundaries of where they live for their growth and protection. It is fun for them to be with other children on the Dome. Even though it is a fun time, the children still miss their parents. The Science team knows children's emotional state and provides designated times to communicate with their parents.

While Drake waits for the connection to clear between Earth and the Dome, his heart hurts. It hits him hard. He looks forward to hearing his children's voices. Hearing them brings the normalcy of family back to him. He reflects on his deceased wife, Corinne, and their children's tender moments while in the comforting station. It is the place she loved reading and singing to them before bedtime. When she read to her children, you could always count on hearing them cackle at some point during their time together. Drake realizes he still misses her. He knows his kids miss her as well, and they need him. He is the children's only family on the dome except for Javelin, Corinne's best friend. It is Javelin who tends to the children when he is away. Drake finally talks to his children and is happy that they are having fun at camp and seem to be ok with him not being there. He did not tell them about meeting Wren. He kept their conversation about camping, gathering new species for research, and the berries he ate as he walked through the woods. After their family communication ends, Drake focuses on his duties and how glad he is to come to earth in one of his self-designed modules.

His Module is one of "Drake's deluxe" versions of his design. He has things he likes that are not an option for modules sold to others. All of his designs usually have multiple purposes. The occupants can use them for general services and security purposes. He also particularly loves the creation of the skylight in his module above his bed and the monitors that rise from hidden compartments extending up through the roof. With a flick of a button, the outside monitor records sound taken from the outdoors to the indoors. He enjoys the tranquility of the woodland sounds. He likes positioning his module near the trees. The trees sway ever so quietly one moment and escalate to abrupt episodes of applause the next. Anyone usually listening would find it relaxing, but in his circumstance, at this moment, all it is doing is providing background music that is stimulating his mind to think about Wren. He keeps replaying his recent interaction with Wren. Finally, he realizes it gets him nowhere closer to resolving his unsettled state and decides to get some rest.

He takes one last drink of his beverage, punches his pillow, and attempts to sleep. He purposely rolls over, forcing his eyes closed for at least 15 minutes, a technique he uses intending to cause slumber. Drake doses off, waking up a little less each time. He still has insecurities about being in a new location and has yet to find a sense of familiarity, which generally comes when he spends more time in a new place. This time he is startled from his sleep due to the wooded noises that cause him to be alarmed and on edge. He finally decides to turn the monitor off and puts his security in the hands of his robotic sentinels. He closes the skylight, and with the stopping of the sudden interruptions of nature's tunes and the sentinels' activation, he finally can put his self-preservation mode to rest and before drifting off to sleep Drake replays the encounter in his mind with Wren and takes the encounter to another level.

Like viewing a movie, the sun's rays highlight Wren and her majestic horse coming through the trees. Drake finds it challenging to process. In his mind, he first reasons to handle her intrusion with aggression, yet he yields. He becomes intrigued to see what may come of this encounter. He chooses to move out of his comfort zone and allow himself to become more acquainted with this trespasser. Now completely honest with himself, he is delighted she wants more of him. If she were a spider, he would be the prey caught in her web. Drake dreams.

"Jump on up if you think you can."

"Oh, I can jump up there," Drake quickly adds, pointing to an area near the high grass.

"But, how about going over to that rock behind that grass, so I can jump on as you did."

Smiling, she directs her horse Ginger to return to the rock from whence she mounted. She seems amused and impressed with how observant he is. He walks towards her as she comes back from the grass. He takes her hand and mounts the horse sitting behind the saddle's cantle, putting himself near her but not right up against her due to a tiny sliver of the blanket he can sit on. It helped to buffet his bottom from directly sitting on the horse's hide. He had to admit to never having ridden a horse before. It felt exhilarating to ride behind her. He speculates that she notices his firm body and the heat-generating behind her.

It felt proper that he was separated from her by a slither of space between the saddle's back lip. After all, they hardly know each other. Drake puts one arm behind him, firmly planting his hand on the horse's rump; the other hand hesitates where to place it to help him stay stable. Wren must have picked up on his moment of contemplation because she nods at him to access the saddle horn in front of her. He carefully maneuvers around her waist and grabs the saddle horn before her. Softly speaking into her ear, he whispers.

"Are you sure you want a strange man sitting behind you on a horse?"

Startled yet in control, Wren appears unafraid, yet he knows as if he can read her thoughts. Though she responded in appearance as not being afraid, he knew her stomach was saying,

"Be afraid, be very afraid!"

She responds quickly.

"If Ginger and I expect trouble, we certainly know how to handle it."

Ginger snorts as if she understands what they are discussing.

"Can you do me a favor, please?" Wren asks.

"When you meet my Uncle Spence, don't let him know I allowed you to get this close after first meeting you!" Grinning, Drake speaks again into her ear playfully,

"Wow, two secrets in one day!"

That made Wren smile. He distanced himself from her ear and knew Wren felt quite relieved. She had to feel the electrifying feeling of having him breathe and speak so close to her neck. He is a breath away from touching her; she has to feel the heat in his breath.

While they trot back to her family's ranch, Drake inhales the fragrance of her hair. Though it flew in his face, he deemed it pleasure more than an irritant. He is delighted to have impulsively agreed to the meeting of her kin but, more importantly, to have the opportunity to get more acquainted with her. He attempts to create conversation in a non-threatening way.

"Good healthy hair!" he shouts."

Wren jumps a bit from his sudden vocal outburst and suddenly feels reckless that she did not take thought of her hair flying freely behind her. It must annoy him, flying about and whipping him in the face. Considering everything, she tells him,

"Oh, I am so sorry! Picking up an extra rider on her excursion is not normal, and this incident is the first time I have ever let a stranger ride behind me."

"That makes me feel special!" Drake blurts out. She quickly pulls back the reins to a halt and thrusts the reins into his hand, holding the horn. She points him in the direction of the ranch so she can gather her wayward locks and bounds them with a band on her wrist. Trying to steer the horse towards the ranch and watch her simultaneously is entertaining but stressful. She quickly pulls her hair in a tail off to the side and gives him a nod of appreciation for taking over the reins. Wren rescues them back from his hand and allows him to resume his hand position on the horn before her. She guides Ginger with a nudge of her foot and a squeeze of her legs while vocalizing a clicking noise.

"I usually only hear the swish of the horse's tail and the sound of a horse walking when I head back to the ranch." Responding, Drake amusingly adds one last comment before they arrive at the ranch.

"Yes, I bet this is an off experience from the norm."

Silence resides for the rest of the trip. He realizes Wren must wonder if he is projecting a comment in fun or a judgment on her for being so open to allowing him to be so close after meeting him.

"Boom!" a loud crash of a tree branch falls onto the top of the module. Drake's eyes fly open, and he sits up sweating. He grabs his pillow and throws it across the room as if it had a bug crawling on it.

"Get out of town. That could have happened!"

Drake then recalls why he awoke so abruptly and checks his sentinel's incident report, and has them scan the place of the occurrence to determine if any damage has occurred to his dwelling from the fallen branch. He decides to move his module to a more open space the following day, which would present less chance of it happening again.

He is grateful all is safe, and it is only minor damage being reported. He can repair it in the morning. He plops himself in a corner chair, thrusts his fingers eagerly through his hair, and leaves his hands there. He hears himself say,

"I have not had anyone touch my soul like that in a long time."

She is creating a feeling of anticipation for the want of more. No one since his departed wife has had that effect on him. He realizes he has an opportunity to find out if he can put himself out there again. He can not believe that she has this hold on him. He has just met this woman, yet this vivid dream calls him to action. He has heard of couples knowing it would be special the first time they met, but he did not believe it possible until now.

"This is some crazy cosmic mojo that's happening."

He pulls back on the thought of them together and

decides to lay low for now. He eventually returns to his bed and finishes his night's sleep.

He rises and saunters into the kitchen galley. He lifts a panel cleverly camouflaged on the counter and pushes a button. A door opens immediately, and a hot beverage extends toward him on a small plate. He takes it out and takes a sip of his beloved coffee. Carrying his steaming brew, he heads to the relaxing cove located in front of the fireplace. He realizes he has to decide if he will take the opportunity presented by pursuing Wren or remain in the state he grew accustomed to before meeting her, which is single. He reflects on Corinne. He notices that her memories are fading, and the pain of the loss is less severe by far. Pulling up a picture from the Luna port gallery, he opens recorded dialogues he had with her before she passed. He smiles at the beauty of her voice and glistening eyes. He turns it off and reflects.

Drake, in his thirties, is in a personal debate. He tosses around the idea of further investigating who this Wren is. It has been four years since his wife moved on to another realm, and it has surprised his friends and colleagues that he has not found someone else already. Maybe this Wren is just a catalyst that catapults him to a new dating season and perhaps finding someone special to share the rest of his life with.

Drake turns his thoughts to his mother. He wishes she was still living so he could consult her. She had the most significant impact on her son. She is one of those that did not brag or seek recognition for her successes. She was a hardworking woman displaying many good character and humility attributes. She was honest, kind, and not lazy. There is not likely another woman on earth like her, Drake renders. She is one of a kind.

This meeting with Wren has caught him off guard. She unknowingly enters his world and brings warmth and laughter in a different way than his children or working accomplishments can give. She unexpectedly slips into his life and releases a glimmer of hope that someone might be out there for him, someone extraordinary.

CHAPTER 4

DRAKE'S JOURNEY

Drake is an only child that grows up in the company of adults and robotics. His parents impose their beliefs that God is a God of Science. Believing God to be the ultimate scientist, they feel that all advancements man comes up with directly come from the Creator's DNA. His parents each impart an awareness of the world's rapid decline. They see the fall of humanity and want to be a part of saving the future of humankind. This strong stance led them to join a movement called "Procure Earth Society." This group unifies people from all walks of life. They influence the group to use scientific advancements to help humanity live on. Drake's choice to join his family's fight is a no-brainer. He chooses to work alongside his mother of whom becomes a significant part of finding a solution the P.E.S. seeks.

Drake's mother's training gives him his scientific foundation. He learns how to engineer robotics and use botanical remedies to heal the human body. His mother becomes a sought-after scientist. She starts her study to unveil the mysteries of God's creation and uses that revelation to find new solutions to complex problems. Her robotic advancements are way ahead of any other designs out there at the time.

The government notices her and seeks to use her research to incorporate robotic innovations into farming and military areas. Her prototypes are suited to serve the communities on a small scale and eventually expand production globally. The approval comes from the need to establish efficient production not hindered by a lack of workers due to sickness and quarantine. Robots do not get sick, demand pay raises or vacation days off, and do not need medical leave or insurance. Robotic manual labor is the most feasible answer to the shortage of workers.

The government also hopes to implement robotic support to help grow food to feed the hungry population and use the robots for police patrol. Working alongside robots could ensure better community security assistance, alleviating most police fatalities. They want to use this robot security core for riotous outbreaks driven by malicious intent. Once these robots prove functional and effective, they plan to develop a line of robots to use as sentinels. She agrees, presenting the stipulation that she hires as an outside contractor. She is given access to the base and supplies without restraints.

His mother has a secret lab on her property, and no one except her family members and droids can enter. This government connection gave her access to government supplies with no red tape. Now she has "the more" she needs to research and produce on a grander scale and her terms.

Her lab is well hidden from outsiders of any kind. It is a well-thought-out plan on how to make the layout of the construction look inconspicuous. The central portion of the lab is below ground level, and a tiny bit sticks above the ground. The above-ground section connects to the wind silo and greenhouse. Both solar and wind provide sufficient stored energy for her lab to stay off-grid. Being self-sufficient allows them to remain inconspicuous about what otherwise might red flag them using power from public utilities. They use the public utilities and some backup reserves from the windmills. The utilities must appear appropriate for the resident part of their home to keep them disguised as an average user for a family of three. She depends solely on wind and solar power to operate her lab. The lab is accessible from the basement entrance of their residence, and two additional possibilities of access to the lab are at the other end of the tunnel connecting to the silo and one in disguise in the greenhouse. The last two mentioned are backup entrances they could use to enter if needed. She developed a line of personal robotics to assist her with lab duties and sentinels designed to protect the occupants and research in the facility.

Drake and his mother share the space. They often work into the wee hours of the morning. It is not all about robotics; his mother also researches botanical specimens. She finds it essential to make it a way of life to grow and gather newfound food sources to consume and promote health and healing. She and her son's contribution to the world impact its betterment. The shared knowledge is not unlike a pebble thrown into the water, causing a disturbance. That disturbance produces a ripple effect, generating small rings that progress into larger circles. Her ceiling would be Drake's floor. Her ripples birth a vast expanse of breakthroughs that her son will advance when she no longer can.

Drake's father is the more practical parent, and he keeps his mother grounded. Socialization regarding simple everyday conversation is not his mother's cup of tea. Talking to others outside her field with petty banter is not her forte. These gatherings cause her to get agitated, and the stupidity she flags in their conversation is brutal to look past. He ensures not to stray far from her at events and stays near enough to check on her discussions with meddling people. She would glance at her husband during difficult moments, and he would wink back at her, giving her a sign that she could say what was on her mind with a smile and walk away. People are unsure if she is serious or just having fun. She would wander over to her husband, and he will make an acceptable way for them to withdraw from the social event and whisk her away.

His father, Troy, is a college professor with a natural flair for writing and speaking. He uses his talent to bring a fresh perspective to societal issues and awareness of environmental decline. His voice motivates others to act on behalf of what is occurring around them in nature's revolt. He hopes to produce independent thinkers and world changers when he is teaching. After retiring, his life becomes more flexible, so he pursues freelance writing. In Drake's younger years, his father helps oversee him while his mother works long hours in her lab. When Drake's father travels for speaking engagements, his mother brings Drake into her Lab. He eventually spends more and more time with his mom and begins picking up skills that lay the foundation for his scientific advancements.

During the timeframe of Drake's graduate work, his mother passes away. She becomes sick and eventually dies from a heart attack. Drake decides to dive deeper into his studies and powers down his mother's private lab. He packs up her files, ties up loose strings, and closes the deal with the government. They have all they need to complete their objectives at this point. The government monitors him, speculating he might have pertinent information he could share with other oppositional government forces. They wonder if he, too, will continue his mother's work. But, the loss of his mother leaves him with grief he does not know how to deal with. He hopes to return someday, maybe later in his life; he will merge his acquired knowledge with his mother's work, but not now. He diverts their speculations by pursuing his architect engineer dreams and producing mobile vacation modules. The government loses concern regarding his sharing government secrets with others. It appears he has moved on and found his niche in life.

Drake loves time spent with his father. Drake's studies in Psychology help him bond with his dad. One activity they enjoy together is" people-watching." This leisure activity exercise hones their skills in reading people. They can ascertain personality types in a brief amount of time. They generally choose a public location where conferences and workshops congregate. They both use three categories to assess people. Each one takes a turn interpreting mannerisms, dress, and walking. Drake and his Father scope and predict the potential line of work with the accuracy of those specific persons they pick. The casual interaction with the people gives Drake and his father the information they need to support their speculation. However, they know the norm measurements they apply do not fit everyone. You know, kind of like the warning about depending solely on your side mirrors. It says something like the images may appear smaller than they are. They develop an article together for his Dads' writing agenda; it is something to do together that promotes a sense of enjoyment.

Drake and his father speculate that most people genuinely fall into one of three personality types: Low-key, Mid-key, and High-key. All three categories have good and bad qualities attached to them.

The Low-key personality type is a laid-back personality. They find it difficult to perform a task with much intensity, but they see it through. Their performance is due to their contentment at hand. They feel there is no need to make a fuss about anything. They operate out of the motive of just getting it done, which suits them well enough. They choose to apply themselves in a more straightforward frame of mind toward life. Perfection is not a motivating factor. They are more about operating out of a sense of freedom and allowing time to play. They would work, but only as much as they have to. It is not a joy to them to focus on working just for a paycheck. This personality type's duration rate is set aflame for a short period as needed and then put out. Because of the short spurts of stressful expenditure put forth, their life expectancy is prospectively longer.

The Mid-key personality type operates out of both the Low-key personality and the High-key personality type determined by motivation. These personality types must have a drive and purpose or reasonable goal that makes sense to be willing to perform to their end goal. They have to have interesting work for them to want to engage. They perform with quality efforts in both modes and can transition to the next gear of intense performance once they find something worthwhile to engage in. Given reasonable timeframes, if they have a practical purpose and logical goal aligned with their skill levels and interest, they will focus on that task until completion. They know how to juggle between work and play. They have the most balanced personality type. Their energy level moves at a steady burn. Their life span expectancy is typically labeled the normal range.

The High-key personality types are those that press themselves beyond expectations. These types are the most productive of all three-personality types. They have an intense passion for producing their best and are typically labeled perfectionists. It is hard for them to relax and turn off their creative minds. This personality type must intentionally schedule personal and family time. They are the ones that will forget to eat and sleep and fail to feed their children if the children do not remind them that they are hungry. They must incorporate breaks for good health. They are not likely to go to parties and naturally deflect socialization. They are the ones who sacrifice family and friends to finish the task to perfection. They have an instinct that insists on putting all their focus into finishing the job. Once the mission is complete, there can be a release of satisfaction. Scheduled downtime for self-health benefits and maintaining personal relationships must be in place with workable time restraints. Their life expectancy is shorter than the other two personality types. They are like a candle that burns at both ends.

Drake has a high rank in the "Procure Earth Society." They highly value his inherited and self-built expertise, skills, and wit to procure a better life for all humankind. Calculating where Drake falls under the three personality types, you would be correct if you placed him under the high-key personality ranking. His mother is a high-key personality, and his father's rank is a mid-key personality. Drake cannot produce any other product that falls "far from the apple tree." What passes down genetically and instructional through his parents is beneficial. Beyond genetics, his genius results from both parents' influence on him in their work. They contribute to who he is, and Drake appreciates both parents.

On his own, Drake moves forward with great faith to transform his ideas and ideals into a reality. It is typical for Inventive people to have High strung personalities, so Drake has to force himself to relax, disengage from his work, and ground himself with his family and friends. His mind is constantly in gear. He has to schedule quarterly periods where he purposely withdraws from creative thinking and takes time off to a remote location. It proves to refresh him.

At first, he would travel alone; however, later, he incorporated his family. He enjoys areas where he can interact with peaceful natural surroundings and pursue his hobby away from human contact as much as possible. His hobby is different from following a particular sports team or handyman projects. His hobby passes on from his mother, who would search for natural resources to promote good health and scientific advancements. His favorite vacation locations are where he can camp and search for specimens. He likes to go places with very little commercialism to distance himself from the noise and light that civilization generates.

Drake's dream is not far from his parents of ultimately creating, protecting, and extending humankind's life and procuring ways to preserve their world. Drake goes about it differently. Drake grows into a uniquely gifted and intuitive man. His knowledge expanded, and he obtained doctorates in both Automated Engineering and Architect Design. He has a master's degree in Biology, with a concentration in Botany, and has a minor in Psychology. He is motivated by making a name for himself, not just the notoriety of being his mother's or father's son. It gives him more options as to how he wants to contribute. He loves architectural design and creating mobile units with the advantages of incorporating new technology. His Architectural talents make him shine, and it adds another skill his family offers to the world to make positive changes for humanity.

Aside from the residual allure of the pinning of his parent's accolades, the "P.E.S." arrays on him, Drake prefers the attention he gets from the general public concerning his Architative module designs. He blends colors and textures that nature displays and adds innovative technology using minimal space. His models are highly sought after, and the people who purchase his designs find reprieve from the hustle and bustle of everyday life.

Drake uses his getaway module for the same intent but has special robotic assistance the general public does not have. These automated assistants and fully equipped lab are things he needs but hides so he can keep his true identity under wraps. He designs his outer shell like those he sells to the public using camouflage. He has a more complicated side undetected inside that the commoner would not suspect his module being any different than those he sells to the general public. It is one of these modules; he takes and uses it for temporary residence when he happens upon Wren.

CHAPTER 5

THE DEVELOPMENT

Biotechnology birthed new avenues for scientists and dreamers to solve sickness and disease. Their advancements enhance one another's existence and not eliminate it. The Procure Earth Society has become much more proactive and influential than the public can handle. The P.E.S. group wants to merge the natural attributes of botany with robotic enhancements. The general public view is starting to turn from thinking they have an excellent solution to it being a Frankenstein thing to do to people. They would have no part in tampering with The natural design God made. This leads the P.E.S. to find a place to continue their work without confrontation.

A financial team is formed and seeks to pull top-ranking market entrepreneurs from across the globe. Drake's father is one of those that contribute as a private investor. Since "Space Exploration" is halted on Earth, Elite Government personnel approaches the group with an option to use the abandoned Space Station. The Elite Government has authority and access to the Station's maintenance. The General governing sectors are uninformed and unaware of what the other higher levels of government do. The Space Station called The Dome and its based facilities on Earth are all disguised. The Space Station has mechanisms designed within its programming to detect and reflect any probe coming across them using a cloaking device. Any attempts to discover them from the earth are not likely.

Some contributors that fund the P.E.S. group choose to remain on Earth, while others go to the Science Dome stationed in space. Funds are generated, allowing the movement to place their scientist and equipment in the abandoned Space Station and the exodus of P.E.S. scientists and families from Earth's population to board. It is handled with discretion so the general "Commoner Government" cannot trace it.

The P.E.S Society scientists seek out Drake identifying him as a valuable addition to their dome group. Drake is one of the first Scientific Architect Engineers to go to the science space dome in the outer atmosphere above the earth. Who knew he would go from working alongside his mother in her private lab to working on the Dome in space? Though he has excellent architectural skills, and that's his field of preference, the P.E.S. society finds him to be a vital piece to their puzzle because he can access his mother's work. They present to him the importance of continuing and expanding the work his mother initiated. Only Drake worked alongside her and could access her work and secret lab. With his fresh mind and genius, The "Quiet Scientists" are optimistic about him bringing the breakthrough they seek.

He would work for the Quiet Scientist because they hide from the general population's view. With their obscurity, they operate to create a better existence for humankind through technology and obscure anomalies beneficial to healing. Whether or not the scientists ever come up with the formulas they are searching for, they know it is feasible, and all it needs is the right person to connect the dots. That in itself ignites their hope of seeing their vision through. Drake is a scientist they hope will reveal the missing link. Their scientist's objectives are not only interested in enhancing human life but in helping human life exist beyond life expectancy.

No one else could come close, in their opinion, to finding the formula to enhance the life of humankind than Drake. He is making progress, but it is not until after a tragic event that he drives to the point of finding the essential elements needed to succeed. The despair causes him to dig deeper into finding the solution to the science dream he and his mother have worked so hard to achieve. To escape the pain of losing his wife, he dives into his research and makes it his purpose to find the solution. If it had been in place before her death, maybe he could have prevented the loss of his beloved. Out of tragedy, hope replaces feelings of helplessness.

He expands upon his mother's research and makes it possible for humans to evolve into a race with more vitality and longer life expectancy. Drake is the Ace in the deck! Joining the "Quiet Scientist" team of experts, the P.E.S.

Dome's dream eventually comes to fruition. He is the science team's answer they have been hoping for. He brings the advanced technology he and his mother created. His experienced hand in developing robotics and formulas to enhance health is the sole purpose of finding a breakthrough. They are incorporating technology along with the natural workings of the human body.

The delicacies and uncertainties of the new science motivate the secret society to create a safety protocol from which to operate. There are questions they have to address. How would individuals be approved to participate in the science project? What statutes should be implemented so only willing individuals can participate in this new science? How do they properly prepare individuals that want to take the journey of becoming a Hume-au-tic? These persons will be the pioneers that evolve with regenerative abilities incorporated along with technology. Hume-autics could be free from death and decay. Although uncertain, they could possess a life that has no end.

The Procure Earth Society mostly lives on the Dome, leaving a few on Earth. On Earth, remote regions are specifically zoned, and Scientists can work in these zones or the Dome without fear of harm or interference. Approved members can travel back and forth to location sites spread out all over the earth.

This new scientific breakthrough carries the weight of the consequences of their meddling with the main design from the creator. A challenging and dangerous journey lies before them. Scientists must learn how to navigate the ripples that will likely occur, considering it is a new science. This science has never been done before, as far as they know. Good and bad results are up for review, and wrinkles need to be ironed out. It takes a multitude of deliberations among the team before they can generate a safe plan and list. They commence the journey of advancement not done before. The transformations' responsibility and after-effects are to be observed and altered as needed in a controlled environment. That is where the Space Dome needs to look deeper. The repercussions of the science team changing and tampering with things that have been sacred since creation are objectionable to most.

Changing the road we have only known to travel or entertain will lead to contentious and heated debates. Questions like: (dinosaurs): What would it be like today if someone had tampered with the ancient creatures' significant role in the evolution of the environment here on Earth? What if they never died and were still roaming our lands today? These questions provoke more and more questions. Scientists know they have to tread lightly and cautiously for the safety and management of the human race, their environment, and the cyclic rotation of life for all living things created. The Creator's "ancient cycle of life" method worked. The new replacing the old causes one generation to lead the next generation to move into higher levels of existence.

It must be addressed, however, that the resources needed for survival will eventually be exhausted. Since pollution and advancements continue, more than the recycling campaign is required to maintain a healthy environment that affects all life forms. Another conflictive proposal is the question regarding creation living longer due to the work of this new science. How would the world's population respond to the likely capacity limitations? In addition, it is most likely the government that would take control of the scientific breakthrough would gain immense power. It would leave room for someone to become a world leader and use this science to propel their reign. This leadership could use the knowledge to regulate unfavorable citizens. They might control the population by allowing fewer babies to be born or setting a life timeline of maturity allowance. The latter would mean that humanity might have a specific "time frame" to live. Not the Creator's designated time frame, but the flesh and blood man or woman in power. A "life to live" or not approval of the individual holding the highest rank. If sinister leadership decides this new wave of technical advances beneficial to their reign, it would be a travesty.

The limited resources available in a world that uses this new life science could mean life without measure. It would create definite conflict. Any environment and its variety of inhabitants could only safely handle a specific capacity of living creatures at one time. If the "normal cycle of life" is up for debate, and more individuals live longer, it becomes a "too much, not enough scenario." The lack of nutritional resources to sustain a healthy life for the larger population has always been a concern. With this new science, a dash of expansion that takes more resources and space makes the idea of longer life spans alone produce panic. One common expectation of the reactions to the new science among the population is that it will most likely provoke innate interactions with each other. A natural competition already present in the population's DNA will ignite as the "Survival of the fittest mode." It has been written repeatedly in history how the advantages of those more intelligent and assertive have no hesitation in thinking they have the suitable superior ranking to take what they want and annihilate those they take it from.

Movies from the past have covered some of these concerns. One film addresses the population and food shortage issue with a scenario of how an albino race living underground uses the humans that live above ground as their cattle. Those residing in caves below supply the inhabitants living on the Earth with food and comfortable lodging for a younger race of humans. These humans above ground living a "Garden of Eden" lifestyle becomes a satire: "fattened calves," so to speak. They effortlessly have all their resources given to them, yet, not without a sacrifice. This elaborate lifestyle is lived only up to a specific age. When the age limit matures, these humans are called to march into an opening in the mountain. It is as if they all are in a trance, numbly walking to the tune of a pied piper. Once they are beaconed to come, they enter a dark cave with a vast door closing behind them. Their loved ones and friends never see them again. It takes a time traveler from another time to witness the oddity of their population only having young people. He investigates and discovers the horror of what is taking place. He chooses to intervene and educates humankind. The people retaliate against these so-called keepers, and the survival of the fittest mode plays out.

Another movie deals with the dilemma of overly large populations by offering a way out. The setting of this movie starts with gray colors reflecting the atmosphere drained of life. It lacks beauty and the things that would please our five senses. It has high crime and oppression in this movie. The concern this filmmaker has is the overpopulation dilemma. In this film, they place the viewer in a position of "the what if's."They propose in the movie to give people the liberty to live or die. The reasoning is that there are always those that do not want to live anymore. (The depressed, mentally ill, elderly, and deceased.) So this government makes way for that to happen.

Willing participants enter an environmentally pleasant facility and sign an agreement. The world within this timespan has little or no experience with the beauty of seeing trees and flowers. The recordings of past times when things were once abundant appear across the panoramic view, and it is like a type of heaven to them.

People are ushered into a private room and asked to lie on a comfortable bed, having already chosen a panoramic scene. Music plays, and the scene starts playing on a screen surrounding them. Curtains are drawn. Using an intravenous drug, the willing participants pass into eternal sleep. Though this seems humane and acceptable because they were not forced or pulled from society, what happens after they pass is disturbing. After their lives end, these individuals are processed and made into food. They are distributed to the unsuspecting hungry population by truckloads. The trucks received by the people believe they are being taken care of by a compassionate government. The government is blindly trusted to supply food to the starving population. The truth is that the trucks deliver crackers made from recycled corpses unbeknownst to the receivers.

This period of time is one where having one jar of

jam in your cupboard is a luxury. The elite people are among those that know the truth, and only those being of high-ranking governmental positions have access to natural meats and preserves. The "black market" distributes rare food commodities to consumers where they can make the most profit. Someone exposes the truth to the people, and you can figure out the rest.

Both these imaginative but disturbing movies send a message from the artist observing and one thinking outside of the box to make their take on what could happen to humankind if they do not pay attention. The authors are hoping to get their point across. They consider what the consequences of their environment's neglect could entail. The first question is the effect the transition projects on the morals of humankind. They bring the reality that comes into play when humans must choose the options offered. What would you do to continue humankind's future existence in light of our growing population? How would you propose to meet the lack of resources to meet the needs of all living things? If, by some extraordinary means, we could solve the capacity issue and the exhaustion of resources needed to live through migration into space, then perhaps using the expanse of Space is not such a bad idea. It may be the answer to overpopulation, and the lack of natural resources needs addressing.

The P.E.S. group must require at this time for the science team to follow bi-laws that are only to transition fully mature adults who are psychologically fit Individuals. Children are not allowed the option to transition, and adults aged between 25 to 45 years old are the only ones allowed to engage in the transformation. This age requirement is necessary because the natural growth of human reasoning and coping abilities must already be naturally developed. Adults who choose not to transition can live out their days naturally but with some constraints.

Those not participating in the new scientific frontier will be treated fairly. The science team will address the issue immediately if an individual has an at-risk feature for a disease or weakening bodily function. Even with health monitoring, individuals operating at the optimum function in the natural realm cannot defer the inevitable decay that the "Creator of all creation" put into place using the Cycle of Life perimeters. The expectations of living a longer life among those that choose the natural function over enhancements are cared for, allowing natural decay to occur. Their DNA is the timer that determines the quality of life they will live. There are limitations to what interventions are available to help the body extend one's length of life. Those that chose not to transform would have to understand that their choice means their life will come to an evitable end. Their human body functions are operational for a span of time that only God knows how long.

A panel of scientists is assigned to monitor the acclimation of the advancements of persons choosing to become Hum-au-tics. The board makes sure they have emotional support as they transition. The physical health of all individuals on the Dome gets monitored. So whether one chooses to transform or not, individuals can still live long, productive lives.

For the citizens of the Dome, independent health monitoring devices are made readily available at will. They can gain personal updates on their health status.

This health module is a place of simplicity. No blood is withdrawn using needles or surgical invasion of the inner parts using scalpels. All intervening health repairs incorporate the use of supplements into their body through the ingestion of food, liquids, and laser-altering treatments.

It is essential to the P.E.S. to ensure no physical deficiencies occur among humans in their care. Take, for instance, the function of the heart. Science today recognizes, through extensive research, that the heart beats a specific number of beats before it stops. One heart doctor seen on TV believes the best thing to do for the heart, knowing it has a limited time to function, is to take a nap. There is an end to this way of life chosen, whether accidental or by design. All-natural humans will eventually die, and only The Creator knows how many beats an individual's heart is allotted.

Those already in their science dome who choose not to transform must accept that they cannot return to Earth. The team must take protective measures. These individuals could leak out the Procure Earth Society's location and secret agenda. In the past, humanity has shown limited positive reactions to change. They are not inept at readily accepting this kind of scientific breakthrough. Mayhem will most likely take place. Already the movement has experienced resistance and threats to their dream being attainable. That is why The P.E.S. chooses to go into seclusion.

A few individuals at a time are all the science team chooses to work with. Realistically, you must remember that the number of Hume-au-tics would increase after a while, and the dome's capacity will need to increase. Inevitably, there will only be logical occupational room for them to receive any more individuals than they had room for in the science dome. They would have to consider migrating elsewhere in space.

Stragglers that unexpectedly stumble upon one of their bases on Earth are taken into their custody. The Procure Earth Society secures them because they cannot risk exposure to the P.E.S. In those instances, the secret society has no other option but to keep those who stumbled upon them in the care of the Science Dome. They will return to a different lifestyle than they are accustomed to, and there is a sacrifice they have to incur for their haphazard intrusion. They are relocated to the Dome or other earth-based facility to respect their right to thrive.

Drake has clearance to travel back and forth from Earth to the Space Dome. He takes his health breaks from his job, using his personally designed mobile transport. He can travel to a vast number of locations secured by P.E.S. He uses this time to pursue more scientific resources for research, but just as importantly; he envelopes his experience to do things that relax him. Having no one around to distract him, he finds it rewarding to pursue his hobby in less human-occupied areas. On his excursions, he prepares by stocking his supplies with ample food for when he is designated to be away but always incorporates gathered vegetation found on site. He will venture into nearby communities to meet his needs if his supplies are dwindling.

Drake uses his robots as personal assistants and his security. When venturing out of his secure dwelling, he carefully selects public areas of low risk. While in a public setting, he has to be careful not to stand out to ward off exposure. Designing his dwelling, he uses a blend of technology disguised in natural-looking materials inspired by nature's environment. These specially designed pods allow him to venture into faraway worlds he otherwise would not be able to go.

The site he chose to camp when he encounters Wren is a new location that just got added to the list of safe zones. The Dome personnel designated it as a safe region to travel to. Drake schedules a mission to help the Waters install security. Security is put in place to ward off unauthorized individuals or groups, and Wren is one of those they would hope to ward off. Drake thinks how nice it would be if outsiders would only obey signs and stay within the borders of their property. If it were the case, the Waters would be more secure and have less chance of discovery by the violent opposition.

Drake is familiar with reactions the human race has with one another, repeating the same mistakes and sins of ages past. He knows how emotions affect actions and proves how people value what is important at that moment. Man's actions are never genuinely predictable. There will always be Wrens who, if dared, have no restraints to crossing lines. Among a few, she has no fear of stretching the limits and journeying across lines drawn meant to keep out intruders. Wren, of course, is one of those few who do not always follow the rules. If a practice does not make sense to her, it can open a window where she will allow herself to cross the line. Knowing this, he rarely encounters intruders who venture into his space. There are procedures that these getaway locations have to follow. The nature of the intruders that cross over is typical, those paying no mind to any trespassing boundaries posted because they reasoned that they are the exception to the rule. Number two, intruders are usually trespassers that grow unhealthy vegetation to sell for illegal profit. Therefore, property owners commonly use spy drones and security beacons to scare intruders off. Electric fences have monitoring cameras and heavily posted warning signs as standard property security equipment. In addition, security personnel will usher out intruders as needed.

Drake's father, Troy, remains among Earth's population living in hiding as much as possible. Though being a witty person, he takes the dangers of humankind seriously. He proposes not to live in the secured zones and chooses to live among the general population. He feels his writing will help promote change in how the common folk addresses the seriousness of the world's decline.

He uses a ghostwriter's name to remain anonymous and avoid direct public scrutiny. He hopes to reshape the population's mind in a way that helps them find better solutions for societal dilemmas. He uses wit, laughter, and psychology to buffer the harsh words of reality. He manipulates words and emotions to bring slight reprimands as he fills it safe to approach. He has mastered the language of saying complex things with a smile. He promotes positive thinking. He strives to impart to those that might listen to make a difference individually for the betterment of humankind. He holds to his conviction of being a voice to prepare the way for the future as long as he can operate on safe platforms.

Drake saw his father face to face only a few times after he went into hiding. When they did connect, it was a valued connection. They commonly use the "Lunaport communication system." set up on the moon base. It is risky for Drake to visit his father due to his involvement with society at the dome and the traveling back and forth. Drake is under strict protocol not to draw attention to his mysterious coming and going. There are specific times of the year when space modules are highly undetectable. Fall is commonly the best time to visit Earth, and it has something to do with a seasonal transition that clarifies the sky and transmissions. The standard population did not find any ties of Drake being with the undercover Society or his father because it would most likely be subjecting them both to harmful and deadly consequences; to get them to disclose the location of secret bases.

CHAPTER 6

INFLUENCE

Drake meets Corinne at a resort on the Dome. She coaches alternating groups on applying a healthy lifestyle to their hectic schedules. She trains to incorporate moments of relaxation and fitness into the everyday routines of her clients. She is like a breath of fresh air. She brings energy to her surroundings with beauty, wit, and joy. Corinne's hope is always to guide others toward healthier physical wholeness. Her strategies incorporated good eating, exercise, and relaxation to maintain good health. She particularly likes to bring others to the value of relaxation. Under her care, Corinne maintains records of each case and educates her constituents. Her goal is for each client to obtain a workable solution to help them shed bad habits and replace them with healthy ones. Laughter is a crucial element she imparts to her clients with a keen sense of humor. She believes it to be a natural release. Drake connects with Corinne after class.

"Hey, you are really into this fitness stuff, aren't you?

Corinne is surprised when he interrupts her while she focuses on putting equipment away. He jumps in to help her.

"First, thank you for helping. Your Dr. Silverman?"

"You may call me Drake." Corinne acknowledges him with a smile.

"My answer is yes, I am! It helps to know the whole dynamics of what makes a person tick. Learning how to relax and apply healthy eating and exercise habits promotes stability. I teach the intricacies of the unseen and seen parts of the body and how they have assignments or job descriptions that they must fulfill individually. Each unique part of the creation is custom-made with a purpose or job description. If one is not doing their assigned job, it negatively affects some other function. It leaches from others throwing everything out of kilter. They all need each to function in harmony individually to function as a whole." Drake is impressed.

"That is why I am here. My superiors have directed me here to gain a balanced lifestyle, and I guess they want me around to find the solutions they are pursuing. They say the pressures of work cause stress."

Corinne chuckles at his comment. She finishes putting on her backpack and heads toward the exit while replying to Drake.

"Yes, it does indeed! Unmanaged stress will cause health issues. To every action activated, there is a reaction that responds. Stress has a mode of defense that our bodies use to help relieve it. If it gets overburdened, it will take from something else to attempt to compensate and cause multiple areas to be depleted and become the root cause of many illnesses." Drake likes her certainty.

"Oh yeah, something to do with the hormones. I read about that. If you keep stress untamed, the hormones will not have enough time to build back up the reserve supply before another bout of stress presents itself." Corinne is surprised he knows about it.

"Yes, that's right! It will permeate bad energy to the depths of the bones within the human body and affect how well the body functions."

"That's interesting. I heard laughter is good medicine. Is that something you know anything about?" Corinne smiles.

Drake thinks Corinne is intriguing and wants more time with her. He opens the door.

"Corinne, I find you intriguing. Would you join me at the entertainment quadrant for some amusement later? They have a band and comedian presenting tonight. Since laughter is good medicine, I think it makes for a good time." She smiles and chuckles at his wit.

"Drake, that sounds doable. I have a few things to tend to, but I should be able to meet you there in a few hours."

They head out, stop and take another glimpse of one another and wave before heading in opposite directions. Drake makes arrangements for his date, calling in a favor from a friend to ensure they get a table. Corinne reschedules a date with someone she has acquaintance with through a friend. Drake seems nice, and she likes the vibes she is getting from him.

Corinne meets Drake later and sits down at a table Drake is already sitting at. She gets up to go to the counter to order some snacks and healthy drinks. She returns, and Drake is amused with what she has chosen for them to snack on. He admires her healthy frame of mind in work and play.

"So I see you have chosen a lighter version of food we are to eat."

Drake looks over the wontons she brings to the table with vitamin drinks. He helps her remove them from the tray and thanks her.

"I know It is a bit forward, but since you are in my class, I took the liberty to help you practice gaining a solid base for promoting a healthy lifestyle even when you go out for entertainment."

She takes a bite and continues to expound.

"Knowing how the body, mind, will, and emotions come together is important when determining a plan that best fits each individual. The combination of how nerves intertwine to the bone alignment and the influence of what types of food are ingested within the human body's cyclic process to regenerate itself supports one another to obtain optimum performance."

"So, can you look at someone's outer persona and see what's happening within? You know, with your trained eye?" Corinne raises her eyebrows.

"A map of what we are doing on the inside eventually shows up on the outside. It can be a warning sign. You can look at the condition of the skin, hair, nails, and even the eyes and see something is out of balance. If not addressed, it could be the onslaught of disease and health issues."

They take a moment to eat and watch the entertainment. Drakes realizes that Corinne's physical beauty and disposition combined make a potent combination. Drake enjoys her company and begins thinking about how he can make this meeting last longer and how to keep it going after this time together comes to a close. Perhaps the entertaining Dome Sports competitions and musical presentations are the events he can line up. His thoughts are interrupted by Corinne.

"Hey, Drake, you want to whirl on the dance floor? I love these nostalgic tunes."

"Well, not that I have any aptitude in this area; I would be happy to try it?"

Drake wants to learn more about her and discover what makes her tick. After a few dances, they return to their table and notice drinks waiting for them. The waitress comes by and points to a fellow at the bar, raising a glass to them. Drake recognizes his co-worker to be the one he called to secure him a table. He salutes him and turns his attention back to Corinne.

"A fermented drink this time and salted treats. Are you up for it?"

Corinne recognizes his friend and is a bit embarrassed since he is the one she ditched for another time. She shrugs and gives a sheepish grin in his direction while Drake looks at his Menu. She mouths, I'm sorry, and he nods and returns to his date. Apparently, he takes no time to recoup. Corinne responds to Drake's question about the drinks.

"I suppose it will be good, considering this is a night

of introspection for the both of us. I see you are looking at the menu. Are you going to order something?"

"Wow, I was not going there with the introspection yet, but maybe I will when I return to my quarters."

Corinne pauses to align her thoughts, contemplating what he might ask her next. She figures he will start asking for deeper details of her life. Drake takes over and orders more food.

"I am going to order us some more off the menu. Is this ok? Salty snacks are not enough."

Corinne approves and gives him her full attention preparing for his onslaught of questions.

"So tell me about your family. What influenced you?" Corinne jumps on the bandwagon.

"Let me see how I begin. I grew up in a household that encouraged me to think outside the box. My father is a business consultant who brings opposing sides to one unified solution. My mother's field of work is preserving historical documents. Her job is to preserve what is in the depth of the pages read. Using modern technology, she creates programs that duplicate historical events using realistic holograms. People can talk to the holograms and ask questions. The hologram experience is a new wave of storytelling. She hopes it will help humanity make connections to history they could not get in the old ways of teaching history. She says that history is cyclic and that man tends to keep in motion. She truly believes that unless the human race can heed the past and learn from it, humanity will not be able to break the repeat cycle and advance."

Corinne has her eye on him. Though Drake is inwardly figuring out how he will proceed in this encounter with her, Corinne makes the first move of suggesting they go on another date together. She is not interested in a playmate but in finding a partner to raise a family with.

Corinne and Drake court and genuinely love doing life together. She becomes Drake's biggest fan of his accomplishments, and he is hers. Together Life shows to be full of hope and wonder. Drake's success is a triumph for her. She fits nicely with him. Both of them use their talents to impact the world to be a better place to live. It is not hard since she is in the area of coaching a healthy lifestyle. She is a positive energy that spurs him onward. She loves that Drake has the same passion as his mother and carries her legacy.

Corinne's career gives her a sense of fulfillment though not at the level of Drake's notoriety. She loves how down-to-earth he is and not arrogant, as one would expect him to come from such a family line as the Silvermans. Corinne appreciates the organic and non-organic science that Drake brings to the table, and Drake appreciates the insight Corinne brings regarding proper nutrition, exercise, and rest. Both contributions are expressions to help others in need of a healthier lifestyle. She finds joy in having a purpose and being known as a positive influence in her client's life.

She works primarily with high-functioning-minded individuals since she is a part of the "Procure Earth Society" movement. She provides her clients with feasible plans to implement. The science foundation endorses promoting a healthy lifestyle for its group. They use Corinne and others like her to help the Dome residents to obtain their optimal potential. This line of work suits her, she finds it very fulfilling. This job is how she met Drake. He came in for a complete evaluation. While activating his plan, she finds him appealing. His first initiating conversation was impressive. She has always been able to keep her professional and personal life separate, yet this time things change. She likes that he has a zest for making life better. His passion aligns with hers.

Corinne and Drake eventually marry and, within three years, give birth to a little boy they name Jesse. Drake and Corinne are ecstatic about having a family. It is like uncovering a treasure. It is as precious and dear to their hearts as they ever thought possible. Both Corinne and Drake hold tight to the duty and responsibility of a parent to protect and nourish this little life given to them. The power of love that washes over them for this baby is a wonder. The protective mode instantly merges with great joy and yet with intense responsibility. No longer is the operation of their home about only Corinne and Drake, but now focused on the little life they are to raise. They both agree with what they wish to impart to Jesse. They want him to grow up to be a balanced man that becomes a productive, positive citizen of life on Earth and in space. The grand opportunity to pass on "the gold" they have uncovered in life to Jesse and any possible children who are part of the next generation is exhilarating. They are optimistic about the future.

Choosing the right baby name is essential, especially for Corinne. Her mother taught her that a good name is a valuable label to impart. Her birth name meant "beautiful maiden." A name is important because it imprints and declares an identity. It places an anointing and value on the person. Therefore, Drake and Corinne chose Jesse's name for their firstborn son because it derives from the biblical Hebrew definition: to be a gift, oblation: one who is. When anyone spoke his name, Corinne saw it as a declaration to the Universe. It is a name that offers the creator a heart of thankfulness and dedication, from decreeing that they would raise their child with the standards and love of the Creator of which he wants his children to operate. They want to honor the Creator for the beautiful gift and not take it for granted. Corinne is more in tune with the Biblical God. Drake has a hard time perceiving that the Creator is anyone more than a scientist.

Two years go by, and another child arrives. They name this baby girl Abigail. Drake suggests the name this time, and Corinne agrees it is good. He researches the name and finds that it derives from Hebrew and means: Father rejoiced or Father's joy. Abigail is born a beautiful, healthy baby with no defects reflecting the likeness of her mother. She has Corinne's plump lips, a tiny nose, and light hair. However beautiful the moment is to them, an immediate change to the course of their life together changes.

Corinne begins to show signs that prove to be concerning to her husband. While the assigned health professionals were doting on the little one they placed in the incubator, Corinne showed visible signs of distress beyond the norm after a healthy delivery. Drake calls for their attention, and the medical team sees the urgency unfolding and jumps into action. The newborn baby "Abigail" is swiftly swaddled up and laid aside safely in the nearby incubator. All attention then goes to tending to Corinne.

Complications came swiftly to the forefront and propelled Corinne into a dangerous decline. Drake helplessly looks on. He is aware that something went wrong during the birthing process. As soon as her declining health condition is understood, it is not enough time to intervene and have the outcome turn out differently. Immediately, the atmospheric celebration of new life transitions from a miraculous moment of giving birth to a moment of mourning for the one that ushered in that new life. The unrestrained medical team works to stabilize Corinne's rapid drop in her blood pressure, confirming that the team suspected it had to be a rupture. There is no rhyme or reason that this would occur to Drake's way of thinking because Corinne lives a healthy life. With all her health guidance for others, no one suspected this scenario to play out for her. It was astonishing and devastating how fast her descent occurred. It is like a ferocious storm coming out of nowhere and hovering over their room. It is pretty disturbing to all that witnessed her death. Teardrops stream from the medical team's faces as they handle the occurrence with hospital protocol and sadness. This event came in suddenly like a bank robber and stole away a young mother depriving her endeared ones of her physical presence.

Daunting numbness consumes Drake like "the soulmate of death," covering him with its wings. The very one that helps him through difficult times is now non-existent. He immerses his sorrow deep down inside him. He is shaken and angry and blames God. How could God allow this? He is momentarily incapacitated with anger and tears. As quickly as he feels anger, he knows he has to leave it to God. He did not know how he would ever recover. He takes a short leave from the room and finds a secluded hallway where he can put his true feelings before the Father of his Corinnes. He seeks her version of the creator's comfort. He entrusts all things to Heaven's perfect will, as she would have wanted him to. However, he is human and demonstrates the frailty of that garment. Though he knows all the right and good things about God's plan and intention for his children. He knows the right way to respond, but he cannot now. God's grace must cover his difficulty while dealing with the loss. His pain is immense and travels deep to the depths of his bones. He knows he does not appropriately respond to others while suffering from losing his best friend, partner, and mother to his children; he can only hope they understand and give him time. He withdraws from socializing and uses his research to distract him from his sorrow. He takes his already high key personality to a new level of intensity and drifts farther away from having fewer conversations with God. If Corinne were present with him, going through a dark time of losing someone dear to his soul, he would be better at coping. Yet, he has no Corinne to do that.

Their close friend Javelin immediately takes on the task of looking after his two children. She is Corinne's best friend and loves her family. Javelin knew Corinne's motherly aspirations. At that time, it is suitable for her. It helps her heal the loss of her precious friend by diving into the nurturing of her children in Corinne's and Drake's absence. Her intervention gives Drake the support to process and appear strong to his children during their crisis. Javelin brings peace and calm to their home, comforting the children and Drake. His emotional state exuded empty responses. He manages to walk among the living, existing, but not knowing how.

Drake has difficulty looking at his children and finding the strength to see past all their losses. He no longer has his adoring wife, and his children no longer have their mother. He struggles with the validity of it all. He feels as a father figure to his children should portray strength. At this moment in his fathering journey, he chooses to avoid grieving in the presence of his children and finds other ways to cope. He starts staying at work later, and later, he leaves Javelin primarily to nurture his children. It becomes a common day-to-day occurrence, choosing not to participate in the rearing of his little ones. He feels inadequate and amputated from the one person that made sense to him. She is the reason he has his children. After losing her and putting his children into Javelin's stable, loving hands helps him regain some sanity and continue with his and Corinne's life's passion; to procure and help make the world a better place. Receiving Javelin's Help is the only logical way he can function with his vulnerability. He uses this time to regain his sight and stop the spinning in an upside-down emotional experience.

Sitting at his desk in his lab, he reflects on his late wife's notable traits. He recalls her positive outlook on life. She operated from her motto, "Each day living in the present brings more value than the weight of the past." She was content with her life and appreciated the days she was ordained to live. She imparted encouragement and support wherever she trod. She could make you abruptly laugh at the least expected times.

Having relaxed at his desk with a brew and sandwich,

Drake sinks into deep thought. He sifts through his recollection of how things went down in the maternity ward and focuses on precious moments he had with her. After raising his hot brew to his chest, "heart high," positions himself to bring back the warmth of her touch. He recalls feeling much joy being with her and their new baby. What a highlight it was seeing her hold Abigail and remembering her delight. It brought a smile to his face. He quickly remembers how rapidly the light of joy flashing across her face faded. Darkness begins shading her face as her countenance drains away. It appears as if she slips away in a blink of an eye.

He remembers how his heart hurt for her and his newborn daughter and toddler son. They did not even have that time allowance to develop a bond a mother and child should experience. He remembers how she smiled softly for her husband and new baby girl. The medical team stood by and gave the couple time to transition from what was inevitable. Corinne knew she would not recover and mustered all the strength she could in her condition. Drake joins Corinne by gently lying on the bed beside her. He cradles her in his arms and tries to encourage her not to give up.

"You are not leaving; you hear me!"

Tears drip down his cheeks like soft rain. He strokes her head and declares over her,

"It is all right; you will be ok!"

Drake draws close enough to her so that he can hear her last wishes. She whispers in his ear words that she will never speak to him here on earth again. At last, sensing her time was drawing near; she whispered one last time to him. She informs him she will be in Heaven soon and that he needs to find strength in God to raise their new baby girl along with Jessie.

"They are our gifts from heaven! They will be your joy."

She reminds him of her request in the "Will " that her best friend Javelin can support him in this. She grabs his shirt in desperation to hear his verbal agreement. She needs to listen to him say it aloud, so he will do as she asks. It was as if hearing him say it would give her peace. He remembered how hard it was to breathe and how hard it was to process the thought of losing her.

Dabbing her tears from her eyes with a handkerchief, he tucks it in his shirt pocket and kisses each closed eye and forehead. She was gone. He shutters at the remembrance. He attempted to take every attribute of her face while she sank softly into her pillow, empty of the life he once knew. She passed on to the eternal threshold a promise to God's children of faith. Mother and wife lifted to the jubilant arms of the Heavenly hosts. He had heard that angels accompany those who departed from their earthly vessels. Looking up to the ceiling indicating the Heavenlys were listening, he shouts.

"You take care of her, you hear!"

He reads in Ecclesiastes. To heaven, death is a time of jubilation to have the children return. If you think about it, it does make sense that the Father would be happy the suffering of this world was over for His child, and their life now is in His presence. All those left behind must presume "The Comforter" will be sent to help them deal with the trauma. His friends and family petition God's comfort. A chaplain enters and imparts some advice.

"Only the Father can disperse the peace that surpasses our understanding. He knits together the open wound. May God send ministering angels of comfort to blanket your family."

A nurse steps forward.

"If I may, I want to suggest that God might send an ordained bird or animal to bring a sense of comfort. It might come through a child's laughter, a word, a touch, a song, a smile, or a fragrance. Whatever his approach, he has many ways to bring comfort." The Domes chaplain interjects.

"Yes, thank you, sister. It is known in our faith that there are seasons we live joyfully and seasons we may suffer. I want you to know that when we experience the death of a loved one, and we know they are His child, it is comforting to know that they will be going to a better place. They are redeemed from sin and dwell in His presence. Knowing that a loved one is with God and that it is not their end becomes a great comfort. There is a life after death, and aligning with the Father's heart gives us hope to see our loved ones again. Heaven is a place where pain and suffering are not. It's a place of beauty, light, and everlasting love."

Drake knows the promise of life after death for those who believe in His son Jesus should be happy, but happiness is subdued; by the shadow of grief. Even knowing all the ideals encompassing Heaven, Drake feels great anger towards the injustice of his loss. He does not deny that Corinne is in a better place, and it's the wreck left behind due to her going to a better place that is more weighty.

He, his children, and her family are now without a wife, a daughter, a friend, and a mother.

First, he could only remember to breathe in and out. Eating is a forgotten pleasure. Darkness shadows his face. Thoughts of how he will continue functioning without Corinne loom over him like a perpetual dark cloud. He thinks of his future in these weak moments, certainly looking bleak. His "great love" is gone. He feels as if the color has drained out of the world. His existence feels in comparison to a broken vase. Javelin helps Drake tremendously. Knowing she will provide the children with a female presence gives him peace. She will provide them with the nurturing that only a woman can give. She will be more sensitive to their needs.

Acting alone now as a single parent is difficult for him. Javelin proves to be a great support. Both Javelin and her father suffered that loss when her mother passed. When Drake would leave for work, Javelin would impart words of comfort. She reminds him,

" There will be phases of grief: anger and denial, and they are all part of a process God put into place. It sounds cliche, but time is the ultimate factor in emotional healing from losing a loved one.

It is ok not to be so hard on yourself during this time."

He looks at her with gratitude but also irritation. How can she truly know how he is feeling? Sure, she lost her mother, but how does that compare to losing a spouse? She sees he is not getting it.

"Drake Corinne's God is your God. God knows how much you can handle and what you are going through."

Drake nods in acknowledgment of her meaning well. He leaves for work, pondering things.

At first, his mind processes things slowly. He knows he is not thinking clearly. But he knows things will get better from what others are telling him. Hearing that gives him hope he will see the light at the end of the tunnel eventually. The healing process will progress, and he will gain better functioning with time. It's not like an ailment; you can take an antibiotic, and in 7 days, you're cured. It takes months, even years, to work through. There is a reason the experts suggest not making any major life decisions during the first year after the passing of a loved one. He notices that he has bouts where he cannot recall colleagues' names. He gets through those embarrassing moments by extending a "hey," when passing by them in the corridors of their work environment.

Drake adores his son Jesse and daughter Abigail. He hopes it is true what the experts say regarding the resilience of children. He did not want this temporary situation to thwart their development. Because of his heart for them, he decides he needs higher help. He begins to pray, pursuing the Father's solution. He is asking that his failures and fumbling during this recovery will not harm his children but only strengthen them.

The Dome health professionals assign a team to monitor the family. Having a team helps Javelin tend to her personal needs and not get so caught up in someone else's life that she loses her own. The children's daily schedules contain activities that promote a healthy frame of mind and physical strengthing.

Javelin and Drake agree with Corinne's plans to join

forces to care for the children. This situation poses a problem. The Dome counsels are aware of the dynamics. They counsel the two to remember what is real and what is not. If the two develop an intimate bond as two adults, It will jeopardize other relationships. Drake and Javelin know what others might think, including her fiance and his family. They agreed to keep their relationship platonic. They love one another, yet in a different way. Neither one, out of respect for Corinne, would ever consider their relationship to go beyond friendship. Even at that, they did have a close call. It was during one night when the two were celebrating one of his breakthroughs. The children were in bed, and they were drinking champagne. They hugged each other at one point, and it became an awkward moment. Drake kisses her and throws them into shock. It was purely innocent and expected. They back away from each other, and Drake apologizes. Holding onto their drinking glasses hovering over the rails, they toast his accomplishments. They chatter about the kids and his workday. It is a relief they have things to talk about. They stopped when Drake replenished their half-empty glasses. They look intently at each other, rapidly mulling over what would or would not occur. There is a moment of doubt regarding their agreement for friendship. However, with their mutual respect for Corinne, they did not.

"It is good to know you have room to love again, and you can move on." Javelin noted.

"I have someone and do not want things to get complicated." Embarrassed, Drake responds.

"Yes, you are right. It would be a bad idea to pursue a relationship with our friend. I know the kids would not be able to handle that, I am afraid, and you are right. You are engaged."

Both distance themselves from each other. They chuckle at a few wisecracks Drake makes and finely return to their quarters. She cannot work her regular job while caring for Drake and Corinne's children. She is given compensation from the security funds between Drake and Corinne. Javelin never stays in their quarters unless Drake is gone, and she is only there for the children. She has designated time to be with her fiance. She has to make sure to nurture her relationship with her fiance. All who care for her want her to marry and have a family.

Javelin accepts his proposal with the condition she has time to help her best friend's family transition to a healthy place first. In time, Javelin marries her fiancé Zack, and Drake and his children participate in the ceremony. They quickly have a family and become Drakes and his children's extended family. They become like an uncle and aunt to Drake's kids, and their kids become like cousins to Jesse and Abigail.

CHAPTER 7

ON THE MEND

While Javelin is supporting Drake and his family, the Science Board is carefully monitoring how he is processing his mourning. He has to be under health surveillance and administered authority-prescribed nutrients appropriate to sustain a healthy life. He has mandated appointments scheduled for psychological therapy. The science team is sorry that he lost his wife, but the reality is they need him. They are so close to finding the missing links to the science his mother worked so long to achieve. He is a vital source of their growth and scientific advancements. It would be a tragedy for the Society of P.E.S to lose the momentum they were operating against time to complete the process of finding solutions to saving humankind.

Drake does follow the board's guidelines to maintain a healthy life. He seeks counseling and takes vacations. As a father, he loves his children and celebrates life with them to the best of his ability. However, it is work that he finds himself having some point of normalcy. This part of his life is his area of expertise. Work gives him a sense of value and purpose, and it just makes sense to him.

On the other hand, child-rearing is challenging, not predictable, and makes no sense. He found no manual written that could teach him the perfect things to say or do for his children, and it is a hit or miss daily. However, on the other hand, he knows he can do his research excellently, what to put in, and what will come from his input.

Drake feels he is on the brink of finding the ultimate scientific breakthrough. He wishes Corinne was there to share it; he misses having her beside him. No one should have to deal with the loss and kind of pain he and his children have to suffer through. Yet, this traumatic life occurrence drives him to find the breakthrough his science team seeks. Therefore, looking at things positively regarding her death produces good things despite only dwelling on the significant loss. He chooses to forge ahead past his grief, pouring himself into something he has some understanding and control over. His creative, innovative home technology designs benefit the future way of vacationing. His advances built upon his mother's research have led to a new wave of living with life-altering discoveries.

It takes precisely two years for him to take on the full responsibility of raising his children. He keeps up appearances as if everything is ok, but his spirit is waning. Those two years, he knows, are not his best being there for his children. He did not always return home promptly and relieve Javelin initially, but he eventually came to a stable point where he could wean Javelin and the children from each other. He did not want to impose on Javelin any longer and take advantage of her kindness. He started looking forward to coming home and shared his day with Javelin and the kids. Javelin starts leaving sooner, and then he begins bonding with his children. They love playing games together after their evening meal.

The family enters the soothing family station as the night draws near bedtime. There, they spend precious time together listening to their mother's voice previously recorded. She lived a life having a relationship with the Lord before her death. She prerecorded bible stories and several others she liked as a child. She shared cherished family memories incorporating stories of how she and their daddy met. She sang and laughed with them as she told silly jokes. Her laughter filled their hearts with joy. It soothed them, and they often fell asleep, all cuddled together. After they fell asleep, Drake laid them each in their beds and returned to the soothing station to listen to her until he fell asleep. Jesse often would get up to use the restroom and cover his dad with a blanket. He never commented on his excellent jesters to his father. Self-taught, he thought it was not the right thing to do to bring attention to his hero's vulnerabilities. Sadly, maturity comes quickly to young Jesse with the loss of his mother and concerns for his father.

The transition that helps Drake and the kids break free into their routine apart from Javelin is the excursions they go on. He takes his family to his favored locations using one of his designed techno pods. Drake's top destination choice is Planet Gustus. At this time, Drake passes on his mother and their grandmother's passion to Jesse and Abigail. They learn how to forage for food and study the significance of the greenery and attributes suitable for healthy consumption. He teaches them how to make notes and drawings in their journals to help tag and categorize all types of plant life. He taught them how to maintain their crafts and small robotics.

Hiking is one of the children's most enjoyable activities. They trek through rugged terrain, which helps build physical strength and endurance. An additional bonus for Drake is teaching them how to map unknown territory. Water abounds on Gustus, and they filter it. They all gain a closer connection during these excursions. Jesse and Abigail learn a lot from their father during these excursions and hold them dear to their heart as cherished memories. Their father is their hero, and they love him dearly. They are a united family scarred from life's blows but made stronger because of it. Whatever may come their way, they are tougher and prepared to meet that challenge.

Time does heal. The intensity of his loss did weaken. Drake succeeds in finding a path he can comfortably provide a new life for his family of three. The children must take responsibility for looking out for themselves and sometimes intervene for those around them. There are dangerous lifeforms that reside in all habitats. Ethically, the natives have first rights and claims to their native habitat. His children's first moral code of world exploration is to maintain respect for all environments and habitats of native entities. They will have to adjust to threatening situations at a moment's notice. Their safety is the top priority. Acknowledging the life surrounding them in any location equips them to remain actively alert. Most urgently, they had to be on alert for Non-native hostile life forms visiting the same planet.

Specific things to be aware of are indeed luring to the eye but may be dangerous. Swamp areas containing bubbling waters are inviting attractions where most non-residential life forms migrate and find their end. Beyond the borders of the beautiful vegetation also lie waters where the native occupants live in the depths. Those creatures render eminent danger to any entering or nearing its waters edges. The expansive mountain ranges on Gustus radiate seemingly innocent lush vegetation but could also render danger. Anything they might encounter, even those things that seem endearingly small and thought insignificant, could very well be deadly. Likewise, they could come across something that appears ominous and of no threat. In any case, being aware of your surroundings will help prevent a potentially deadly outcome.

At times, the mountain tops have a frosty topping of haze, giving way to soft orange beneath. Just below the orange formations are carpeted lime green and white grasses that glow at night. Various vines, trees, and shrubbery serve as an expansive canopy that other life forms find suitable for refuge and a place to call home. Numerous amounts of unique vegetation stretch out beyond what the eye can see. Dangerous caves and dark holes litter the expansive terrain. These are very likely havens of dangerous inhabitants. These common areas are places where rogue aliens or native critters hide. They fear the ramifications of their most recent altercations they fled. Realistically, if they think you have something they need, they will attempt to take it with no regard for your life. Your only value to them is but another resource for their subsidence.

Jesse keeps a journal of their adventures. He values his father's heart and knows that the strict guidelines and standards his father put in place are to procure their safety out of love and respect for others.

The landing pad and its selected boundaries must be "all clear" before claiming an area to set up camp. His father will first check the planet's activity against threatening weather conditions. Next, the item he checks off is ensuring the area is clear from potential enemies his news sources would suggest possibly inhabiting their location.

Drake selects a space previously mapped area that is clear of imposing danger. He launches beacons to create a safe perimeter for them to land. After the Pod is positioned safely on the landing pad, Beacon Bots transition to security mode. They are equipped with lasers to stun and designed to discourage intruders from coming too close to them.

Security works in different phases. Once the desired perimeter is occupied, Bot Security will observe the outside area from the pod monitors inside. If the bots detect possible danger or intruders, they notify Drake via cellular communication and changes in pod lighting. The lighting variations inside the pod signify modes of safety. It is a necessary tactic to give occupants inside the module ample time to take defensive measures.

The bots' mode of operation is the same type of small aerodynamic bots once used in the lab he and his mother used. Proceeding to the intruder's location, the alerted protectors quickly maneuver to set themselves up to monitor the perimeter. The orb's glow activates through a rotating pattern of flashing lights. The lights are to indicate danger. After flying to any known intruder deemed a looming threat, these bots warn the unwanted trespasser. First, they vocalize orders for the intruders to cease advancing towards their perimeter of claim to stay and move away. The bots already have a pinpoint laser positioned purposely on a vulnerability that renders incapacitating consequences to the imposing threat. These bots have the weaponry to produce stronger shocks than the first perimeter bots. Since the first shocks did not stop intruders and their advances, the last bots distributed shocks to levels of strength that could result in death or severe injury.

For the module's occupant's additional safety, Drake has tracking medallions sewn into the fabric of each crewmember's vests and belts. The medallions send vibrations to the wearer when an intruder is nearing their position. They provide a sufficient warning so the wearers have enough time to retreat to their module. Additionally, their garments carry valuable tools and hidden chips that track the whereabouts of the person wearing the security garments. Belts contain slots that hold stunners, shooters, and warning flares. Packs are prepared with camping gear and scavenger gear to obtain vegetation and other samples. A voice-activated force field bubble device is in a pocket of the forearm sleeve. It has the lasting power of a 48-hour timeframe commonly used to protect against predators if needed until help can come and retrieve them.

Once back inside under the security of their shelter and still threatened by oncoming intruders, the crew is to use powerful resources to ward off those wishing to harm them. Blue Sentinel droids will go out and position around the pod and set a netting of protection in the form of outward laser beams creating a dome of protection. Shock waves pulsate out to the perimeter lines set. Those shock waves produce a hot, tingling sensation and will toss intruders off their footing. It is with the expectation that it will send intruders away with but a small exposure of discomfort.

The next phase of protective security is the activation of the defense sentinels. These bots have tracking capabilities and defensive means of eradicating those who continue their aggressive behavior toward the pod's occupants. The last phase of security is incorporating the pod rocket fire. It comes from the top of the Pod to maneuver at all angles. Monitors inside the pod provide a visual for the crew of any intruders. Shields activate with the ultimate safety measure against attack. It is the tactic to "tuck tail" and safely exit back to space.

CHAPTER 8

SPIRITUAL ROOTS

Wren credits her parents and family for shaping her into who she is. They all are spiritual people and have imparted that to her. The most beneficial thing she feels they have imparted to her is that God wants to have a personal relationship with her and wants her to want to spend time with Him. Nothing is too small to bring before Him.

William is not just a father but the Ranch's CEO. He promotes unity in the family. He believes in prayer and earnestly intercedes for his family, community, and world. Both Wren's parents, Caroline and William, have a solid relationship. Her dad taught Wren how to hunt and Cassidy how to use a crossbow. He has no sons, and having daughters to pass his hobbies on to was awesome. Her mother, Caroline, is a renowned artist. She leads with strength and independence. She encourages her daughters, Wren and

Cassidy, and all women to appreciate who they are and be empowered to be a woman. She respects her husband and hopes not to fall short of making known his value to her. Their goal as godly parents is to train their family in a way that produces individuals of good character. They want them to be lights that pierce the darkness making the world a better place. Their Christian standards are to be the driving force of producing people of integrity and excellence for their Heavenly Father's Glory.

Grandfather Theodore and her Grandmother Lola pioneered the ranch. They decide to pass the ranch on to the family. Guidelines direct a percentage of the funds from the farm's profits back to them. It will help support her grandparents as they travel. They handed over the ranch after first making a few smart investments. They have a nice nest egg. They did not want to cause any strain on the ranch's financials, and it gave them the freedom to travel and support their missionary son and daughter-in-law, who are ministering to the people of St. Lucia.

The remaining funds are to provide the funds to operate the ranch and its families' financial compensation for the jobs they individually are responsible for. William oversees the ranch's overall operation, ensuring new growth and productivity. William divides the ranch acreage into sections for family living, ranch livestock, and ranch farming. Other jobs on the ranch go to the rest of the family.

Wren's Grandparents, Tod, and Mary, on her mother's side, also live with them. After losing their home to a forest fire in Colorado, they relocate to the ranch to be actively involved in their grandchildren's lives. They live in a wing addition they renovated on the upper level of the main house. They had an elevator installed so they could continue to use the wing if they ever had mobility issues. They are responsible for the cooking, carpentry, gardens, and chickens.

Uncle Spence is one of Wren's favorite people. Her mother's brother is provided a cabin on the land designated for the overseer of the designated wildlife preserve. All kinds of birds are taking sanctuary here. He has created paths to walk and bird-watching towers. He chooses to live a minimalist life. He built a platform on the third level of his cabin so he would have easier access to the feeders. With this setup, he can sit in his living room and watch the birds feed and thrive. A mic attached outside his cabin allows him to hear the sounds of birds and other woodland noises while observing through a one-way tinted glass. The one-way window view is so the birds are not spooked, providing him with entertainment to watch and hear them.

He has many sides to him, as most people do. But he particularly loves teaching Defense Training. He has a watchful heart concerning his nieces and nephews and gives them advice.

"The world is beautiful, but you must always be alert to what is happening around you. Hidden dangers can lurk within some things that appear harmless and attractive. Being caught off guard can lead you into a dangerous situation. It is helpful to gain an understanding that will help you walk with confidence living without fear in a troubled world."

Her Aunt, Sari, is a sister to Wren's father. She moves

to the ranch after the loss of her husband. Having a place for her and her children is a God send. The other ranch families transform a barn into a home. It is an open-concept and modern dwelling suited for each of her children's needs. Ty-Yung, her adopted son, has a loft to support his photography. Ty-Yung latches on to Wren's uncle Spence since their move to the ranch. Since the loss of his father, Spence is someone that took him under his wing. While hanging around Uncle Spence, he is learning to care for the cattle, seeding, and harvest. He enjoys supporting Uncle Spence with the nature reserve. That is a bonus for him because it gives him a resource for his photography. He loves to take pictures of wildlife and greenery in the protected land. His loft displays photos posted on his walls and strings strung across the room. He uses the preservation zone to perfect his photography and catalogs his finds. To Ty-Yung, art is a practice of rediscovering things long forgotten or taken for granted.

Aunt Sari takes the position of the Ranches' Financial Administrator, with Cassidy Wren's sister being her co-pilot. Once she accepted the job, the ranch's jobs aligned with what best suited everyone. As part of the ranch family, Liddy's chore is to help both Wren care for the horses and her grandparents with their gardens. In Liddy's spare time, she makes jewelry, weaves bracelets and earrings, and grows potted plants. She likes to sell them. Young April loves animals. She wants to be a veterinarian someday. Her chore is supporting Grandpa with the chickens and feeding and grooming the barn cats and dogs. She also practices grooming chickens for the county fair. She loves watching the birthing of any farm animal. The veterinarian took a shine to her and took her under his wing by mentoring her. He shares his knowledge about the medical end of caring for them. He allows her a special pass to access the veterinarian hospital and helps manage the pets boarding there. He sees great potential in her. She admires him. Aunt Sari and her three children, Ty-Yung, age 12, Liddy, age 16, and April, age 10, are delighted with their new residence.

Being considered a young adult, Wren builds her independence and rides alone to a small mountaintop she calls "The High Place." She loves to spend time with God there, and Wren likes the privacy this place provides her. She can worship, play her instrument, shout, sing, or dance without judgment. Wren appreciates all facets of nature on the mountaintop. She imagines the tapestry of greenery surrounding her, joining her in worship with their fragrance, sounds, and colors. She amuses herself at the thought. She likes to think that nature's praise is hard to detect by human ears, but God, the creator of all languages, understands. Wren chuckles as she touches the wild violets, and she asks them:

"Do you praise the Father?"

Cupping her ear with her hand, she pretends to hear a response.

"What! You don't say?"

A sense of tranquility overcomes Wren. A squirrel is directly above her in the groove of two tree extremities. It is diligently munching on a snack. Small pieces of debris softly float down onto Wren's hair. Though surprised, Wren is pleased to meet its acquaintance. She jumps up using both hands, smacking her head to rid the squirrel's leftovers arrayed on her head.

"Oh, it's like that, is it? Ok, I will find another place to sit."

She continues to wipe away that which remains on her hair. She laughs and resumes her thoughts. She looks at the violets and thinks if they have a language that praises God. The story of Elisha comes to mind. It is a bible story she heard as a little girl. She found it magical. It is the mystery of the things that are present but not seen. She loves reading stories that relay experiences of seeing angels. Sometimes they have said that people can see another realm if God allows it. She begins to share her interesting tale with the squirrel.

"Ok, I have a story to tell you. Once there was a time that a great battle was going on. It appeared as if there was no chance of one side beating the other because they were outnumbered. A God-fearing leader named Elisha was observing the battle from a place he could look out over the expanse of the battlefield. A fellow servant came to report their pending defeat because he witnessed the enemy's great number of warriors outnumbering theirs. Well, the man named Elisha saw a different picture. God had removed a veil that kept man from seeing the angelic realm. When God lifted the veil, Elisha saw numerous heavenly angels fighting in the field against their enemy. The servant could not see until the man Elisha prayed and asked God to remove the veil so he, too, could see. He saw them! It had to be an amazing experience!"

The squirrel seems interested in her chatter and jumps downward as if trying to get a better look at this strange human moving about beneath it. The squirrel chatters at her.

"Well, now you are quite the talker. Do you know what I just shared? I think that is what happens with the violets over there."

Wren points in the direction for the squirrel to look at.

"I imagine they are displaying their praise to God. Seeing angels is not commonly heard or expected in everyday occurrences. However, Mr. Nutcracker, yes, that is your name now. The Bible says Angels are among us."

She then turns away from it, lifts her face to the sky, and twirls around. She prays that she could see angels someday and hopes to see them before her passing. The squirrel stops and pauses before it leaps lower and lower from branch to branch. It finally reaches the bottom of the tree and hurries off to a new location beyond her scope of vision. Wren responds to the squirrel's departure with.

"You're likely acquiring another nut to crack."

She smiles at the pun she let escape from her lips.

At the ranch, Wren's parents discuss her departure from the pasture. Her parents know she escapes now and then, and they are ok with it. Their parental wisdom understands that both their girls need room to test their boundaries. They purposely step aside so their girls can fly. They know they will not stay in the nest forever. When they leave the ranch, they want their daughters to soar.

CHAPTER 9

THE DANCE

It has been a few days since Drake first encountered Wren. It is difficult not to think about her. Their meeting is amusing initially, but now his thoughts of her are disruptive and annoying. Not that she is doing anything worthy of being called annoying, and he would have to say, he is annoyed more with himself for not being able to stop thinking about her.

Thoughts of her riding the horse with her glistening hair and long legs tormented him. He is not able to sleep without dreaming of her. It just is not good to have any more contact with her, and he wishes to abandon any thought of pursuit. Yet with all his attempts and despite his logical assertions and the wrestling with his self-made guidelines, today, he will put that logic by the wayside and plans to investigate higher ground. He gives himself a reasonable excuse to find her secret place. He exhausts the low land resources, so why not move up, he told himself. Yes, there is no doubt he will attempt to find the location Wren descended from while he is moving up. If she fusses at him, he will tell her his truth. He might come across that charming place she mentions since he is in the area.

Drake wonders why Wren would risk getting in trouble for trespassing. It has to be a place of beauty. He finds himself moving more aggressively through the brush. He bends down, surveying the ground, and pauses to pick a few wild berries. He feels the texture of the leaves and takes in their fragrance. The variations of the colors indicate which ones are ripe. As he places one in his mouth, more questions come to mind. What place would embrace her heart and entice her to free the music from her soul? What place would beckon her to go alone? The path she came down was ahead. All he would have to do to help find her sacred place would be to follow parallel to the beaten path. He kept within visual proximity of the trail but reasonably hidden.

He decides to take a laid-back mode, using the cloaking of the greenery to stay out of unexpected eyes. It is a secret place, and he suspects Wren would not likely approve of his intrusion. Drake proceeds with a twofold quest. One part is to look for herbs and new species unknown to him, and in that, two would be the chance he might stumble across the cherished location of Wren McCarthy.

Drake successfully finds things to put in his pouch, but he is more into the hunt to unveil the mystery of Wren's unique haven. He eventually comes to a place where the path appears to end. Coming out of the brush, he stands in a forked location with two looming obstructions. A large group of red boulders and a rock arch hovered over a trickling stream. Humorously he becomes aware of an innate pulling that stirs up an urgency created by the sounds of nature. The sound of a trickling stream brought to his forethought the need to find cover and release the now-pressing issue. That "nature call" easily remedied itself by quickly stepping to a nearby tree and taking that moment needed. While in that process, he verbalizes without thinking.

"Oh, how amazing simple pleasures are by taking the timeout to look and listen."

He always feels that true beauty is in the natural. He discovered once the noises of man's expansion of the hustle and bustle of life are gone beyond ear reach, nature reveals its splendor. He takes a moment to look at the height of the trees. His senses take in the woods' sounds, scents, and textures. Wind moving through the trees seems to sound like the ocean. If you listen, you can hear the trees creaking, birds and crickets chirping, squirrels and chipmunks scurrying along the ground, and woodpeckers echoing their food hunt by rapidly hitting the wood hard in search of insects. He could smell green, wood, and earth by applying deep breathing exercises and closing his eyes. He feels the wind's caress against his face and imagines Corinne touching his face with her hand. Using all five senses, he takes it all in and savors the variety from nature's menu.

Leaning against a pine tree, he notices the pine needles on the ground and that they prove to be a natural weed preventer, a natural mulch. He stops and starts gathering large pine needles. He learned how to weave them into a small basket. He experienced making one in the camp when he was young. He will tuck it in his pouch and make a basket later in his module. He realizes he got distracted.

"Ok, now let us get back to our hunt Drake," he tells himself.

Being able to laugh at himself is healthy. He returns, searching for signs of a path she and her horse may have taken. Animals like deer and the like always left narrow worn paths that humans could follow. That may be what he should use. He looks down at the base of the rock archway and discovers a narrow path, believing it is big enough for her and her horse to follow. Looking down at the clay earth, he bends to look more closely and sees faint markings of horse prints.

"This might be it, dear Watson." He moves the debris and notices horse hoof imprints.

"This may be the place she let her horse drink."

He stops and ponders the possibilities of how to find her secret location. One idea comes to mind. He could return early in the morning and find a place to have a stakeout. Then he could follow her unbeknownst to her. He combs his fingers through his thick hair.

"No, that would not be right. It would look like I am stalking her, for Pete's sake! That could be perceived the wrong way."

He did not want to offend her or her family. In addition, he wanted to avoid bringing more attention to himself. He decides to remain distant and just find the place himself. He tracks a bit more and concludes he went as far as he could for the day. At least he felt it possible to find her place with his lead on what direction she took. He has to retreat for now, but there will be another day.

Not far away, Wren struggles with thoughts of the man she met in the clearing. It is earth-shaking to her now as she thinks back on the event. She asks herself why she is so stupid to have approached him. She is putting herself at significant risk. She should have high-tailed it back to the ranch and let her uncle investigate him. She thought it frustrating that no matter how trained or prepared you are, you still might respond incorrectly to unexpected situations. She wonders what it is that made her put aside the red flags. She must be more careful and not allow it to happen again. She knows Uncle Spence is not a "happy camper" and might take matters into his own hands and confront Drake. Oh, how she would not want to be present for that.

Her parents contact the neighbors and have them over for beverages and dessert. Their topic of discussion on their invitation is to get to know their new neighbors better. The Waters have their plan, but they soon find out and are suspicious as to why their neighbors invited them. They know how to play the game, and they each will only provide information as deemed necessary, nothing more. They are not looking to make friends but do not want to make enemies. Her parent's hidden agenda is to find out who these neighbors are and find out why these people are on guard. It is an essential factor in securing safe perimeters. Her parents did not divulge their daughters' or cowhands' past occurrences of having crossed onto their neighbors' property line occasionally. They want a better idea of what their neighbors plan to do with their property and why they are withdrawn and secretive.

The Waters explained that their business was a unique bed and breakfast, and it was a business made available only to a specific clientele. They told them their property would have out-of-towners occasionally staying at different locations. Some clients will be at the bed and breakfast, and some will be on their land using other accommodations. They tried to assure them that their clientele was thoroughly checked and was not a threat to the community but just wanted privacy. However, they asserted while glancing at Wren, who was drinking a refreshing iced tea at the kitchen counter. They are making it quite clear that their clients need their privacy, and it is their job to ensure they get it. They did not purposely appear withdrawn or cold but shared that their security would soon be operational. They wanted to warn them, so to speak, of the consequences if trespassers violated their postings.

Wren is trying to look aloof and uninterested in the kitchen. She thinks she appears to be there only to get a drink and snack, not to listen to their conversation. She looks up at one point and sees them looking directly at her. What else could that indicate to Wren but that they knew she was the trespasser? She inhaled the tea down the wrong pipe and coughed. Wren is flabbergasted! She takes her glass over to the sink and clears her throat. Looking out the window above the sink, she wonders if he has told them.

"He must have! How could he? "

Realistically, he needs more time to return and start relaying her details of trespassing. However, they distinctly look at her. Somehow, she believes they got their information from Drake, for he is the only source they could have relayed her story. Boy, is she mad? She dumps the rest of her tea and ice down the sink and puts her glass in the dishwasher. She feels so uncomfortable being in the vicinity of the Waters. She leaves out the kitchen door to find solitude in the gardens.

The gardens are a tranquil place she likes to go when she needs a space to breathe and relax. While there, Wren concludes she must go and investigate Drake's hangout. She senses the Waters are hiding something. She thinks through some possible scenarios and keeps returning to the neighbors, saying that their security is not operational yet. She recalls her uncle saying he saw Drake heading out to town. Contemplating everything, she took advantage of the moment and presumes Drake will not be returning anytime soon. She takes off for the barn. Her uncle Spence will be busy teaching his survivalist class, so he cannot stop her from going through this impulsive quest. She knows he keeps a watchful eye out for her, but her curiosity and defiance mode is pumping through her veins. It is giving rise to righteous anger. Fighting for "the good," she tells herself. She must expose things in the shadows and shine a light on the unknown. She is to find the truth of the matter. It demands her to act. It is now or never. She must defy the imposing restraints and investigate before the neighbor's security system thwarts her inquisitiveness.

Wren casually walks to the barn from the fenced gardens. Again, she appears as if she has nothing particular to do. She approaches the hired hands, Jake and Charlie, that she would be taking Ginger out to check the fences. She had a section of the fence she pulled back so that she had access to the neighbor's land. She must go after the cattle when needed. At times, the cattle would break down the fence and escape where they thought the grass was greener, she supposed. When cattle break free from their property boundaries, locating the down fence is the first job Wren must do. A temporary fix commonly used is a rope tied to the side of the saddle. It is done to restrict any further exiting of livestock until the down fence gets appropriate repairs. First, when livestock stray, the ranchers must proactively find the stock. Then the ranchers corral and put the stray back with the main herd. The ranchers then fix the broken barricade.

The moveable opening in the fence that Wren accesses is to cross onto the neighboring property. To retrieve lost stock is coming within range. She has often used this section in their ranch fencing to provide fast and safe passage for horses and riders to rustle back lost property. This adventure would be the last time she would cross the property line using this gateway. At least, that is what her neighbors are attempting to convey. However, things happen, and ranch hands will, in the future, have to retrieve the cattle from their property lines. Whether her neighbors like it or not, they have yet to learn how to deal with ranching. After mulling the situation over, she converses with her Heavenly Father while trotting through the ranch's pastures.

"What can we do, Father?"

An idea pops into her mind when the words come from her mouth.

"Double fence."

"Wow! That would be a solution worth trying, she utters."

She thought having a road around their perimeter but within their boundaries is an excellent idea. It is so good; she will share it with the family. The double fence might be the perfect solution that keeps the animals contained on their property. If they break one barrier, then the second fence will deter them. It may be expensive, but the ranch could start putting in the fence on the side between them and their neighbors and progress the project as money becomes available.

After crossing onto the neighbor's property one last time, she arrives, where she first recalls seeing Drake. It is where she and Ginger again jump over the downed trees. She dismounts and feels it best to leave her horse to graze while she takes the rest of her journey on foot. She totes her gun in case of danger. Her digital camera hangs across her chest so she can retrieve it easily to take pictures of things that inspire her and that she might deem odd. (Like things people may have put in the woods that would provide an answer to the folk in those parts) The papers might even fancy a story with some pictures. They might be asking the same questions that she is. What might their business be? Why did they buy this particular property? The enquirers want to know. What are these neighboring folk doing with this property? She senses something is not aligning. She did not buy the picture her neighbors are trying to portray, that the bed and breakfast are legit and for specific clientele.

Her emotions are raw, and she feels the adrenalin rushing like a flash flood. She is aggravated with Drake for letting the Waters know, somehow, that she has been on their land. Even at that, she processes concerns of wondering about Drake. He bothers her, and she does not understand why she cannot let it all go. At that point, she takes on a serious demeanor, finding realness in her heart. She decides to take a moment to poise herself to contemplate it all. She pulls out her compass and maps, hoping to help her navigate her neighbor's property. The map gives an eagle view of her neighbor's property. It shows a cluster of trees close to where she first met him. Wren uses this opportunity to find the "hidden haven" in the woods. Precisely, Drake's den. Now she is tracking a suspicious individual's whereabouts, not her family's cattle. She notes her location on the map and ponders what direction to investigate first. She ties her neck scarf on a nearby branch and begins her hike deep into her neighbor's wooded property. She goes farther than she ever ventured before. She knows there could be consequences for her choice to proceed.

Wren is determined to enjoy the last exploration of this portion of land. She knows she must find answers now, or she may never have more opportunities. Tomorrow the security will be operational. She wonders what that means. Will it be cameras, dogs, guards, or an electric fence? She wonders what will happen if she travels over the line of limitations after security is up and running. She wonders if her new neighbors will press charges. She stops in her tracks after discovering something in the clearing within a short distance. She maneuvers closer, keeping cover behind the brush. It is an odd-shaped dwelling. How on earth would someone get something of that size through the woods into the clearing? She moves closer to gain some sort of conclusion but finds herself in a frozen state of fear instead. She takes a moment to listen and thinks she can hear someone humming. She could swear it sounded like the melody she played the other day in the High Place. Gathering her wits, she musters up some audacity to move in to attain more Intel. She needs answers. She sees him. It is Drake. Here is the very person who was not supposed to be there! He is outside doing something. She closes in to get a better look, and to her surprise, he is taking a shower outside his quarters. "Yikes, he is naked! She should have looked away, but Wren finds herself intrigued by the situation. Frozen in her thoughts briefly, she decides to advance and maneuvers to a large barrel. She whispers aloud,

"Of course, Drake is naked and taking a shower."

She feels the untamed heat traveling. The evidence of embarrassment is racing up her neck. Wren tells herself that she must gather her wits and finish the task. She must have taken too much time enjoying the woods and snapping pictures because she thought she had plenty of time to explore before he returned from town. She recalls creeping out of the brush to reach the other side of the module. She remembers thinking she would keep out of sight. She is trying to remain incognito, and so far, it is going well until a twig snatches her shirt as she ducks for cover. She ducks down to hide.

Now she is holding her breath while placing a hand over her mouth. She waits to see if he indicates that he might have heard her. The shower still sounds like it did not halt its flow. She hears him humming still, thus again thinking it most likely would be safe to move forward. She has no choice but to advance and not retreat. This one opportunity is the only time she fathoms obtaining the answers she wants. She needs to gather evidence of his elusive presence there. Assuming that he did not hear her, she proceeds with caution. Her first goal is to get to the other end of the module. There she will be able to get a better glimpse of the campsite and take a few snapshots to verify his purpose. Then she will silently retreat, return to her property undetected, and look over the photos later. She moves in stealth mode and arrives at the point she wants. She takes cover behind a small vehicle she thinks he might use to get around. She takes a few snapshots of the camping area. Now that she is there, she wants to look inside, but it would be too risky. Abruptly Lights start flashing. She senses that it is time to get on her way. She knows she is pushing the boundaries. She started easing away carefully, and then her intuitive warning alarm went off. Goosebumps popped up on her arms, and a flutter in her stomach. She can feel someone behind her. Fear causes her to drop her gun. She slowly turns around, cringing.

"Well, what do we have here?"

When confronted by Drake, Wren lets out a scream, and he instantaneously grabs the camera in her hands. In those moments, Wren beholds Drake's nudity; due to being interrupted by her uninvited visit. He had to abruptly shoot out of his shower in pursuit of an intruder, which made her flush exposed to it.

"Oh, oh, Wow!"

She starts rambling by looking down at his feet so as not to view his body unclothed.

"Drake, I took one last excursion in the woods before

the Waters activated their security. I overheard the neighbors talking to my parents. They were telling my parents that the security system was nearing completion. It popped the cork! I just had to take this opportunity to explore one last time."

Wren points at the camera dangling from his hand. She continued to explain why she was there.

"I was taking pictures of interesting things I saw in the woods."

Wren pauses in her thoughts while processing her words with the conviction of the Holy Spirit.

"I was not lying about using my camera to take pictures of nature. I am not revealing the other reason I was using My camera: to take pictures of anything that might lead to a better understanding of who Drake was."

"I came across this unusual dwelling, yours, I take it?"

she said, stammering. Now gaining control, she spouted out,

"Goodness! Anyway, can you please put some clothes on? I do not care to see your stuff, Mr. Drake." Wren quickly retrieves her gun while Drake is distracted.

He pulls the towel from his shoulder and loosely wraps it around his waist. Drake holds it in place with one hand while the other holds onto her camera. He is dripping wet.

"Well, Miss Wren, since you are intruding on my privacy, I think it more fitting for you to ...."

Drake abruptly stops his comment mid-sentence due to reacting to the rifle pointing at him.

"Don't get funny on me, Mr. Drake!"

Drake instinctively responds to the danger of the gun

by holding up his hands. He drops his towel but hangs onto the camera.

"Oh, for heavens' sake, come on!"

Still keeping her gun on him, she tells him to turn around. He complies, and she again flushes with the embarrassment of seeing his nakedness. She puts her hands to her mouth and whistles for her horse as she backs away. She aimed to establish a safe distance away, where nakedness is no longer a threat. He heard her walking further away. Countering her withdrawal, Drake responds with,

"You pulled the gun!"

He pauses to listen for a response.

"I can't hold up my towel and raise my hands, now can I?"

Ginger came running powerfully to her call. Hearing the snorting and heaviness of the horse's feet, he knows she is getting ready to mount and race back to the ranch.

"This is not over, Ms. Wren."

"It is for me, Mr. Drake,"

She trots off in the opposite direction from whence she had come.

Getting back to the barn is all she wants right now without further altercation. Sitting on a hay bale by Ginger's stall, she giggles at the remembrance of Drake dropping his towel.

"What a cocky guy." She mutters.

"He has no qualms about revealing his nakedness; by the Grace of God, I could think clearly and high tail it out of there when I did."

She wonders. What is he going to say to the Waters? She decides she needs to put it aside for the moment and starts to muck Ginger's stall and replace it with fresh straw. It's no biggie; she has developed a daily routine of caring for her horse.

Wren opens the small fridge, pulls out a few carrots, and feeds them to Ginger before heading home. She takes a few moments to reflect a little bit more on Drake. She talks to herself as she walks to the house. Would he turn her into the Waters? How frustrated is she again, getting into these embarrassing scenarios with him? She has never been in a similar situation or experienced anyone like him.

Drake feels safe enough to stand down and gather up his towel for coverage. He is ecstatic that he was able to confiscate her camera. He returns to his temporary home, freshens up, and changes his attire. While fixing himself lunch, he attempts to understand what happened with Wren. He finds himself restless and commences meandering through his quarters. He paces like a cat while glancing at the camera on his chair. "

He grabs it and begins examining it as he paces. Finely stopping, he plops in his comfortable chair, lifting his feet to settle on a stool. He looks at the camera studying it as if it is a new unknown object. He begins to poke and prod, trying to figure out how to pull up her pictures so that he can see them. He finds the on button, and yes, it comes alive. After a while, he can finally figure out how to retrieve her pictures gallery.

"Ok, she is telling the truth. She did take pictures of things found in the woods, and this dwelling is a picture she feels worthy of capturing..., and oh, looky here. Nature is not the only thing she is intrigued to take pictures of; my camp also seems intriguing."

He disagrees with her explanation of why she had been in his camp. Studying her pictures, he jumps up from his sitting, shouts, and starts pacing.

"I do not believe she is as innocent as she puts on! She purposely searched for my dwelling. How could she just happen to fall upon it, and why would she take a risk coming here alone?"

He assumes she would have had to suspect he was there somewhere. The odds of running into him this far in the clearing are likely. Maybe she got wind of me heading out? Too bad for her, I decided to make it a short trip.

"So, she must find me worthy of investigating!"

Laughing aloud, he looks further at the gallery of her pictures. He finds enjoyment in looking at them. He sees her family pictures, pictures of students picking pumpkins, and various classroom events. She even has selfies of herself taken out in the open range. He notices her holding a violin. Is this the picture she took of her violin in the location in the woods she spoke about? Perhaps it is her secret place. He looks closer, enlarging the image. He must figure out what to do about her unexpected visit. It is pretty humorous to him how she caught him showering and exposed. Her reaction was endearing. She appears innocent and likely has never seen a man exposing his personals. He liked her awkwardness and found her a challenge. With a determined mindset, he agrees he would like to get to know her.

Nevertheless, it has to be on different terms from how they have already encountered one another. Now he has a personal quest. He wants to find her secret place. Fair is fair. He gathers his backpack filled with supplies, pulls on his hiking boots, gathers up her camera, and heads out. Having her camera could be fun. After deleting the snapshots of his dwelling and camp, he becomes amused with the idea of him "turning the tables." He gets an idea. Why not take some snapshots of her secret place? Of course, it would not be as innocent as that. He will add a bit more to the photo. He will be in them.

Drake plans to go to the same area he tracked prior. He looks for horse hoof imprints near the stream in the soft clay mud. The following day he rises early and follows the path that takes him higher. He reaches the top, where it levels off, and sees an area half surrounded by a rock wall. Ferns are growing out of small crevices. Water is drizzling over the rock, falling into a pool of water. A large tree looms over the cliff above. Smaller trees are baring their roots near the pool basin and expanding their canopy upward to reach the benefits of the sun. The sound of dripping water soothes his thoughts. The air feels crisp and clean. He continues looking around, taking in all it has to offer. He locates a rock that presents itself as a perfect place for sitting while playing the violin. The canyon is the ideal acoustics to echo back whatever vocal or instrumental voice someone might use. It is a fantastic place! She found a treasure in this place. While there, he pokes and prods around, looking for specimens he might still need to gather from his stay there. He finds quite a few. After finalizing his last sample and putting it in his bag, he walks to the rock, placing one foot on it while leaning on his hiking stick. He admires the view and stands to his feet. He wants to play with the canyon's acoustics. He cups his hands to his mouth and shouts a declaration to the canyon to the ears that listen.

"I will expose you, Ms. McCarthy! You have not seen the last of me! You have started something that has to come to an end."

He lets out,

"Woo-ee....!"

It echoes back to him, and it brings a smile. It is a type of happiness he had forgotten he could have. It was a moment and a place in his emotional state he had not experienced in a long time.

"Now it is time for some pics."

He commences with some photography therapy.

Wren finishes brushing Ginger with a coarse brush and casts off dirt and debris. She softly runs her hand over her warm coat. She takes notice of a scratch that needs to be tending, and she figures she must have obtained it when the horse ran through the sharp brush; to her aide. Wren opens the medic box and puts some salve on it.

"Ginger, I am sorry I put you through that girl! However, I do thank you for coming to my rescue!"

Hugging Ginger, she smiles while pulling out something to eat hidden in her grasp. Ginger sniffs and nudges her hand to reveal the treat. Rubbing Ginger's soft nose, she opens her palm, exposing an apple, to Ginger's delight! Her soft nose touches her hand as Ginger gently nibbles hesitantly before grabbing it totally and chomping away.

"I have to go inside now, girl. Have a good rest. Thank

you again for being there for this silly human today. I can always count on you."

She laid her head against Ginger's neck and stroked it. Wren kisses her nose and parts ways to head back to the house. Her dad startles her.

"Hey, Missy, where have you been? Did you check the fences, or were you just clearing your head?"

"Hi, Dad. The fences look fine, though we must permanently fix the area used for entering our neighbor's property."

"Yeah, that is true; we must get on that."

He looked at her shirt, noticing it was torn.

"Did you run into some difficulty?"

"Yeah, a tree thought it wanted to play tug of war with me."

"Thank the Lord you just got tugged on by a tree. Did you see any wild critters or of the like (referring to Drake) while you were out there?"

He was raising an eyebrow now, attempting to get her to share her thoughts. She is embarrassed to tell her dad what she did come up against, and she tells him part of the experience and not the whole.

"I crossed over the boundary, Dad. Hearing what the neighbors said, one last exploration was in the making. During my last excursion, I found a dwelling in the woods."

Her dad cleared his throat.

"The fella you came across in the clearing?"

She embraces her father.

"I did not expect him to be there, but he was. I am extremely sorry, Dad. I do not mean to disrespect our family."

She pulls away from him and begins to pace while continuing to share the situation she is dealing with.

"He has the right to his privacy, and the Waters have the right to protect their clients with their chosen means. I keep making stupid mistakes lately and do not know what has gotten into me, and I was so mad at him."

"Well, first, I would like to know if he was inappropriate or hurt you in any way?"

"No, Dad, Though I find him a little smug."

Her dad raises his eyebrow as Wren continues with her experience encountering Drake.

" I am drawn to him for some reason. The problem I keep having is when I speak. When I open my mouth, that is disturbing. I cannot seem to move past a few sentences with him without making a blunder of it. What's worse is, I think he told the Waters about me crossing over on their property. He gave me his word, and he would not expose me."

"I suspect you overheard our conversation with the Waters?"

"Yes, I did, and after I made a fool of myself over the kitchen sink, I took to the garden to gain my composure. Yet, I couldn't shake my need to strike back. I impulsively took off to explore because I feared I would not get the chance again. What if he does not want to see me again? I pulled my rifle on him, Dad!"

"Sounds like you are in the middle of a dance."

"A dance? What do you mean?"

"It's when you dance with a partner, and you have to

decide who will lead and who will follow. If two leaders are trying to dominate simultaneously, both just get their toes stepped on. The dance, as you call it, is then blundered. Someone needs to know when to yield to others leading. There is always a suitable time for each person to lead when needed. I believe that when you find yourself dancing with another leader, there has to be a determining factor as to how they will agree. What will it take to operate and function to maintain that both parties stay on their feet? Who is going to lead in that instance? Both leaders are valuable, but both must choose and accept their role in that relationship for the dance to work. It does not always appear on the outside what a person's whole is on the inside. Let this fellow have a few more days. He may need a few days to figure out how to dance with you. If This guy does not attempt to connect with you in that period, it would be wise to let it go. You are special, Wren, and it takes a special guy to appreciate your uniqueness. At the same time, you must find rest in the reality that sometimes we want things to be ours. Your faith in the one above needs to come into play. He will guide you."

Wren's father takes a deep breath and exhales before continuing.

"On another note. I know you are independent and have your way. Please try hard not to put yourself in compromising situations!"

"Ok, Dad, I will try to be more responsible. Thank you for coming out to talk with me in private." They hug, and he pats her on the back. He suggests they head back to the house for supper. Wren is happy knowing she has her family and they have her back, bringing warmth to her heart. Perhaps that is why they say (home is where the heart is.)

Wren's mom emerges from her art building, waving at them as they emerge from the barn.

"Hey, guys?"

She looks at her daughter and husband and teasingly interacts.

"Wren, what a handsome man you have walking with you. What you two up to?"

Dad points to Wren, allowing her to discuss her situation with her mother.

"Oh, Mom, it's a long story. I will tell you later. I am so hungry! I will jump ahead of you two if you do not mind. I need to get cleaned up before dinner."

Wren bounds towards the house.

"Ok, dear, but I do have something I want to show you. I finished a new piece, and I want to get some feedback."

"Sure, Mom, I would happily give you some feedback. Is after supper good?"

"Sure, sweetheart, that will be good if your father doesn't mind."

Her father responds.

"No, of course not. You two go at it. I have a game of chess, your grandpa, and I need to get to." Drawing his love close to him as they walk towards the house, her mother laughs and kisses his cheek. She leans near his ear and says something that leaves a big grin on his face.

It is a small gathering tonight at the main house. It will be her mother, father, grandparents, and herself. It is not the family night that everyone living on the ranch attends. It is a day that everyone else on the ranch eats at their dwelling. Tonight is the designated time for individual households to spend time together. Wren's immediate family is grandma, grandpa, mom, and dad. Wren feels such a joy to have time with them. Grandma's cooking is impressive. It is always something to look forward to eating. Wren sets the table, and Grandpa; helps Grandma bring the food to the table. Wren's Dad shouts out as he pulls out his chair and takes a seat,

"Meatloaf, Mom, it all looks delicious."

"Homemade biscuits, too,"

Grandpa points out.

"Is the butter your experimental honey butter, ma?"

"Yes, it is, made with love just for my favorite son-in-law."

All laughter subsides, and they join their hands and bow their heads reverently as Wren's father blesses their food. After dinner, everyone clears their place and commences to assemble the kitchen. All share the duties of putting the kitchen back in shape. It always ends with the sweeping and mopping of the kitchen floor. Once they feel all is in order and complete, they congregate on their favorite place, the front porch. Her dad and grandpa go to the play table at the circular area of the porch, while grandma and her mother take to the white rocking chairs. Wren likes to claim the porch swing. She fluffs and places the pillows so she can lie down, positioning one bent leg leaning against the back while the other lengthy extremity hangs over the edge of the seat. Gently she swings herself back and forth. She intently looks up at the sky. She has thoughts of her sister wishing she were there. She would love to get her sister's input on her situation with the new stranger she finds herself at constant odds. Wren sighs, remembering that, soon enough, Cassidy will be visiting. Wren hopes she resolves a few things concerning Drake first and thus has positive things to share once she arrives.

After some time passes and the family gathering on the porch disperses. Everyone departs their way. Wren and her mother head to the Art barn together. Her mother instructs her to close her eyes while she guides her to the hidden art she wants to reveal.

"Now open your eyes."

Wren is speechless and overwhelmed with emotion. Tears drop slowly down her cheek. The subject her mother chose for this work of art is priceless. Gathering appropriate words to reveal her amazement, Wren speaks.

"Oh, Mother, this is beautiful! You captured my heart!"

"Yes, I hoped it would get that response. It will be displayed at the county fair in your honor for working with special children."

Wren ran to the piece looking closely at each detail and running her hand softly across it.

"You created the piece from the students on our ranch exertions!"

"Yes, I took photos from your camera and used them for inspiration."

"You captured their delight! Mom, I love it!"

"I hoped you would. It will be finding its home in front of our community library, and you are the first to see it."

Wren embraces her mother.

"Oh, Mom, you are so amazing!"

"Did you see the words? Children are gifts from the

Lord, and the scripture that moved you to serve in this field?"

"I do see it!"

Wren reads it. Speak up for those that cannot speak for themselves.

"This is the best gift you could have given me!"

"That makes me happy."

Her mom kisses her forehead. Lifting one of the tarps, she asks.

"Now, help cover the sculpture back up. I don't want anyone seeing it until the ceremony." Wren helps cover it up, and Wren hugs her mom. They both smile, and Wren grabs her mother's arm and silently walks to the house.

Drake needs to confer with someone he can trust about Wren. It is a lot to ask his father to meet him. He has not seen his father in person in a long time. Lunaport communication is typically their only means of connection due to security reasons since his transition to the P.E.S. Dome. Now on vacation and in close proximity to him, he thought it a reasonable time to take a chance and meet in a safe setting. He can use the local phone to get together. He needs his dad's counsel regarding Wren. Pondering letting Wren in his life, he needs his dad's fresh perspective. He looks to his dad and wants to glean from his wisdom and insight. His father's perspective and approval are essential to him. He decides to make arrangements to meet up with his father. Pulling out his cell phone, he calls.

"Hey, Dad, it's Drake." His Father answers.

"Hi, Drake. I've been thinking about you. How are you doing? Are you enjoying your vacation?" Drake laughs at the rapid-fire questions his Father is putting out.

“Yes, Dad, I am enjoying my time here. Listen, can we meet? I know it is not the usual way we converse, and you might have things going on, but I need your input.” His father is delighted at the thought of seeing his son face to face.

“Sure, son, I would be happy to meet you. Where do you want to meet up, and what time?” Drake is relieved and thrilled he will have a chance to connect man to man.

“I will send you the directions soon. Let us make it about 9 am in town at the Bluebird Café. They serve tahini and Greek coffee, and I know you would enjoy the menu. They also have many other Mediterranean options if that does not interest you.” His Dad is happy to meet him.

“Sounds good. I’ll see you at 9 am.” Drake is already feeling anxious.

“Thanks, Dad, it means a lot to me.”

CHAPTER 10

MAKING AMENDS

One of the most appreciated landmarks of the area in their quaint town is its gorgeous mountainous backdrop that encamps the town's population of 23,000. Hikers and campers come to the State Park, known for its beautiful trails that lead to Water Falls and Canyons. The community college is the other draw, and its presence propels local businesses to keep up with the trends and upbeat vibe.

This town has an artsy vibe. During the Spring, Summer, and Fall seasons, freelance artists of all types sell their goods on the square. At the start of school each Fall, family vacationers head back home. The college crowd keeps business rolling from August through November and January through May. Vacationers tend to visit the quaint town June-Aug. December through March are quieter, with the locals mostly having it themselves.

It is now the tail end of Spring, and new life returns to the town. Hikers and Cabin dwellers start to return. Business looks forward to the College students coming out of their winter hibernation. Cassidy is visiting the ranch for a few weeks. It gives Wren a distraction from thinking about Drake. She wants to make things right with Drake but needs to figure out how. Perhaps Cassidy will help her find a way. Wren and Cassidy like to go to town during the opening season. They enjoy people-watching. It is interesting to watch how hair and fashion trends change. They feel ancient compared to the new kids. When they get their fill, they do their next favorite thing, head to the Café and prepare for shopping. They love to head to the Bluebird; stopping here before they start their shopping excursion is a ritual.

The Bluebird itself is a quaint yet nostalgic café. Since the owners' Cal and Tamara, are Greek, they decorate with a Greek flare intermingled with American nostalgia. The interior design of the building displays arches, wood, and stone. Every nook and cranny evokes a feeling. Local art decors the white-washed brick walls spotlighted with canned lighting. The stained shiplap walls are the inner walls providing privacy and places for more art displays. Above the internal walls are arched pocket shelves that provide room for sculptures and draping greenery. Dashes of color are present in the furnishings and decor.

The menu of the café includes various authentic Greek sandwich combos, fruits, meats, soups, salads, pizza, bread, and dessert pastries. Their delectable Greek pastry baklava, made with chopped nuts and honey on layered filo pastry, is one of the favorites customers like to order. The Café owners purchase vegetables and herbs from a section of Wrens Ranch called "McCarthy Organics." Other food needs are acquired elsewhere and delivered, but the Café attempts to buy locally.

Tamara is the mother hen of the cafe. She makes their customers feel at home. If she feels a customer needs a word of encouragement or advice, she has no problem boldly advancing respectfully and offering her special sauce. Their business is family run as well. Their daughters and son help serve the customers, and only a few outsiders balance out their employee's needs. Even Cal and Tamara's surviving parents have joined the team. Jasper and Maria are both widowed and have become good friends. Neither Jasper nor Maria chose to marry after losing their spouses. They, instead, choose to support their existing family. All the grandchildren on both sides are grown, some away at college and others living independently. Both grandparents find solace in each other and have become best friends. Looking from the outside, no one would ever know the depth of their friendship. You would think they are a couple. Cal's and Tamara's daughters and one son work at the Café. Still single, they connect with the young crowd. People of the ages of young adults to retirees feel comfortable hanging out at the Café because someone there can usually connect with them from the same age bracket.

Wren and Cassidy love to order the lamb gyro plates and love sitting in the nook by the window overlooking the front of the Café. Before grabbing their seat this day, Wren drops off a few bags of herbs and vegetables at the counter and settles the bill. While Wren is doing that, Cassidy visits a few pals she spots outside the shop. Finally, both women sit and catch up on the most current news. All around the café, chattering customers enjoy one another's company. Wren notices Tamara conversing with some new customers sitting on the green couch. She leans over to Cassidy.

"It looks like Tamara has found a couple of unsuspecting newcomers. Isn't it funny how new people tend to gravitate to the couches by the fireplace?" Cassidy responds.

"Yes, I think they find it cozy, but I noticed that once visitors become acclimated to the family-built atmosphere, they begin to venture out to other spaces that are more open."

During the summer months, customers like to sit at tables in the seating area located on the side of their building. The sidewalls connected to the Café are glass, and the doors slide in between the walls when opening to outdoor seating. It provides customers with outdoor dining during the warmer seasons. Adjusting comfortably in her seat, Wren glances over and notices the strangers getting up from their couches. She recognizes one of them shaking hands with Tamara. She looks away and begins to fidget. Cassidy becomes aware of her discomfort.

"What is the matter, Wren?"

Pointing in the direction of Tamara, Wren discretely whispers to Cassidy.

"Well, that is one of the things I wanted to talk to you about. See the fellow wearing the navy blue ball hat and gray tee shirt?"

"Yes, I see him; what about him?"

"Well, he is our estranged neighbor's visitor. He is staying on their property in their woods. I came across him while riding Ginger near my High Place, and I have just made a mess of things."

"What? In the woods, is he a Hobo?"

"No!"

Cassidy responds with a chuckle.

"He is camping there."

"Aha, I see. Tell me more."

Wren points to herself.

"Primarily, every time I talk, I make blunders that cause moments of conflict. For example, I impulsively did it when I met him wandering near our Ranch."

Cassidy is stunned and quietly listens with amusement while Wren explains.

"When Drake responds, it's embarrassing! I exit on that occurrence and trot back to the Ranch. The next time we cross paths, it happens like this. I overheard he was in town, so I took the opportunity to snoop around to get a fix on his camp. However, he is not in town long to my demise, and when I come across him, he is naked and unaware I am there."

Cassidy abruptly grabs her sister's sleeve and shouts where all can hear in the Café.

"Come on! You need to back up?"

Meanwhile, it took little for Drake to notice them sitting by the window. Her sister's loud reaction to whatever Wren was talking to her about alerted him to their presence. Wren looks in his direction to see if he heard her. They have eye contact. She quickly looks away and looks down at the table while she mumbles to Cassidy:

"Oh shoot, he sees us!"

She plunges her hands across the table towards Cassidy. Again, she is in trouble needing her sibling to rescue her. Looking up at Cassidy, she implores her for assistance and points to herself.

"This person is causing me great anxiety."

Cassidy looks and notices him staring at her with a smile.

"Well, Wren." Cassidy is smiling.

"He seems pleased to see you. Perhaps, you are not as outgoing as you might think. Wow, here he comes. Just breathe, and let your responses to his conversation come naturally."

Wren is frustrated at her current situation.

"What? I blunder natural responses. That is what has been getting me in trouble! Can't you help?"

Drake approaches before Cassidy can answer her call for help.

"Hello, Wren. I would like to introduce my father, Troy."

With a gesture of pleasantry, his father reaches out his hand, supporting Drake's introductions.

"Hello, Wren, It is a pleasure to meet you."

"Hello."

Wren points to her sister, who is sitting across from her.

"This is my sister Cassidy."

Her sister quickly responds.

"Would you like to join us, Mr. Silverman?"

Wren is flabbergasted. How could her sister put her in such a vulnerable position? Drake notices her anxiety and graciously bows out. He directs his attention to Cassidy with the comment he has some business to do with his father and maybe another time. Drake turns his focus back to Wren.

"Could you dismiss yourself and talk with me privately?"

Wren stammers around. Cassidy belts out directives.

"Of course, she can. Your dad and I can chat while you two have a moment alone. Drake looks at Wren.

"Wren, is that alright with you?"

"Yes, I guess."

He takes her hand and helps her out of her seat while his father slips into the spot she vacates. He starts chatting with Cassidy. Drake directs Wren to step out before him and guides her toward the door. They momentarily stand in front of the Café window where Cassidy is watching. Troy figures he will help Drake by giving them privacy. He drops his hat down on the table and gains her attention. He starts asking Cassidy questions.

Drake and Wren are standing by the bench near the front of the diner. Drake begins with,

"Wren, first off, I want to say..."

"Wait,"

Wren interrupts.

"I have to say my piece first. I am sorry I intruded on your privacy; I was out of line."

"Well, I have something you left behind in your haste." Drake pulls out his pouch. He opens it and pulls out her camera. Handing it to her, he attempts to make amends.

"I am sure you did not want me to have this."

Wren was so relieved and took it from his hands.

"I am so grateful. I do not know what to say."

"How about, thank you for starters. I want us to clear the air and start over on better terms."

Taking her hands and encouraging her to sit down on the bench by the curb, he continues.

" I know you are sorry, but I am sorry too. I should not have come out at you in a towel and certainly not have dropped it."

Wren chuckled.

"Well yeah, it was quite a shock."

"I hope you can forgive me. I had to act quickly. I had an intruder then, so drying off and getting dressed was not an option."

"I understand."

Wren turned on her camera and pulled up her gallery. Before she looks at the photos, she explains why she was at his campsite.

"I took a few photos of your camp. I deducted you were up to no good, and I was trying to find proof."

Wren looked down at her camera pictures and noticed some unusual ones she did not recall taking. She is now crunching her forehead and is about to complain.

"Hey, wait a minute, that is you in my high place."

She jumps up and is about to release some bad mojo, but after looking at him, Wren sees how distressed he looks; she sits back down and calmly turns off her camera.

"Drake, I see; I invaded your privacy, so you did my privacy. Fair is fair."

Drake ran his hand through his hair.

"Well, I thought it was fair at the time. I wish I did not, and I hate that I might have ruined your special place. I like you, Wren, and I would like to get to know you better."

Wren smiles.

"I would like that. How do you suggest we do that?"

"Let's start over. Meet with me for dinner this week."

"I would love to. When?"

"What day, and I will make it yours?"

Wren pauses for a moment.

"Well, I need to check with my family. I am sure we can work something out."

"Good!"

Drake hands her a piece of paper.

"This is my number. "

"Ok, sure, let us insert numbers in both phones in case I lose yours."

"Well, since it is a temporary phone that other customers will use, the Waters ask us not to add numbers, take pictures, or add apps."

"Oh, I did not consider that. Sure, I will put yours in."

Wren takes the paper Drake gave her and flips it over to write her number down for him.

"Drake, thank you for returning the camera and allowing us to correct the disturbance between us. I am delighted we bumped into each other."

Drake responds.

"I feel likewise, Ms. Wren."

"Ok then, that settles it, I will call you with a suggested day that will work for me, and you will call if you do not hear from me in a few days."

They both laugh. Wren makes a suggestion they head back.

"Drake, we best return to our posts and rescue your father from Cassidy. She will talk his ear off."

After briefly visiting everyone, Drake and his father say their goodbyes and head out. Before Drake and his father are out of sight, Drake glances back at Wren and finds her watching him as they leave. They exchange admiring looks before the door shuts behind them. Once they are gone, Cassidy grabs Wren's arm and pulls her back into the seat. Drake looks around at Wren through the window; he can see she is already conversing with Cassidy. Troy startles him with a smack, and they head down the street. Cassidy rapidly drills Wren about Drake with multiple questions.

"Ok, out with it! What did he say? Did you blunder it"?

"No, I did not blunder it this time!

She grabs Cassidy's arm while putting her hand to her mouth.

"We did apologize for our misgiving encounters! We agreed to meet for a date! Though the time and place are not yet to be determined."

"Eeek!"

Both of them laugh together. Cassidy tosses her hat up into the air above them.

"Wow, how amazing things are turning out to be."

"Yes, let's see how things pan out. We do not know each other yet, and I hope things go well." "Well, observing the non-verbal signs, he is definitely into you. I got into his father's head, and he shared that his son is entertained and intrigued with you".

"Excuse me, did you say I entertained him?" It is not surprising to Cassidy how Wren responds. Cassidy tries to reason with Wren.

"Wren, do not make a mess out of this. I see your

wheels turning in that head of yours. Do not raise the red flag before you even start the course. Positive things can come of this." Wren replies with genuine feelings.

"I'm not thrilled with the implication that I am entertaining, and I do not want him to think I am a joke."

Cassidy stands up and bends across the table to grab Wren's arms before speaking.

"Really? Wren, you are the entertainment!"

They both crunch their noses at each other. Wren throws her cloth napkin at her, and Cassidy sits back in her seat.

"Thanks, you have managed to make me feel foolish."

"Yeah, I do it well, but that's what sisters do in love." Both the sisters giggle, and Wren gets started on coming up with ideas for a date.

"So, where would you think a good place for a date would be?"

"It must be in a public place since you do not know him yet. A place where you can talk without others listening, and a place where you feel your conversation is private."

They both take a moment in silence to think about possible locations to go on a date.

"I hear Uncle Spence's influence in your advice."

Smiling and ignoring her comment, Cassidy responds:

"How about Bob's Place over on 2nd Street? They have amazing sandwiches, long vinegar fries, an ice cream fountain counter, and fun games at the same location."

"Yes, that might suit us. It pushes a fun vibe. I will present it to him and see if he likes it, but shouldn't I have another option in case he does not like that choice?"

" Ok, well, how about Swifty's Steakhouse?"

"I think that will suffice. It has a pleasant atmosphere and a beautiful stone fireplace.

"Also, what do you think about the Mill Restaurant? It has great homemade food, an old rustic feel, and an outside garden that seats people at tables near the stream."

"That's true. I have a good selection now, Cassidy. Thank you! I will text him and let him choose."

Wren texts Drake. At the same time, Cassidy waits. She gives him the three date options to mull over while checking her family schedule, and Wren turns her focus back to her sister.

"Since you have been away, you can choose what store we will shop at first," Wren yells.

"Why not check out "Debbie's shop?"

"Oh sure, I like her stuff. She has a knack for arranging things!"

Cassidy stops for a moment to think.

"I would like to surprise Mom with some new placemats and a centerpiece for the family table."

"I think that would be great. She would love that! However, don't you think we should also pick up something for Grams? She needs to be blessed too."

"Maybe we can also check out the Artist display at Triumphs in the Cross Center and see if Mom's Art piece has sold yet."

"What piece is that?" "

"Oh, she sculpted a beautiful piece of the family on the porch having a good time. I think it is a reflection of us."

"Oh wow! I might want to buy it. How big is it?"

Well, it is a small one and one you could put on a table or mantle."

"I don't think I could afford it, most likely."

Looking in a store window, Cassidy gets caught up in the animated display in their front window. Having seen it many times, Wren casually scans what is happening around them. Her sister enjoys the window display while Wren catches a glimpse of someone she thought she would not see again, and It chills her. Still hearing her sister in the background yip on about the window, she gets lost in the moment. All Wren can do is breathe. She finds a vacant bench and sits down. It is a person she thought she had already processed out of her mind. She finds herself being both surprised and agitated by this occurrence.

All activity around her becomes a blur, and observing his actions seems to move in slow motion. Memories flash flood through her mind. She recalls the two of them shopping during a prior Christmas season. Wren can see it as if it just happened. She and Cole were laughing and causing minor mischief, and she admits she misses those times. Everything seemed well in their relationship. She thought it was about to come to a pinnacle season with the expectation of a proposal at their holiday dinner. She is left in a state of confusion because he does not ask her to marry him. She continues to backlog in her mind and look to see if any signs might have indicated something different than what she thought she was experiencing. She opens her Jeep car door and drives home. The house is empty due to everyone going to special holiday events. Wren retires to her room, changes into her comfy clothes, and pulls out her journal. She writes in it and reads her entry out loud.

"Well, diary, I thought this was the night I would get engaged, but apparently, I was reading things all wrong."

She finds out the next day from his brother that he has left town in the early morning hours. He had ended their relationship with no goodbyes or explanations. It would be good to get some closure now, face-to-face. Yet she fears the journey might pose an emotional breakdown. She does not want to go there. Wren chooses to leave the situation with him well enough alone. She will tuck this moment away for now. If he decides to clarify his leaving to her, that would be up to him. She stubbornly would not instigate the conversation.

As quickly as she had decided how to handle his sudden appearance in town, she looks up, and their eyes connect. He sees her. Wren flushes and starts having instant anxiety. He raises a hand gesturing in public recognition of her. She responds with a stiff, robotic wave and grits her teeth while attempting to smile. Their reunion quickly takes another turn, and she disconnects her glance. She notices a lovely woman coming out of the year around Christmas shop, with which he turns his attention. He glances back, but Wren jumps off the bench and ducks into the nearest shop. Wren peers out the shop window. She sees him looking back at the place she was sitting. He seems disappointed.

"Of course, he moved on, she says aloud, reprimanding herself."

The shop is a nice cover for her. The shop owner put one-way filters on the windows so the customers could see, but no one could see in and invade their privacy.

Cassidy was suddenly aware that she had lost where

Wren was. One moment she was beside her, and the next, she was gone! She called her on her cell phone, leaving a message:

"Where are you?"

Wren did not respond, and Cassidy sent another text.

"I am heading to the Knick & Knack store. Come and console your flustered sister when you decide to quit playing games. For real, let me know that you are ok."

Wren flops down in the nearest available seat by the window ledge. Wren texts her sister back and tells her she is ok.

"Just had to duck out for a minute."

She gives Cassidy the go-ahead to shop without her and meet up with her shortly. Wren's Mom is concerned.

"Hey, Wren, are you alright?"

Wren looks up and sees her mother. She is in Billy Joe's Pizzeria.

"Mom, I just needed a breather."

"You look like you saw a ghost."

"I did!"

"What?"

"Well, you might as well call him that."

"Oh, you saw Cole."

"Yes, how did you know?"

"We bumped into each other yesterday. I hoped he would be gone by now, and he must be sticking around a few more days, probably visiting his folks."

"What?"

"Well, you know Wren, it would happen eventually; it is where he grew up. He has a lot of connections here."

"Yes, and one he forgot to disconnect."

Putting her fingers above her head, she uses them to mock his lack of doing what is right concerning her. She continues,

"He vanishes without even an explanation!"

"Yes, Wren, your frustration is evident. Perhaps this is the time to clear up things. Can you muster up the courage to confront him?"

"Mom, I do not know if I will see him again."

"Well, I heard he will be at The Gathering Place tonight."

Wren is now holding onto the seat.

"The Gathering Place, why?"

"Well, a poster over there says he is singing tonight."

Her mom points to a poster pinned to the community board. It's where anyone can post things for the public. Wren looks.

"Well, there he is. Huh, he's a professional singer?"

"Yes, and quite good, I hear."

With that, Wren decides she is at her limit of overwhelming news. She could not deal with any further information about her old boyfriend. Wren feels it's time to get back to Cassidy. She stands up and excuses herself. She tells her mother she will see her later and kisses her cheek.

"Oh, I want to discuss something else later."

Mother and daughter hug, and Wren steps through the door back onto the strip, flowing amongst the tourist shoppers.

Wren tries to make sense of Cole coming back. She knows she should not keep Cassidy waiting longer because she will worry. Wren processes her conversation with her mother while walking toward the Knick & Knack store. She pulls out her cell phone and calls Cassidy letting her know she is on her way. She doesn't notice Drake observing her. He is leaning against a light pole. He wonders what is bothering her. She appears in deep thought. He impulsively bolts away from the light pole he is leaning against to follow her. He quickly maneuvers behind a few folks to conceal his presence. He watches her as she walks haphazardly, bumping into shoppers. She would abruptly apologize and move on with haste.

The remembrance of that sad part of her life with Cole causes her to lose clarity. The incident shakes her up and forces her to lose focus on all the good things in her life. It is as if the color had drained out of her and everyone around her. She sees everyone in black and white. She knows she is being ridiculous and has to get back her stride. She stops by the brook and sits on a bench taking a few moments to gather her wits. She begins to feel more stable and confident. Prayer brings a calming that soothes her anxiety. It returns her to a balance. Peace comes, and she can return to her normal mode.

She gives herself a pep talk, telling herself she is strong, and if it does not work out with one person, it is for a higher reason. Her hopes are in God's provision. She laughs. She does not want to blunder or miss what God may send her way. She trusts God to operate in all timeframes.

She enters the store, and Cassidy quickly whisks her behind display cabinets.

"Hey girl, are you ok? I assume you freaked out. Did you see Cole?"

"What, Cassidy, you know Cole is here too?"

"Yes, you would be right deducting that, dear Watson."

"Ha-ha, I like that!"

"Sorry, that happened."

Cassidy continues.

"The family suspected it would happen eventually. Are you going to be ok?"

"Thank you, Cassidy, and you are right. It is silly. It has been a long time since I have seen him. Besides, it has already been a done thing. I will not let this pop-up appearance rock my still waters and take away my joy."

"That a-way, sis! Good to hear you have moved on. How about getting back on track and getting your mind back on shopping? I saw something Grams might like."

Dusting off her shoulders as a statement of moving on, she found solace with her sister and put her energy towards inspecting the items her sister found for Grams.

Drake chose not to follow her into the store. He, instead, plopped his tail down on a nearby bench, thinking of the insanity of following her and wondering what his next move might be. He asks himself,

"Should I invite Wren to meet up at The Gathering Place?"

The Waters told him it is a place where the locals go for live entertainment, so Drake texted Wren.

"Hey, I noticed you were still in town. I am planning to head to The Gathering Place tonight. I thought we could meet there?"

Wren felt her phone vibrate and peeked at the message sent to her. Looking at Cassidy, Wren says,

"Cassi, it's Cole!"

"Well, what does he want?"

"He says he will be at The Gathering Place tonight and hopes to see me there. He hopes we can have a moment to talk, and he wants to clear some things up, being how he left."

"Well, now, this could be your desired answer."

"What should I say?"

"Tell him you will be there with bells on."

"Now, I don't think I will sound that enthusiastic!"

Wren texted him back.

"Yes, I already planned to go with Cassidy, and perhaps they could have a few moments to catch up on things.

Wincing, she hit send.

"Aaah, what am I getting into?"

"You will be fine, sis. You are a grown woman, and there is nothing to fear."

Her phone buzzed again.

"Goodness, what star is shining on you today?"

"Wow, it is, Drake; he wants to meet us at The Gathering tonight." "Wow, this should be interesting." "Well, of course, we can meet them both." You are not going on a date with anyone. You are going with me." Wren texted Drake back and told him she was going with her sister and would be happy to connect at some point. She told him where she typically sat. After getting her response, Drake returns to his module and looks forward to meeting up at the Gathering Place. Observing Wren in a social environment will help him gain more information about her. What better place than amongst her pals? Wren and Cassidy tidy up their shopping and head back to the ranch to prepare for the exciting night ahead at The Gathering Place.

Wren and Cassidy arrive and find a table they claim for the night. She looks around immediately to see if there are any signs of Cole or Drake. She sees Cole sitting at a table near the platform where he will be performing. That table has set reservations for the entertainers, who get free food and drink. Her Mom filled her in on his disappearance reason, and though she is not very happy with how he handled it, she is more at ease. She looks around to see if the girl she saw him with earlier is still there, and she is not. It was odd. She hopes to find out more when they get a chance to talk.

While singing, Cole locates Wren's table and takes the liberty to head over to their table, where she and her sister are sitting after he performs a few sets. He moves over to their table, grabs a vacant chair nearby, and pulls up next to Wren. After a few cordial howdy-dos and polite talk, Wren's sister finds it suitable to let them have a few moments alone and joins the line dance. Cassidy fills it as the perfect opportunity for Wren and Cole to clear the air. After a few moments of talking, the awkwardness settles, and they head to the dance floor. A slow song transitions couples to the dance floor. Lights are dim, and Cole takes that opportunity to draw Wren close. He holds his hand out while asking Wren to dance. She gets anxious and looks at Cassidy exiting the floor for support, and Cassidy gives her a thumbs up and whispers her advice.

"Go for it. Find your closure, sweet sister."

Cassidy heads back to their table.

Drake strolls through the crowd and finds a place to position himself to observe. He sees people of all ages. Kids are running about holding hands, and the elderly generation is sitting on the sidelines, laughing and cutting up. He sees couples and singles. Everyone seems to be at ease and having a good time. He sees Cassidy talking to a few friends and is anxious because he knows Wren must not be far away. He cannot find her as he visually scopes the perimeter around the dance floor. He turns his attention to the dance floor and is startled when he sees her. She is with another man on the dance floor! He is taken back a bit and finds himself getting a little testy. He did not entertain the thought that she may have a man.

"Well, why not."

He scolded himself.

"She is a beautiful doe, and it would be Ludacris to think there would not be any other bucks out there seeing what he saw in her."

The dance ended, and Cole tipped his hat to Wren and returned to his singing platform. Wren returns to her table, where Cassidy cuts up with some folks sitting near them.

"Well, did you get anything for closure?"

"Yes, my assumptions are correct. Nevertheless, we are on good terms, and he has a career and no time for romance. According to him, what I took as a blooming future between us was a connection to pass the time until he had to leave town."

"Boo, harsh sis, so sorry! "

"It is alright, and it will not happen to me again. He asked for a date, and it was a no-go."

She wipes her hands off using her shirt.

"Why waste time on someone only interested in a filler? I am not interested in someone who uses you to get them through a short stop in town?"

"Cheers to that! Hey, there's Drake!"

Cassidy waves him over to join them. Drake moves over to Wren.

"Is it a good time? May I join you?"

"Sure!"

Cassidy chimes.

"Grab a chair."

Drake looks for Wren's approval. Wren smiles and replies.

"Nice to see you could make it."

"It's a nice local place to kick up your boots safely. Did you come alone?"

"Well, yes, I did. How about you? Did you come with someone?"

"My sister. Oh, I suspect you saw me dancing with him?"

Wren points to the stage.

"No, he just wanted to dance."

"You looked like you knew each other."

Cassidy breaks in.

"Oh yeah, he's from this town. He had Wren's heart at once, but it is not to be."

Wren kicks her under the table.

"Oh yeah."

Wren is rubbing her leg out of agitation while looking at Cassidy with her big eyes. Cassidy gets Wren's drift.

"I am sorry. I should let Wren tell you her war stories; I stepped out of line."

"Oh wow, I am sorry to bring up a bad experience

Wren; I would be stupid to think you never had any relationships. You are a beautiful woman!"

Feeling a little flushed, Wren fumbles to recover.

"Well, thank you, Drake. Can we talk about something else?"

"Yes, we can!" " What do you do for a living?" "Do you only work on the farm? What are your dreams for your future?"

"That will be a good amount to discuss!"

"Working on the ranch is a full-time job, but I also work in the Special Education field.

" I gather that it was the kids in your photo gallery."

" Yes."

Cassidy excuses herself. She wants to visit some old friends at another table. Chuckling, Wren attempts to answer some of his inquiries. They talked for two hours straight. Cassidy returns and suggests they get going. She reminds her that they have to get up early for farm chores in the morning. Wren replies.

"Well, time flies when we're having fun. We need to get going; we do have to rise early. Enjoyed our chat." Drake replies.

"Enjoyed our conversation as well. Wren, I can't wait to hear more. Let me know when you would be available for our next excursion." Wren likes that he still wants to see her.

"I am looking forward to it. I will let you know."

Both are smiling ear to ear. Cassidy interrupts their smiling activity and jostles Wren's shoulder.

"Come on, Wren, time to head home."

Wren is embarrassed. She waves back at Drake over her shoulder and follows Cassidy out.

"Hey, Wren!" Cole hollows."

Wren whips around to see Cole walking toward her.

"Huh?" Cole catches up to them and asks her if they can talk.

"We did talk, Cole. I have moved on, and it is time you do too." Cole does not give up.

"Seriously, I need to talk to you; can we meet soon?"

"If I am around, and we bump into each other, maybe that could happen, but don't hold your breath."

She and Cassidy hightail it to the car and head back to the ranch.

"Wow, Wren, way to show him!"

Wren focuses on the road ahead while responding to Cassidy.

"Funny, I just have been there and done that. I have no desire to allow it to happen again! Now, help watch out for deer or critters who may jump in front of the jeep. I don't want to injure another animal."

"Yeah, it sucks! Nevertheless, that is what happens in rural areas. You have to toughen up, Wren, and not allow an accidental hit to cause you to move to the city again?"

"Yeah, the last move; I ended up teaching there the whole summer."

"You must pay rent when you're not living on the ranch."

"Yes, I know, but it did allow me to expand my experiences. It is not without its pluses, and I saw how city folk live, love, and laugh." Cassidy playfully raises her eyebrows.

"Oooh!" Both are amused. Wren starts talking.

"I discovered what things I prefer and what kind of life I want to pursue. It is here on the ranch near friends and family; I need to be. This ranch and town is the place to make my stamp on the world. And it is here I hope to raise my family someday. So yeah, I have toughened up, but I still want to avoid unnecessary collisions with small or large animals. So keep your eyes peeled."

"I am on it! You have to say, you had attention tonight, and you had Cole and Drake both making efforts to connect."

"Yeah, but Cole does not count. He is out of the arena, and I do not want to waste more time on someone who does not want to stay here. He desires to travel and pursue his career, and I will have nothing more to do with him."

"It looked like you enjoyed the slow dance. Did I see things right?"

"I was caught up in the moment. I remember when I knew he never intended to commit to one girl. He played me, and I have reevaluated things and don't think it is all bad."

"Yes, you had good moments and bad, but you had to step out and try! You never know until then."

"I know, but seriously he assumed I would welcome him back with open arms. That's crazy!"

"Got it, so what about this Drake guy? Do you think he might be one to take on the dance floor?"

"I think I would like to risk it. He has gotten under my skin."

"So, what did you guys talk about?"

"Well, he has been married before. His wife passed

after delivering a baby girl; he has a boy and a girl. Never pursued anyone since her passing, he says he has not ventured out to pursue anyone until now."

"Well, woohoo! Where are the children now while he is here?"

"They are at camp." Both are silent for a moment. Cassidy continues.

"What else?"

"He told me he works a classified job and has to take breaks from the intensity of it occasionally. He is an Architect-Engineer and designs modules that blend with nature using the latest technology. He also researches edible sources that may promote healing; he calls it a hobby."

"Do you think he designed the module in the woods you saw?"

"Do not know that. I guess I have to wait for an invite and inquire."

"Yeah, that's true." Stomping on the brakes, "Hey, didn't you see those masked bandits?"

" Yes, but in my defense, they were in disguise."

"Funny, seriously, keep an eye out!" Cassidy humorously pokes at Wren.

"Hey, they just popped out of nowhere! Yes, a Raccoon family. There must have been three babies. You would think they would train them better not to frolic on the roadway, which could only lead them to the end of their precious life. Maybe the adults were teaching the young. Yeah, that's it! The critters just might be giving them a dry run."

Wren looks at Cassidy with those eyes that say, "Really?" Wren, however, does chuckle at Cassidy's wit. Cassidy continues.

"Now, hear me out. The woodland creatures would know that normally drivers try to avoid them. You know, Animals sense your intentions."

Wren smacks Cassidy's leg.

"You're a buzzard!"

"What? I bet the mom and dad bandit is trying to teach them how to scurry off the road. A near miss probably scared the dickens out of them; I know it did me."

"Let's just get home; we can talk more later."

Cassidy opens up the moon roof and stares at the stars while Wren focuses on the road and the sides of the road for other animal encounters. Wren pokes fun at Cassidy.

"You better hope an owl doesn't swoop in at your head. Sticking your head out the roof is like putting out a beacon for them!" Cassidy blows her comment off.

"Not likely. I have my hat on anyway."

Wren quickly grabs her cap she had stuffed in the counsel and puts it on. They both are not taking any chances. Cassidy chimes in.

"When did you become aware of owls going after heads?"

"I overheard a conversation between a few guys in a booth behind me. One guy was sharing about a creepy thing that occurred with an owl. During a routine security check, they had to wear shiny silver helmets. One night they were outside doing routine checks from building to building. One of the security guards saw this huge winged thing hovering above them on the ledge. It was looking down at them. He said It creeped him out! One guy shouted out at the other, asking what it was.

The next thing he knew. Cassidy interjects her suspicions.

"It attacked his helmet!

"Yes, he threw the hat down and ran inside to escape. That is how I got that information about the owls. They like shiny helmets, maybe even heads protruding outside car roofs. I am not taking any chances!" Cassidy somberly responds.

"That's a bad experience. Good thing he had the hat on."

"Yeah, not sure if the owl saw a reflection of himself thinking it was another owl or just felt threatened by shiny objects in the night."

They both stop talking, and Cassidy pulls the window shut above her. They both ride in silence the rest of the way home. The sky is pitch black, but it is the perfect backdrop to show off the stars and constellations. Not one cloud obstructs the view of the stars. Cassidy is the first to break the silence as they pull onto the ranch property.

"I love the night skies! It is so big, and we are so small."

"Cassidy, you have always been intrigued with the night skies. You like the veiled mystery. On the other hand, I prefer to know what's coming."

"I know, Wren, you are on a trip! You need to learn to trust and enjoy the creation around you. It has so many joys to give; you just have to take the time to unwrap it and take hold of it. The sky above us is only a window inviting us onto a new frontier. We would have no advances or improvements if everyone were afraid of change. Thank God above, some individuals fearlessly pursue the unknown to find solutions that lead to a brighter tomorrow.

CHAPTER 11

LIBERTY

Drake needs to give Wren some space, and he hopes she will be able to gain her family's approval for her to meet him for a dinner date. In the meantime, he has many things to distract him from thinking about her. He has the security system to finish at the Waters and collect the new specimens he hoped to obtain.

The Society assigned him to get the Waters security set up and running. The last details of the security system on the Waters property are now completed. In return, he can use its accommodations to refresh and pursue his hobby. After he arrived, the Waters shared how they had difficulty with their neighbors adhering to their no-trespassing postings. He advises installing security measures and offers some advice from previous experiences on promoting good neighbor relations. Considering it is a zone created for refreshing and relaxing, he hopes that contentions will resolve so there will be no issue with their connection to P.E.S.

Early evening, Drake is sitting at the kitchen table reviewing the latest report completed by the Waters. Upon hearing laughter, he looks out the window and takes notice of a large campfire emerging on Wren's family ranch. He moves to the back screened porch to observe while waiting for the rest of the report to print. It is a good time to take a break and look into the neighbors' business. Going out to the deck, he obtains a clearer view. He considers his snooping justified because it is the gathering of pertinent details that can give a clearer picture of who a person is. He picks his binoculars up and zeros in on the partakers at the entertaining fire.

Mr. Waters notices Drake's fondness for their neighbor's daughter, Wren. It seems odd to him that Drake would take a liking to someone that crosses lines and jeopardize the Procure Earth Society's need for privacy. He walks toward Drake on the Deck and starts a conversation.

"You know she is a pretty one, a natural beauty. Don't you think?"

"Yes, Walt, she is." Walt gets more serious.

"She's a wild card, and I see you are growing fond of her. Do you think it wise to get involved? I mean, the living arrangements you both have are worlds apart?"

That stung a bit. Still, Drake held his observing stance without wavering. Walt continues.

"How will you protect the P.E.S. Society?"

Drake steps down and faces Walt.

"Walt, I am carefully taking one step at a time. It's a personal place I have not experienced in a very long time.

I am fully aware of Wren's reckless actions of crossing the lines of this property. She is a spunky gal, but I am getting to know her better and think she is quite a reasonable and intelligent person. If you take the time to listen, Walt, you can gather a lot about a person."

Walt realizes Drake is a little testy when he talks about Wren. He backs down.

"Well, I hope, for all our sakes, you are not playing with fire. I will not yet report my observations of this situation between you and Wren."

Drake certainly hopes he is doing the right thing. Walt continues.

"I will give you time to sort this out, but If I feel it is becoming a security concern for our society, I will have to send a note to our superiors." Drake is a bit agitated now but understands.

"I hear your concerns, and I promise I will be careful." Walt takes it on a lighter note.

"Her family is tight-knit, aren't they?" Drake signs because he thinks he is done conversing

about Wren and her family.

"Yes, it appears so." Walt attempts to smooth over the bad feelings he may have caused with Drake.

"What do you suppose those girls are up to?"

Drake hands over the looking glasses, and Walt observes.

"Looks to me like they are having a female pale wow. I see hotdogs and s'mores."

"Yes. The women appear to be enjoying themselves, that's for sure."

Walt hands the glasses back to Drake, and Drake takes

one last look when he takes notice of Wren picking up a violin. She plays her instrument while moving around the fire, and the other girls clap and cackle. The music brings back memories of how he first met her. She played her violin in "The High Place," as Wren calls it, and he recalls the melody. He knows Wren has a strong will. She crosses over lines, firmly convinced she has the right to. Regardless if her choice is right or wrong, he would not have the pleasure of meeting her if it were not for her audacity. That in itself would be a shame.

The charismatic bonfire is on. After Wren plays her instrument, Cassidy plays the bongos, and then Wren and her cousin Liddy dance around the campfire. Their Grandmother started the tradition with them. The girls keep the yearly get-together in honor of her. Her Mother, Aunt Sari, and her other Grandmother spend the first opening moments of the event with them and head back to the Ranch, leaving the young women to themselves. Around the campfire, hotdogs, s'mores, the telling of stories, song, and dance are what happens. The young women are hamming it up with their dances, singing, and cooking out in the open. Each plays instruments to promote a sense of jubilee, and Cassidy projects loudly.

"Hey, let's play truth or dare."

Liddy, Wren, and April look at each other, shrug their shoulders, and agree. Cassidy proceeds to remind everyone how to play.

"This is our newest version of sharing. Whatever question is selected, the person must answer. If the person does not answer, they will take on another's ranch chore for a week. Chores are chosen from the ones asking the questions."

All Women present stood and smacked hands and bumped hips in agreement.

"Liddy, Liddy."

They chanted while clapping. Liddy pulls out a flag that is fashioned out of a quilt square. She stands and waves her flag. Each of them brought a unique flag that represented themselves. Whoever is getting ready to share is to wave the flag and say:

"By the emblem of what I represent, I agree to the guidelines stated and wave this flag as a banner, giving you permission to proceed."

Cassidy starts the game.

"Truth or dare, Liddy?"

"Truth."

Liddy replies while giggling. Cassidy, Wren, and young April huddle together to determine questions suited to ask. After they return to their log, Cassidy nods to Wren to start the questioning.

"Liddy, we will ask you three questions, and you get to pick the one you want to respond to. Are you ready?"

"Ok, I am ready."

Staying seated on the log, Wren starts her questioning.

Liddy laughs.

"Well, I choose: Have you ever taken anything that was not yours? Yes, I did. When I was age 11, a close friend and I took our bikes to ride the trails by the Canyon. We both wanted to stop at the candy store in town first. While waiting for my friend to pay for her taffy at the register, I took the opportunity to take some bubble gum and slipped it into my pocket. There wasn't anyone that I am aware of who ever knew. I felt awful! I knew for my sanity and wanting not to disappoint God. I had to remedy my stupidity. The next day, I took my allowance, went to the store, and bought ten packs to relieve my quilt. I never took anything again, except one more time from someone in my family."

"Oh girl, now you are toying with us. What is the other thing?"

"Oh no, that is another question. I decline on the grounds; you can't ask any more questions besides the one I selected from the three."

"Ok, Liddy, the next person to question. You get to choose."

"I choose Cassidy."

Cassidy raises her flag. Liddy and Wren read the same questions to Cassidy. The game continues until all take part. The women have fun sharing and laughing together. Closing the celebration, Wren stands and raises a Dixie cup toast to:

"Good medicine, cheers to Grandma's Moto; "a merry heart does a person well." They all unite,

"Good medicine, Grandma; we love you!"

After the girls end their time together, they tidy things up, load the golf cart, and head back to the ranch.

Both Golf carts pull up to the front porch. Wren notices her Father and Uncle chatting about something that seems quite concerning. Cassidy and Wren know their Father and Uncle are in protective mode, watching out for their gals. It is only a matter of time before their protection takes action.

"Hi, Dad. Hi Uncle Spence, we are heading in now. We put the fire out and cleaned up."

Wren kisses her Dad on the head and pats Uncle Spence's shoulder. She crunches her nose playfully at them as she enters the house. Both Cassidy and Liddy follow in sequence as they pass the men. Wren shouts to her Mother and Grandmother, chatting at the kitchen counter.

"We are heading upstairs. Got any goodies?"

"Grandma pushes a plate towards them.

"Here are some loaded potato skins out of the oven and freshly made fruit water in the glass dispenser, along with the glasses you like to use."

"We can always count on you, Grandma! Thank you!"

"You are most welcome, anything for my jewels. Bring back the dishes, and don't forget to clean up when you are done."

"Smiling, Wren responds.

"Will do, Grandma. I think it's Liddy's turn tonight to return the plates and clean up."

Wren teasingly pats her on the back while bounding up the stairs. Liddy retorts: "Oh no, you don't. I did last time, and it's April's turn."

The girls play a few ping-pong games in the game room and head to Wren's room for a balcony view of the heavens. Cassidy is taking in their time together. Since she married and moved out of town, she needs more time with Wren, Liddy, and April. She loves catching up and messing around with them. Wren also misses her, and she misses their sister-talks long into the night. Liddy helps April gather the dirty dishes and takes them downstairs to the kitchen. Wren starts reviewing with Cassidy the game time they shared with Liddy and April.

"I guess that game of truth or dare is good."

Both girls laugh. Wren pushes buttons.

"She should have answered the question," Cassidy smiles and responds.

"Yeah, but some things are difficult to share." Wren spouts back, smiling,

"Yeah, the third round is not easy. We were pushing sensitive buttons on her romantic experience." Cassidy throws a pillow at her. She gets Wren's sense of humor.

"Yeah, but seeing how far we can prod before someone breaks is fun."

They cackle softly about it. Wren closes the conversation about Liddy.

"Aah, she is a good girl. I am enjoying having her around. Cassidy turns the table on Wren.

"What about you, Wren? Are you going to share how you got tangled up with this guy Drake?"

Cassidy gets her stored telescope out of Wren's closet. She wipes the lenses and extends the tripod legs locking them in place by screwing the knobs tight. The telescope is attached to the top. After tilting it to a perfect position, she zooms in on the section of the heavens she wants to observe. Liddy and April return.

"Come on over, you guys. Look what I found."

After they all spend some quiet time peering at the night sky, they decide it is time to rest. They sprawl all over the bed and floor. Wren closes the doors to the balcony and makes sure all the women and young girls have their blankets to snuggle down for a good night's sleep. Tomorrow is Family Liberty Night.

Before the Family gathers, Wren approaches her Father and seeks to see him privately. They head into his office.

"Dad, when we meet tonight with the family, can I bring up something about that guy I encountered in the woods?" Her Dad is kind and considerate.

"Sure, I am guessing you want some feedback."

"Yes, since it is the night for sharing and having the liberty pass to speak freely, I thought it would be a good opportunity to get different perspectives on what to do about him."

"That is a courageous thing to do." Dad pats her back as a signal to join the family in the family

room. Wren is delighted to plop on the comfortable chair beside Cassidy.

The family randomly shares their concerns and allows others to give input. They are there to support each other and enable the family members to express their opinions without crossing the line. There are red flags that each person could visually lift if someone feels it is going too far. Once a flag rises, the conversation halts and is on the shelf. It can only continue again if the person having the conversation approves. And then it may proceed with caution. Once a black flag rises, the conversation is over. Father makes closure regarding it. Private counsel is in his den to be counseled later if or when the black flag rises. In that case, both mother and father unite to keep peace and unity.

Each month allows the family to expand their vision

for the ranch and personal growth. It is a time for creative input, helping one another to achieve their dreams or projects. The open forum leads to group discussion. It's a thinking session to help find solutions. All concerns are valued. Encouragement and wisdom are given to help others gain clarity to reach their desired goal in the Lord. Positive things come out of these meetings, like gardens, habitat preservation, making things to sell, and building homes for families. Many dreams and ideas are birthed and nurtured during this time. The family has a fruitful time together if they are open to each other.

The Liberty meeting is now in session. The family sits in a circle as if sitting around a campfire, except with comfort. During this time, Grandma likes to multitask while listening. She sits in her rocking chair, crocheting baby hats for the local hospital. She frequently makes colorful blankets for sick children. Any sitting time is an opportunity for her to listen and crochet. Dad sits in his comfortable chair with Wren's mom on the arm beside him. The rest of the family sit around on whatever they can claim first.

Their new neighbors are a highlight of tonight's group discussion, and their unfriendliness is a concern. Wren's Father starts the meeting with a challenge of what the family can do to make the Waters feel more welcome.

The new neighbors are resistant to standard ranching procedures regarding strays. They talk about what may be a good solution, like the double fencing around the perimeter that Wren suggests.

"Well, I know I have to stay off their property," Wren freely let out.

Everyone laughs. Father responds.

"Yes, we see your dilemma, Wren. I think double fencing is a good option, and we will get staff to check on the cost of materials and the estimated time to get that done. What else can be done?"

He offers others to come forward with any ideas. Liddy suggests asking them to attend their annual pig roast. After all, they are preparing to advertise to their neighbors and friends. Mom interjects the possibility of everyone taking a day to do something nice for them, and it could be a letter, flowers, food, craft, prayer, etc.

"A welcome month!" April interjects. Grandma offers her suggestion.

"I can make some baked goods."

Spence offers his services regarding the care for their Green Space.

"We could order them a pizza?" Ty-Yung chimes in.

"Cool idea Ty," Grandpa says.

They all agreed. Spence pats him on the back with a sturdy, playful affirmation.

"Let's sign up our days on the whiteboard in the mudroom." Looking at his wife.

"Mother, will you do the honor of setting the format up? The visual schedule will prevent overlapping or repeating one another's good deeds." Dad continues.

"Ok, now we are closing the discussion over the neighbors. The floor is now open for others needing the family's input." Wren lifts her hand, and her Dad explains.

"Wren has already come to me asking permission to discuss her matter; do you want to take the floor? Before that, I want to interject that we can have fun with this.

However, I want you to consider her vulnerable transparency and offer her your input with good intentions. Wren, you have the floor."

Wren stands and addresses the family.

"Thank you, guys, for allowing me to share my situation. I have met a person I am sure you are already aware of."

The whole family is smiling.

"This person is a guy, and his name is Drake Silverman. He has been staying on the neighbor's property of late. Well, it has come down to him asking me out. I like him for some reason, and I want to try it. I know it is odd to ask, and no fooling; it has been awkward, and I do not know much about him. I do not want a summer romance; I have guarded my heart in that regard and am unsure how to pursue someone without wasting my time. I do not want to date just to date. I want to find someone that I can have a future with. I would appreciate your input."

Wren sits down, fidgeting with the necklace her Grandmother gave her. Cassidy speaks up first.

"Well, I know Wren has guarded her heart since her bad experience with Cole. I want to see her step out and take a risk. I would like her to go on this date. Of course, it must be in a safe setting where other people are around. I suggest perhaps they even could drive separately. Then she could learn more about him and see if he answers her questions about possibly being at a future wedding."

All laugh. Mother interjects.

"Cassidy, let's not take it that far."

Grandma puts her crochet down to reply.

"On a serious note, I agree with Cassidy. Having dinner would be a good icebreaker, providing an opportunity to learn more about each other. You could perhaps walk to the ice cream parlor and sit and talk by the fountain." Grandfather pipes in.

"It is a beautiful place." Grandpa gets the group going.

"Yes, that ice cream is not a bad idea at that. I think I will head out and get some if anyone wants to go after our meeting?" All are chuckling. Aunt Sari responds.

"Sure, Grandpa, my group would love to go."

Father stands up and shares his thoughts.

"I respect your openness about it. Spence did conduct a background check on him already, and he did not come up with anything, but that does not mean he is not hiding something. Wren shakes her head upon hearing that Uncle Spence and her Father are already looking out for her behalf. She responds.

"I agree with taking it slow and meeting in a well-populated place."

Her Father replies.

"I suggest you let him pick you up. That way, we can meet him while you are getting ready and see if we can get more of a handle on him. I am interested to know his thoughts on God."

All vocalized in agreement.

"Ok, I appreciate your input. I will take it under consideration."

Mom grabs Wren, kisses her cheek, and whispers.

"Wish you well, sweet one." Uncle Spence speaks to her.

"Yes, it is good to be thoughtful regarding who you allow getting close to you."

Wren ends the discussion and agrees with what has been deliberated, yet Uncle Spence has one more interjection to note.

"Time is needed to get a better feel if he is worth getting to know better. The meeting ends, and everyone heads their way.

A few days later, Spence and Father talk on the front porch at the playing table. Both are playing a chess game, and they check more on Drake Silverman, and Uncle Spence starts talking.

"I investigated Drake, and he has no record of wrongdoing, nor did I find anything particularly out of place that would lead to suspicion. However, I still sense something off." Father responds.

"Me as well. I also discovered that Drake is an only child and attended college. After college, he joined his mother's contracting jobs with the government, and I assume it was robotics since his mother is well-known for that. He returned to school, tallied some more degrees, and his mother died. It appears he traveled the world for a few years and joined the NASA group." Spence spouts.

"That's where the secrecy plays out. It makes sense! He must be a brilliant guy to be into all that."

Father then replies.

"Yes, which is good for Wren. She deserves someone with an intellectual capacity. His mother and father were a part of that group campaigning for a better world." Spence takes up a new sense of concern.

"That movement is still operative, I hear." Father puts his hands under his chin.

"Yes, and I suspect you know who else belongs to it?" Spence shares.

"Our new neighbors belong to it. Don't you think it odd Drake just happens to be visiting with them, and they both have interest in this?" William responds.

"That does connect some dots. But that does not mean they are bad. They are a passionate group setting out to protect our resources and save our planet, and there is nothing wrong with that." Spence continues with a mode of suspicion.

"Yes, that is true; however, I heard this group is also working on bettering humankind. The avenues they are traveling to arrive there conflict with those in the mindset of the normal population." While William is distracted, Spence makes some impressive chessboard moves.

"Keep going. I am listening. What do you mean?" William is hoping it is not bad. Spence is excited to share what he just read about that morning in a journal report.

"Well, the papers are reporting this extreme group is working on finding ways to extend life. They are tampering with human-created properties and using technology and natural resources. They hope to develop measures to mutate our bodies to self-heal but also have no restraints to adding technology to the body to improve life. The conservative population feels it is wrong to mess with the natural order of creation. They had a few uprisings, and it seems the scientific advancement for the world group went into hiding or dissipated. Nothing more has been reported about them again." William finds that intriguing and shares some more information he uncovered.

"I found out that His father is a freelance writer and

supported the movement. Maybe they are still actively operating, and I have to say it sounds like a story for a science fiction movie. Maybe they have an island where they experiment and produce monsters." Spence smacks his right leg.

"There you go. Maybe that's why we feel something off, and Drake is a monster maker."

They laugh at the ridiculousness of the thought. Spence makes another comment.

"It would explain why the neighbors have specific clientele they work with?"

"Yes, that is true; we must do more extensive research."

CHAPTER 12

GETTING ACQUAINTED

Wren's father and mother are sitting on the swing on the front porch. Drake pulls up in his car and parks. He goes up the steps and, nearing Wren's parents, shoots out his hand to shake for introductions.

"Hello, my name is Drake Silverman. I assume you are Wren's parents?"

William gets off the swing and greets him.

"Yes, my name is William, and you can call me Will if you like?"

He invites him to sit in the rocking chair while William sits by his wife on the swing.

"This is my wife, Caroline, Wren's mother."

She extends her hand to shake his.

"So nice to meet you, Drake. Wren is getting ready, and she'll be down shortly."

"I asked her to invite you a little early, so we could have a chance to get acquainted. Will says."

"I see; I expect that you would." Her mother asks.

"So, where are you from, Drake?"

"I come from a small town in Ohio; I'm an only child. My Mother and Father are both accomplished people, and I am proud to say I am who I am because of them."

"Oh, what did they do?"

"Well, my mother was a scientist who contracted with the Military to work on developing robotic prototypes that would serve the population. My father worked at a university. When he felt it time to move on from his position as a dean and professor at the university, he transitioned into becoming a full-time freelance writer and motivational speaker."

"Are your parents still living in Ohio? Wren's Mother asks.

"My mother passed, but my father still owns the property we lived on then. He is rarely home due to his desire to stay incognito. He dithers around gathering familiarity with different cultures all over the world. He rents secluded places suitable for his passion for writing." Wren's Mom replies.

"We are very sorry to hear you lost your mother."

"Thank you. It is kind of you to say that, and I do miss my Mother."

Drake feels vulnerable and clears his throat. Upon seeing Wren appear through the squeaky screen door wearing jeans, a sleeveless periwinkle blouse, and a matching sweater draped over her forearm, he is relieved. Drake rises to greet her.

"Ready to head out? You look lovely." Wren smiles at him.

"I see you are getting acquainted with my parents. Hope they are not asking too many questions?" Wren leans into her father, giving a look that portrays a sassiness.

"Nothing you should not expect from two endearing parents who love their daughter."

"Great, good to hear I am so loved."

She kisses her father on the top of his head and kisses her mother's cheek. Wren turns to Drake.

"Shall we get going, Mr. Drake?" They turn and leave.

They get into a nicely washed jeep and buckle in. Wren starts their conversation.

"So where are we heading to first?

Drake nods to look ahead. He drives Wren down the ranch's lane, lined with white fencing and perfectly aligned trees. As he approaches the main road, he toots his horn at a rabbit sitting on the road and soon picks up speed. Wren's hair flies in the wind. He watches her from his peripheral vision as she gathers her locks and places them in a secure clip to keep her hair from beating her face. He cannot forget when her hair hit his face in his dream. As they travel in the doorless vehicle, Drake clears his throat and responds.

"I thought we would try the Mill. It has a nice place to walk around and get some ice cream."

"That sounds like a plan I can get into!" Wren breathes in the fresh air and raises her arms.

A little time of silence takes place until Drake breaks the awkwardness.

"By the way, Wren. You look lovely tonight, and that

color compliments you." She puts her arms down and straitens her sweater on her lap.

"Thank you, Drake. I think you look very dashing yourself. Aqua suits you! I have always liked Oxford shirts with the sleeves rolled up." They both laugh and return to an awkward silence.

Wren notices Drake's unique watch, which appears to have a multitasked purpose. She inquires about it.

"I like your watch; It's very techy."

"Oh well, yes, I like techy stuff."

"Do you wear a watch?"

"Yes, but it feels confining, so I don't always wear it. My phone tells me the time if I need to know."

"Oh, yes, sure, it can feel that way sometimes."

"Would you like to listen to some music?" Drake offers.

"Ok, I can look for something while you drive." Wren pushes buttons and passes over various stations until she settles on an oldies station.

"Is this ok with you?" Drake is surprised at her choice.

"Why, yes, it suits me fine."

They arrive in town and slowly pass families and couples taking a stroll. Wren shares.

"I like watching people. Look at the two elderly couples sitting on the bench. They are holding hands. Is that just the sweetest thing? I hope to have that kind of love someday."

Drake smiles. He parks the jeep and jumps out heading over to Wren's side politely offering his hand to help her out. She grabs her sweater, and takes his hand while rising out of the vehicle she replies.

"Thank you! I can get used to this kind of treatment." She hoped he did not notice the heat racing up her neck.

"You are welcome." Drake is amused.

He notices her embarrassment at his touch. She seems so innocent and vulnerable, yet he recalls their initial spunky interaction and how she demonstrated that she could care for herself if needed. She is not as helpless as one might think, yet he suspects there are more layers to her personality. He hopes this date will give him some clarity on if she is someone that would work in his family's life. He thinks about how she took notice of his watch. It would be more complicated to explain if he got any signals on his watch, as she calls it. It is his communicator. He will be more thoughtful about concealing that kind of technology. He stops and asks her to wait a moment. He heads back to his vehicle and opens a hidden security compartment, and quickly removes his watch, placing it safely inside before he returns back to where he left her. They take a short walk and view artsy trinkets set out by a vendor before heading to the restaurant. They sit in the upper dining area overlooking pleasant surroundings. A bubbling brook and tiny lights are a few of the restaurant's many details to create an ambiance. Lighted stairs lead down the paths below. Soft music serenades from a nearby speaker neatly tucked away in a pot of greenery.

"This is nice." Wren shares her approval.

" I love being outdoors." Wren shoots back.

"You must like it, considering you are now camping amid nature."

"Well, yes, I do love it. I like gathering new plant specimens; my mother is the biggest reason for that hobby."

"Oh, where does your mother live?"

"She is no longer with us."

"I am so sorry."

The waiter interrupts them.

"Are you ready for me to take your order, or do you need more time?"

"Yes, can you give us a few more minutes?"

"Yes, no problem."

The waiter walks away, and they pick up the menus and ponder what to get. Drank nods.

"Wren, please get whatever you like."

"That's very generous. I appreciate that."

The waiter returns, and Wren goes first with her order."

"I think I am going with the baked chicken and rice dinner." Drake jumps in.

"Sounds good. I am going with the ribs and baked potato. Does It have a complimentary salad and rolls that go with it?"

The waiter nods. Wren interjects.

"We will need to walk around town after this meal." They both laugh as the waiter takes back their menus. Drake replies.

"Yes, and hopefully, you can save room for ice cream." Wren gets excited.

"That is what doggy bags are for. I will make sure I save room."

After the meal, they walk around the town. It is a very quaint and romantic town. Drake takes her hand, and she sheepishly welcomes it as they head to the ice cream parlor.

"So, Wren, what led you to choose a career in education?" Wren clears her throat.

"Teaching suits me. Nothing is more fulfilling than knowing you can make a difference in helping a child bloom. It is an honor to work with children."

"How amazing! It sounds like you got it together. Wren raises her eyebrows and points to herself.

"Oh, now, don't flatter me too much. I don't take on those accolades easily; I am just a woman who works and loves what she does. How about you? Explain what you do." Drake replies.

"I design mobile modules for people to take on vacations. I enjoy providing a safe place for families or individuals to reside temporarily. My modules are designed to reflect the characteristics of nature, but tweaked with comfort and technology."

"That sounds terrific! I would love to see what you have done. I assume the module in the clearing by the woods is one of your designs?" Drake is delighted she can appreciate his work.

"Yes, it is. Perhaps before I leave, I can give you a tour?"

"Oh, I forgot that you will only be visiting briefly. I hope it is not too soon?"

"Well, he hesitantly says, I think we can manage a time for you to tour my dwelling, as long as you do not take any snapshots."

She smiles, knowing he refers to her last escapade sneaking a rough peak at his place in the woods."

"Boom, you got me. Yes, I recall. I learned that lesson already," they join in laughter. Wren turns to him.

"Here we are! Ice cream, kind sir?" Wren extends her arms, pointing to the charming ice cream vendor.

"Yes, beautiful lady, I do! Drake points to a poster displaying an ice cream sundae.

"Look! The cherry on top. It's visual and aligns with how you chose a career that suits you. It is like putting a cherry on top."

She drops her jaw in a surprised look that says it all. Is he for real? She exhales and lets out a laugh.

The ice cream clerk enters their conversation.

"Next! Do you know what you want?" Wren blurts out.

"I do!" Drake pokes with a sense of humor and points at the poster again.

"I want that one on the poster." Wren chirps in.

"I like that choice. Make that for me as well."

Both enjoy their time together, and Drake is taking a shine to her. She, in turn, is fascinated with him. Wren can hardly believe a person like him is in her life, and then Drake gets on a serious note.

"I have enjoyed my time with you immensely, Wren, but I believe it is time to head back."

He kisses her hand, and she flushes.

"Wow, thank you for this. I have enjoyed our time together."

They both walk back to the car in silence, looking at the stars and scenery. They arrive at Wren's Ranch, and Drake walks her to the front stairway in front of the house. A curtain in the front window pushes aside, and you can see her sister Cassidy peeking through them. Cassidy realizes she's spotted and drops the curtain abruptly.

"I see they are waiting for you." Drake playfully responds.

"Yes, she will want all the details." Drake laughs and takes Wren in his arms.

"Don't leave this out." He brings her in for a kiss, and she gets lost. She seems to melt into his arms, and he loves the feeling of her next to him. He releases her, and they stare at each other with endearment.

"Hey, you two."

A male voice coming from the corner of the porch shouts out.

"Glad to see you made it back safe and sound."

Grandpa had been sitting at the game table porch drinking a glass of sweet tea when they pulled in. He is in the shadows, so they do not know he is there. With a bit of embarrassment, Wren distances herself from Drake.

"Yes, Grandpa, we did. He has been very good to me." Drake waves at him.

"How do you do, sir?"

"Mighty good, thank you. Sorry, I do not want to intrude on your goodbyes. I will head in; it's time to hit the hay."

"Thank you, Grandpa. I love you!" Wren shouts at him as the screen door hits him in the bum.

"Love you back, sweetheart. Glad to know you both had a good time." Wren enters the house and waves goodbye to Drake as he leaves down her driveway and returns to the Waters.

Entering the house, Wren sees her sister sitting on the couch, smiling like Chester Cat in Alice in Wonderland.

Their cat is purring on Cassidy's lap while she strokes its fur. Wren's sister cannot contain her need to know.

"Ok, spill!" Wren plops down at the other end of the couch facing her.

"I enjoyed him! He is fun, caring, and makes me dizzy."

"Did he kiss you? Does he want to see you again?" Wren is elated.

"Yes, and yes."

"Yowzer girl, and holy granolas! I am happy for you!" Wren laughs.

"Me too! We are going out again in a few days to hike the trails in the Canyon and have a picnic."

"I hope it all works out. I am so happy you decided to give it a chance."

"Me too! He said he would also let me tour his personally designed module at some point."

"I would love to see it. Do you think Drake would allow me to join you?"

"Perhaps, I do not see why not. It would be more appropriate if I were not alone in Drake's dwelling." Cassidy nods in agreement.

"Right, that would not go down well with the family." Wren jumps up.

"You got that right. Let's head up to the bed and talk more."

The television in her parent's room is still on. They quietly pass by and head to Wren's room. As Cassidy passes her parent's room, she points, she puts one hand to the side of her mouth, and whispers.

"They will want to know about your date in the morning, you know?" Wren winks at Cassidy.

"Yes, but I do not have to reveal everything." Wren is smirking.

"True, some things are private. Thanks for filling me in, though."

The next few days go fast for Wren's family. They all work overtime getting ready for the festival festivities. Mom is wholly absorbed in her secret art project. Dad and Spence are working overtime and gathering needed supplies and structures for setting up their family's barn display. Grandma is cooking up a storm in the kitchen. Grandpa is building exhibits for the ranch booth and birdhouses. He is hoping to sell out, as he did the prior year. Aunt Sari and April are busy painting and printing cards to sell. Ty-Yung is sorting through his photographs to choose which ones he wants to display of the wildlife in their nature preserve.

Wren and Liddy work hard doing their chores. There is little time for personal pleasures for anyone; all crash badly at night from pushing themselves so hard. They have no trouble sleeping. The phone rings, and Wren picks it up with one hand while hanging the horse reins on the peg. She walks out of the barn and heads to the house while talking.

"Oh, Hi, Drake. Yes, I will be ready with bells on. Give me at least 30 minutes to freshen up."

She sees Cole's vehicle coming up the lane, which is unwelcoming

"Oh man, Drake, I need to go. We have an unexpected visitor."

Wren is flustered; she does not want to talk to him now. She quickly heads to the house and runs upstairs. Within minutes, she asks her sister to come to her aid.

"Cassidy, we have an unwelcome guest coming up the driveway. I do not have time to deal with him, and I am getting ready to leave on a date with Drake in 30 minutes. Can you intercept me?"

Cassidy jumps into action.

"Yes, I will see what I can do."

"Hurry up, he is almost at the door, and I need you to get rid of him. I do not want him present when Drake comes."

"On it!" Cassidy dashes down the stairs, ready to intercept and get Cole out of there.

Wren's Grandmother enters through the back door where she had just watered the garden. She hears the knocking at the front door and sees Cole. Walking towards him, she greets him.

"Howdy Cole, what a surprise to see you! Are you in town long?" Cole stops and chats.

"Just a tad. I was hoping to get a chance to talk to Wren. Is she around?"

"As far as I know, she is. Let me see if I can round her up. Have a seat. Would you like a glass of sweet tea while you're waiting?" Cole responds.

"Yes, that would be great! Thank you."

Cassidy is too late; Grandma got to him first. Cassidy darts out the door to the porch, where Cole sits and approaches him head-on while Grandma gets some iced tea in the kitchen.

Cassidy attempts to give him a solid message to clear out.

"Hey Cole, what are you doing here? Wren has plans, and messing them up would not be fair."

"Are you saying she has a date?" Cole is acting put out, and Cassidy does not care what he feels.

Cassidy is looking at him sternly.

"Yes, by golly, I am! Haven't you caused her enough pain without stirring things up again? How about having the courtesy to call first? You need to find out if Wren welcomes your visit, and you don't just show up!" By that time, Grandmother comes through the screen door with an alarmed look.

"Well now, Cassidy, is that how we treat guests?" Cassidy is frustrated.

"Grandma, he is messing with Wren."

"Stop right there. I understand how protective you are of your sister. Let's hear the man's words, and then we can shoo him away if necessary." Cole feels uncomfortable.

"No, Cassidy is right. I should have called first. I do not mean to cause a scene; I will just head out and try another time." Cole starts to turn and leave when Grandpa comes out of the house.

He takes the glass of tea from Grandma's hand and delivers it to Cole. He directs Cole to the barn.

"Hi Cole, good seeing you! Let's take a walk and chat a bit." Cassidy is stressed, and she needs to get rid of Cole promptly. Her Grandma interferes without knowing her dilemma, and then her Grandpa retains Cole further by taking him to the barn. Cassidy bounds back upstairs to inform Wren of her failure, but Wren darts past her.

Wren hopes she dodged the bullet and Cole is gone. She runs down the stairs pulling her cap on her head. She heads to the kitchen to check on the picnic basket Grandma is putting together.

"Grandma, it looks fabulous! Thanks, Grandma, for taking the time and effort to prepare our picnic basket." Wren kisses her on the cheek.

"Quit your fussing. I Love doing these kinds of things. Do not forget the jug of iced tea and blanket."

"I have it, Grandma. Thanks for reminding me."

Wren notices Cassidy acting odd. Cassidy meanders over to Wren and whispers.

"He is not gone."

"What, why is he still here? Drake will be pulling in at any moment now."

"I know! Grandpa intercepted before I could get him out of here".

"Where is he now?"

"Cole is in the barn with Grandpa and Dad, I expect," Cassidy says.

Drake arrives on time and parks his jeep in front of the steps. He notices another truck parked in front of the barn where visitors and clients usually park. Wren quickly heads outside and meets him with the picnic supplies to put into the car, and she hopes to hurry him along before Cole has a chance to mess things up.

"Hi, Drake. These need to get loaded. Grandma is so gracious to put together a picnic basket for us." She hands him a jug of tea.

"Oh! Dang, it. I have to go back inside. I left the blanket on the kitchen stool. Give me a few minutes."

"Ok, I will put this stuff in the back."

Drake places the basket inside the jeep, but first, he peeks at the contents within. Wren is already out of hearing range. She shoots up the stairs into the house before he can respond. He notices she is rushing for some reason; then, out of the barn, he sees Cole approaching. Cole speaks.

"Hi, you must be Wren's date?"

Drake sees Cole as the fellow Wren was talking to at the Gathering. Now things make sense why Wren was bustling around. Drake boldly asks.

"Yes, I am. You are?"

I am Cole, an old friend of Wren."

"Augh, yes, I saw you at the gathering. Are you here for any other reason other than performing?"

Cole smiles and gets ready to respond when Wren abruptly enters the scene. To her horror, she senses that Cole and Drake are at odds with each other. Wren's Dad comes out of the barn and observes Wren's predicament. He quickly dashes over to where the men are conversing and apologizes to Drake for not coming over earlier to welcome him. Her Dad interacts with them, hoping to alleviate any brawl that seems to be brewing.

"Where are my manners? I gather you two are getting acquainted?"

"Yes!" They Drop their defenses with one another for the moment.

Dad looks up at his daughter and gives her a nod of affirmation that he is intervening on her behalf. Wren's father puts his hand on Cole's shoulder and speaks to Cole, and he then extends his hand, which guides them both toward his truck.

"Cole, It is nice seeing you. We wish you the best with your music ventures. Please give our regards to your family."

William gives Cole a firm pat on the back. He directs him back to his car parked by the barn. Cole responds.

"Yes, sir, I appreciate getting a chance to meet up again."

Cole tips his hat at Wren and Drake, jumps in his truck, and revs his engine before heading out. Wren's Dad turns to Wren and Drake and shouts out with encouragement.

"You two have a nice time today. It's a good day to have a picnic. I peeked in the basket and noticed your grandma has a good spread set up for you both." Wren responds.

"Awesome! I can't wait to eat! I am famished." Drake looks at Wren's Dad and thanks him. He turns his attention to Wren and starts the engine.

"Ok. I am hungry as well. Perhaps we can eat first, then hike?" Wren interjects.

"Sounds like we are on the same page. I know a great place we can have a picnic."

CHAPTER 13

THE FESTIVAL

Once a year, the town comes together to appreciate those citizens who stand out in their community. This year it focuses on celebrating unseen heroes and this year's focus is on outstanding educators.

Wren does not get any indication that the community will be celebrating her this year. Her mother gets the ball rolling in Wren's favor. She offers to create a gifted sculpture for the library in honor of her. It is a reminder to all who gaze on it; the imprint one person can make on another for the good of their community. Special-Needs children do not have society's approval, and Wren "steps up to the plate" to help.

The festival is located at the County Fairgrounds. It has an extensive array of tents set among the barns and a large bandstand where derby racing occurs. Vendors line lanes with food a large variety of food, animals, games, crafts, and entertainment. They even have events of competition that the crowds can enjoy, like an area set up for old cars. The cherished smells mark the end of Summer. Their savoring aromas float in the air's current: cotton candy, vinegar-splashed french fries, and fish. Various meat aromas fill the air. The savoring smells bring a smile to many faces.

Rows of entrepreneurism showcase homemade and commercial goods near the Library. Using tented cubicles, the merchants can present their merchandise, keeping the sun rays off them and providing ample room for their displays. Each vendor has an assigned spot. They all are family-oriented professionals and amateurs representing the flare of what they have to offer.

In honor of the educators in their community, a whole barn is set aside to accommodate the celebration. There are portraits of all educational professionals in the local education field, along with displays of pictures, letters, poetry, and video representation of the teachers in the classrooms put together by parents. Children's artwork, creative pre-recorded musical demonstrations, and an assortment of appreciation are evident everywhere.

The student booth representing Wren's presentation is the first display you see. With the help of the parents, teaching aides, and students, a cyclic recorded video visualizes the student's growth and love for learning on a big screen accompanied by music. Each current student she has in her care and those she instructed in prior years impart their heart and reason for choosing Wren to be the town's person to celebrate this year. They share comments as to why they love their teacher. It goes as follows:

"She makes learning fun."

"She loves us."

"She finds something we are good at."

"When we feel small, she makes us feel big."

"She lets us have bad days and still loves us."

"She lets us know we are valued."

"She takes us to places where we get to pet horses, go on hayrides, and drink cider."

"She spends her money buying school supplies, holiday decorations, and parties."

"She makes our classroom feel and smell good.

"She is my friend."

At the end of the video, the children and their parents gather in a group and shout.

"We love you, Ms. Wren. You are our family!"

Wren loves the variety of foods offered at the festival. Her favorite selections are the hot vinegar fries, a hot, tasty lamb-filled gyro, and freshly squeezed lemon/strawberry lemonade. They all dazzle her taste buds with delight. Her sister Cassidy loves the elephant ears with powdered sugar, caramel, and chocolate drizzles.

Wren has been getting lots of smiles and good wishes from the Vendors, which feels odd to her. She does not like accolades, and she feels everyone deserves credit for making the community a place to be proud to be a part of. Some vendors have already given her a free complimentary side which Cassidy knows why. She does not want Wren to know the possible honors getting ready to be bestowed; she makes light of them.

"In honor of our educators?" Cassidy replies to them.

"Wow! Thank you! This is the year for educators."

"We want to thank you as well for your delicious food!"

All are giving nods of appreciation to one another. The girls move on to the Events Tent.

The volunteer Event tent has a full lineup of horse barrel racing, cattle roping, sheep herding, pig and turtle racing, frog jumping, and potato sack racing. It is a tradition that Cassidy and Wren take part in the potato sack race, where they have to put one leg each in one bag and race to the finish line. They laughed so hard the prior year. They were doing well until they came up against a stinky obstacle. They attempted to avoid the droppings an animal left behind that the cleanup crew missed and chose to take a tumble. They almost wet themselves laughing so hard. Kids remember their teacher tumbling. They thought her laughter was crying and consoled her by telling her she could try again and do better next time. This recollection always warms her heart. What she imparts to them comes back at the least unexpected moments. Now, Wren's students recognize her on the line and cheer her and her sister on. Wren shouts out to her students.

"If we win? You get a popcorn movie day."

She winks at them, sealing the deal.

Drake drives to the festival in a classic 1959 red and white vintage car. After parking it among other classic cars in the car show zone, a card with a large black number printed on it goes on display on the windshield, and another smaller version for his pocket to give back when he retrieves the car later. He leaves it in their care and proceeds to meander towards other festival festivities. While leaving the car show section, he notices boxes purposely placed throughout the line of cars so people can vote on their favorite car. First, second and third places are up for grabs. The winner gets a gift card to local eateries and a winner ribbon. It is his favorite classic car. He even complimented the car's iconic connection to Coke by drinking a glass bottle of Icey Coke, wearing rolled-up jeans, a white shirt with rolled-up sleeves, and slicked-back hair representing the time of the 50s. The local newspaper took a snapshot of him holding his Coke cola. The Waters asked him to submit their car in the contest. They had other pressing things at the Bed and Breakfast and wanted to participate in their new community event.

Drake wishes his kids could have been here. Their life experiences living in Space are so different from kids residing on Earth. His children are the children of the future. Drake wanders around and checks out the various booths of goods up for sale. Baked goods, jewelry, candles, art, and the like are available. He notices the McCarthy Ranch booth display and their branding above it being prominent. He heads over to see if Wren is there.

Wren's grandpa spots Drake.

"Well, howdy, Drake. You enjoy the festival?"

"I just arrived, getting the lay of the land, so to speak."

"If you are looking for Wren, she and her sister are most likely at the Event tent. They signed up for some games."

"Alright, I appreciate the heads up."

Drake heads out, searching for the rabbit who took him off course from his original mission for P.E.S.

Drake walks casually amongst wall-to-wall people

and is trying to be careful not to bump into anyone. He does not like crowded places usually, but his feelings for Wren motivates him to suffer through.

"Hi, I saw you at the gathering. Have you been here long?" Startled from Drake's focused thoughts,

Drake realizes a woman is shouting at him from a food booth he is passing. She is selling "elephant ears."

"Just for a little while." He smiles and removes eye contact.

Drake picks up his pace, eager to walk beyond her range of communication. He is uninterested in her flirtation. He gets safely away from his pursuer and resumes his search. He finds himself being under pressure to move with the flow of people. Even though he thought he was well beyond communication range, the Elephant Ear vendor ran up behind him and thrust a card into his hand with her number.

"I am here all week if you want to sample some of our treats."

He did not want to chitchat with anyone then and is glad the flow is starting to move more fluently, helping him to escape her passes. He is familiar with women flirting with him and knows not to play into her maneuver. He has no desire to pursue anyone else.

Drake arrives at the Event tent where Wren is said to be and notices her not being there. He looks some more and notices a group of kids carrying on. He walks over and sees Wren right in the middle of their commotion. He decides to observe. It is Cassidy who first notices Drake, and she comes up behind him, eating a lemon-lime ice slushy.

"Hi, Drake."

"I see you spotted Wren. Those are her students, and they are excited that she won the potato sack race. Last year was a failure, and they were looking forward to seeing her succeed this year.

"They must really like her?"

"Yes, they do at that," Cassidy replies.

Wren notices Cassidy talking to someone and realizes it is Drake. She hugs the kids and dismisses herself from them, and joins Cassidy and Drake.

"Hey, Drake, I was wondering when you would you show up?" Wren says, smiling.

Cassidy realizes it's time to move out of the picture so they can have fun together. She pipes up.

"Well, I suspect you guys will be chumming around now. I will go back to the McCarthy booth and help out." Wren shouts out to her sister.

"It was fun, sis."

"Yes, it was. See you two later, and don't forget the town's reveal. Mom is revealing her sculpture."

"I will be there for sure. Thanks for the reminder!"

"Let's head to the education barn. My students are excited about me seeing what they put together for me." Drake grabs her hand.

"Well, let's go for it. It is good to see you! I missed you!"

"Yes, me too! It has been hectic getting things ready for the festival. She jumps up and gives him a smooch on the cheek."

"Awe, now that is not fair. You missed!" Drake stops.

He grabs her around the waist, lifts her into him, and kisses her. Wren is embarrassed about being caught off guard.

"Oh my, that was something. I like it!"

They both laugh and get applause from the female standing behind her booth that flirted with him earlier.

"Nice catch." Wren is not sure if she is referring to her or Drake. They smile at her and stroll onto the education barn.

"Oh my goodness, Look at what they did here!"

Wren is in awe as she enters the entrance of the barn.

"This is extraordinary!" Drake agrees.

"Yes, I like what I see."

Drake pulls her shirt to bring her attention to what he is looking at. It is a large screen playing a video of Wren and her students. Tears start falling down her face, and a parent nearby hands her a tissue.

"You're a special person, Miss McCarthy," the parent says.

"Well, thank you, my students are my heroes. They make me shine."

Wren leans into Drake's shoulder. She feels silly that she wept in front of a parent. Drake is moved. He clears his throat and fidgets. He parts from Wren and steps over to the booth to vote for Wren. Wren takes his hand and kisses it. They walk through the tent and begin reading the letters from her students posted on display. They are expressing their gratitude to all the educators represented. Wren is pleased. She quickly diverts the attention placed on her and asks Drake to dance.

"Hey, I hear the music. You want to go dancing?"

"I would love to if it is with you alone, but you are such a celebrity now, I don't know?"

"Funny, let's get going before I start blubbering again."

They find the entertainment and sit at a nearby table.

"Hey, there's that guy Cole. Your ex...., Wren holds up her hand and stops him.

"Yes, and we are not considering any confrontation. I am here with you, and you and I are a thing. We have been all summer, and he has nothing to do with our future."

"Wren, you have narrowed it down. Are you sure about me?"

"Yep! I am in love with you, and I do not want anyone else."

"Wow, I am in love with you too!"

They laugh and hold hands across the table. Drake looks serious now.

"Wren, Are you willing to go with me and leave your family?"

"I know your work is confidential. I do love my family. I am sure it will be a transition, but I will go where you go. We become family. Your children are amazing! I have no reservations."

Drake goes into concerning thoughts as she exits their table to go to the restroom. How is he going to make this relationship work? There is the P.E.S. he has to consider. They have to give an all-clear for him to marry her. Then there are his children, a different location out of this world where he lives, and issues of separation from her family. This marriage will have to pull together quickly. He will have to return to his work and family soon. What will he do if the Society says no? What will he do if his children do not like the idea of him getting married? Perhaps if The Society would not allow it, he could return to his parent's property. He can resume his course of research and design a different breed of mobile units more suitable to those nearby. He will also have to face the reality that he could lose her. He just could not fathom it.

"Hey, are you ok? I hope I did not scare you off!"

Drake comes out of his thoughts and returns to his activity with her.

"No, I am just processing things. I have no intention of losing what we have, sweet Wren."

"Good, that settles it! I am yours, and you are mine." Wren looks at her watch.

"Not to lessen the seriousness of our talk, but we need to get going. My mother is having a reveal ceremony, and it's imperative we are present. Let's pick up the pace so we won't miss it.'

Wren is proud of her mother's accomplishments. Drake and Wren arrive in time to see her Mother walking up onto the platform.

"Wren, will you join me?"

Wren leaves Drake with her family standing in the crowd. Her Mother points towards her as she comes up the stairs to the stage. The crowd applauds.

"This is Wren McCarthy, my eldest daughter. I am very proud of her and the field she chooses to work in, serving others. I have been commissioned to create a sculpture to remember my daughter among other educators like her. This sculpture will be set in front of the local library. Before I unveil, our Mayor and school superintendent have something to say."

Wren's mother steps back, and the distinguished leaders move to the microphone. The Mayor speaks first.

"Thank you, Caroline. We are excited to see what you

have created. However, before we do that, we want to recognize our County teacher of the year."

He hands the microphone to the Superintendent of the schools.

"Without further delay, our teacher of the year is our very own Special Education instructor, Ms. Wren McCarthy!"

The crowd explodes with cheers and happiness! Wren cries and gives her thank yous to all the educators, students, and community. Wren hugs her mother, and with the statue behind them, pictures are taken for the local newspaper. Drake and Wren wean from the crowd and head to grab a few coney dogs and onion rings.

Wren and Drake have been together the whole Summer. While sitting in the stands watching a ballgame, he thinks about how he will ask Wren the big question. It is time to get the ball rolling. He is overcome with his love for her and blurts it out to Wren.

"Wren, will you be my wife?" Wren is torn away from watching the celebration of the team winning.

"What? I can't hear you from all the fireworks. Is this not great! I can't believe you won box seats from your win at the festival! Yet, here we are!"

Girls sitting behind them are wide-eyed and covering their mouths in surprise. They shout out in unison.

"He asked you something important!" They giggle, and Wren turns to Drake.

"What is wrong? What are they talking about?"

"Nothing is wrong. I will talk to you later." The girls shout out for him.

"Don't Chicken out!" Drake is trying to keep it low-key.

"Alright, I will!"Turning to Wren, Drake attempts to ask her again.

"Yes, I do have a question for you."

He takes her food and drinks from her hands and sets them down in the box. He takes her hands in his and looks into her eyes.

Wren McCarthy, will you Mary me?" Wren is stunned.

She looks at the girls, who are giddily nodding yes. Wren looks back at Drake and wraps her arms around him before she plants a massive kiss on his lips.

"Yes, yes! I will marry you!"

The girls behind them scream with delight, and popcorn flies everywhere!

"It is not rice, but they are celebrating us!" Wren picks a few popcorn pieces out of her hair, and they laugh. Drake and Wren embrace and kiss again. The girls behind them blurt out.

"Look up there, and you're on the Kissing Cam!"

CHAPTER 14

COMING TOGETHER

Drake steps back and takes a panoramic view of the room. It is all he intends it to be. Once again, it is a fulfilling feeling to share it with someone special. He looks forward to creating memories with her.

Creating an environment where his bride feels honored is important to him! He is going to make use of every opportunity to make her feel valued. Every detail seen in the room expresses his love for her. It speaks without words that he hears her, and he acts on it. Her likes and dislikes are noted. He listens when she converses with him. To create an atmosphere conducive to their special night, he places a silver ice bucket with her favorite pink champagne on the table, accompanied by a tray of light edibles and a box of chocolates. A soft grey throw lay at the end of their bed, playing as a lovely backdrop to randomly thrown pink rose petals. On the mantel above the fireplace, a white envelope containing words of affection leans against the back wall. Accompanying it is a small gift box bound with a white ribbon. Sounds of birdcalls resonate from behind the forest greenery, which then transitions into the pounding of ocean waters colliding against the barrier; it is not to breach. The intensity of the waves cycles first with strength and vigor and ends with a soft sound of receding waters.

Wren is preparing for their wedding night in another part of the dwelling. The delightful rooms she makes herself ready in are unique due to Drake's inventiveness. Wren loves how his large dressing room and bath intertwine with his hidden technological innovations. Taking an in-depth look at her surroundings, she notices lightweight rock materials and greenery in use to establish the feel of an outdoor vibe. The decor accents and flooring are made of natural stone material, with the colors: tans, whites, and grays. From two softly glazed transparent sink basins, flow aqua-colored water from motion-activated faucets. The sink countertop is a clear substance infused with sand and flecks of gold, supported by a wooden bamboo cabinet. A section of the countertop retracts into the wall making it convenient to access hidden storage beneath. Tranquil pictures of forest greenery and streams of rushing water hang above the sinks. The bathroom walls change into a voice-activated viewing screen. The media viewed in the bathroom plays with a broad scope of recorded scenery, weather, and news gathered from all over the globe. Live feeds are accessible, producing sounds and imagery from syndicated places. Drake accesses cameras already in place at oceanic tourist sites, satellites in space, and entertainment hot spots.

Pictures hang above the sink and open like doors. Behind the doors is a shelving unit swivels out for personal hygiene products. Frosted green cylinder vases are hinged to the sidewall next to the sink displaying branches of forest greenery. The vases intermittingly release mists of scents that correlate with the environmental choices made for the room. A commode sits within a wall of rocks in a private nook of the room. Natural lighting beams through the skylights and side windows, eliminating the need to use artificial lighting during daylight. Descending from the ceiling are delicate lights illuminating the room in the evening. A clear resin soaking tub sits in a corner with small lighting dangling at various heights above, simulating stars. The panels surrounding the tub display scenic locations worldwide. The illusion that you are taking a bath in the middle of a desert, on an island, in front of an ocean, or within a rainforest is genuinely genius. Wren likes how the shower simulates a small waterfall.

A large dressing room veers off the bathroom, and it appears primarily empty except for a single oval standing mirror and a lounge couch positioned in the center of the room on the raised platform. The couch upholstery is covered in a shimmering midnight blue canvas, accented with pillows made with shades of greys, blues, and silvers. Wren has instructions on operating the system by vocally requesting help. The dressing room technology is cleverly installed in the mirror panel. Here, the micro-size computer runs the dressing support team. Motion-activated walls light up as you enter, and walls retract behind one other, revealing the garments and accessories available to the client.

A robotic technology team evaluates clothing options appropriate for individuals. The team maintains current and past selections and develops good options. They get to know each client's taste and will pick apparel fit to their liking. Merchandise is pre-ordered using online sites and set aside as options. The client's approval is the final process before making a purchase. Any items chosen are all bought from optimal apparel merchandisers. Articles not selected are returned. Accessories are put on automation racks that move out into the room for optimum retrieval. This time, Wren brings her apparel. Standing in front of the mirror, she admires herself and seeks approval from the last assessment team. The technology considers color, fashion, and enhancement qualities that suit skin tone and body type. Her choice is acceptable to the team. Wren is happy they approved. It gives her confidence that she is right in purchasing it. She takes one last look in the mirror, appreciating the gown's beauty and how it makes her feel.

Her thoughts go back to the day she purchases the soft silk garment. The particular store she finds it in is a high-end store that sells specifically intimate apparel. At the same time, Wren is waiting for her sister to finish getting fitted; she meanders through the store, pulling out this and that until she notices gown and falls gaga over it. It is the newest display. The beauty of the nightgown instantly beckons her. Wren's sister is busy with alterations in the dressing room. Wren questions why it may be captivating her. Perhaps it is in the presentation? The tall antique cabinet has mirrors on the insides of the cabinet so you can see the garment from all sides. Soft lighting and sprigs of greenery, chiffon, and glass crystals are all accessories used to create an atmosphere of intrigue for the highlighted garment. These special touches add a sense of mystery to the display. She feels a tug at her emotion and is motivated to buy it! It is a champagne-colored gown with a matching robe. It conveys both femininity and elegance. The top shoulders of the robe and gown are embellished with soft, delicate embroidery and beads. Wren looks at the price tag, and it reads $999.00. Wren entertains the idea of splurging for it.

Wren contemplates what a purchase such as this will mean to her. She pauses and wonders what other women might do in her position. This type of purchase would seem silly to many sensible women. To spend that kind of money for an event that may never occur. It would be considered frivolous. She rallies herself and declares the gown to symbolize the hope and faith she would privately hold onto that someday she would wear it for her husband. She plans to save it for her wedding night. She wants to be the most beautiful bride she can be for him. No matter how foolish it might appear to others. At this time, she must have it correctly preserved and stored. There is no man at this time. No one among her present acquaintances that are of the sort she is interested in joining as a partner.

Now the moment is finally at hand. The reality of marrying her dream man is here. She and the symbol of hope meant for her husband are here. She comes back from her thoughts and begins humming joyfully. She sways in turns and twists. The gown proves to fulfill all her expectations. Poising herself, she takes a deep breath and slowly smooths down her nightgown against her feminine curves. She takes one last Look at her image reflected in the floor-length mirror. She is pleased it enhances her womanly beauty.

Wren is startled by her husband's entrance. She cannot hide her stirring for him, and he causes reactions towards him that her body cannot hide. He looks so dashing, and Wren cannot stop the rushing of heat pulsating its direction up her neck to her face any more than being able to control the sun from rising.

He cannot believe how gorgeous she is. She is stunning! He takes in her beauty as he watches her move toward him. Her hair seems to bounce in harmony with the song of his heart. Her Honeymoon attire is a compliment to her natural beauty. He is enamored with her. He could not help but respond to the intuitive "call of the wild." She is the one who holds his heart captive from this point on.

Wren runs to him, slipping contently into his embrace. While in his arms, he filters her soft, auburn hair through his fingers as she compresses her body against his. It feels as if they are melting into one another. He marvels at God's creativity, having made this beautiful woman and gifting her to him. She has stars in her eyes, and he notices Wren's stars are twinkling. He is toasty through the depths of his heart. Looking aesthetically deeper into her eyes, you could see that they are the color of a deep mysterious blue with bursts of bronze. After moments of intertwined affection, Drake reminds himself to take things slow and restrain impulsive stirrings.

He interrupts the instinctive behavior and gently pulls back. The fire that is kindling is on hold. He shares how he would like to proceed through the evening. Wren amusingly complies as Drake covers her eyes with a soft silk scarf. He places his hands on her shoulder to direct her to the room he prepared meticulously. Once they entered the bridals suite, Drake removes the scarf. Wren is deeply touched. The thought Drake has put into this moment for them is impressive. She wonders how he transforms a bachelor pad into a romantic environment such as it is. He directs her attention to the gift and card placed on the mantel. She retrieves the card and takes a few moments to process it. An impulsive moment causes her to kiss him. Reading his endearing words deserves no less. It puts an exclamation mark on his expressed love for her.

Wren carefully opens the small ribbon-wrapped package and removes the paper as if she intuitively knew the contents within were fragile. She opens the box and pulls out a necklace. Wren notices three charms on it and a note lying beneath the charms at the bottom of the box. She takes out the note dangling the chain through her fingers. It reads that each charm has three separate significant meanings. The first charm she looks at intently is an opened treasure box containing a single emerald. It represents his birth month. The emerald lies centrally located, surrounded by tiny chips of varied jeweled stones, all representing various aspects of who he is and the vulnerability of his heart. The next charm is a key. It has a single sapphire representing her birthstone. The key hangs beside the treasure box symbol and is what unlocks it. The sapphire is set on a flat surface. At the top portion of the key and the jewels cascade down the length of the key in the shape of a DNA chain. The various chips represent the unique treasure only she carries within. Her DNA chain makes her who she is and who she will become.

The final charm is a ruby jeweled heart. It represents his acceptance of her love and the giving of his heart to her. On either side of the heart are two White gold hands holding it. They represent the creator God encompassing both their lives. The chain has the design of three intertwined gold metals. The purpose is to reflect scripture that says three cords cannot easily be broken. They are made of white, rose gold, and yellow gold. She is speechless at the thought and effort he put into the meaning of each charm. It is one of a kind. Endearingly she smiles while he places it around her neck.

"Perhaps we can create a complimenting bracelet for future charms of significance." Drake shares. He takes out of his pocket one more charm, which signifies anticipation of good things yet to come, and is a star covered with blue jewel flecks. After placing the last charm on her necklace, he directs her to various sections of the bridal suite, where each place has significance.

On the table sits champagne, a tray of meats, vegetables, grapes, cheeses, and crackers. Before they sit down together, Wren slips her hand into the pocket of her robe. Tenderly grabbing hold of his hand, she places her gift into his. Drake gathers it is something personal. Rather than wrapping it in a piece of paper, she has it swaddled in a soft linen cloth. Wren explains to Drake that it derives from her great-grandmother. She explains that her grandmother came across it while vacationing in British Columbia near Mount Hope. It was a painful period for her during that time in her life. Her best friend died. She connected to the sorrow that hurt her heart and chose to channel her pain for the good of others. She committed to praying for others suffering in bad marital relationships.

Her grandmother chose a vacation to meditate and draw comfort from God on the hill. She felt angry. If her friend had listened to wise counsel, she would not have married into a bad situation. It is during this time that being single set her heart to the precedence; that if one day she should marry, it would only be to someone that would harmonize with her standards and values. She did not want to settle for just anyone and be as miserable as her dear departed friend. In her solitude, she raises her voice to the heavens and declares her commitment to God. During her descent from the location on Mount Hope, she notices a local craft and art display set up on the side of the road. She has never seen it at this location before. Though she usually would not consider it, she had money on her and felt pulled into investigating. She thought that she could find a trinket representing her new commitment. It had to be something she could kinetically feel and see and made from articles from Hope Mountain. It was symbolic in remembrance of that day. It ignited an activation of what she had wanted for herself, with God as her witness. It symbolized many prayers and promises of two hearts becoming one.

Wren's younger sister Cassidy married before Wren, which was disheartening to her. Her grandmother presented the necklace to Wren to encourage and give her hope. She is the eldest daughter, not yet married, so her Grandmother gave it to her with instructions.

"This gift is a token of Hope. Wear it until you surrender it to your loved one. This person must guard it until Wren hands it down to another loved one that needs "Hope Ignited."

Drake unwraps the cloth and recognizes it immediately. Wren was wearing the necklace when he first met her. It appears as two different necklaces, yet they are not. They are one because they come together in the back, making them one unit. At the top of a short braided leather, the choker dangles two crystals followed by two delicate stone-jeweled hearts outlined in silver. Two hands give the appearance of holding the hearts. Attached at the back of the necklace is another braided cord around the front, with four single long cords of different lengths. White crystals start at the top of the strands, followed by four turquoise beads threaded onto each strand. At the bottom of each strand are four silver rings with four crystals, preceded by four silver arrows hanging from a silver loop. The arrows are silver; two aim away from the heart, and two toward the heart. Wren is pleased with how he examines the details of the necklace. She continues to share how the hearts and hands visually represent two different lives blending into one. The creator's hands hold each heart. The arrows represent the love that flows in and out of the heart of God.

He knows how significant it is for her to surrender it to him. He kisses her hands and confirms his love and allegiance to the guardianship of their hearts. He gives a place of honor to this necklace and the symbol of surrendered hearts it all represents. She watches him as he rises from the table and pushes a few buttons to reveal a hidden cabinet. A hook descends from the ceiling. He hangs the necklace on a small crystal-lighted hook and presses a button lifting the chain into a lighted glass enclosure. The enclosure disappears into the hidden compartment in the ceiling. Wren is so pleased that he respects and honors her by placing it where it is under protection. He returns to the table, and Drake pours their champagne and toast to their future.

Once they finish their snacks, and move to the couch, settling in front of the fireplace. They backtrack to the memories of how they first encountered one another. They recount how each was thinking at the time. It was important for Drake to hear how Wren developed into the fine woman she is and the significant people in her life. Her experiences are the encounters that make her who she uniquely is. He is happy she trusts him and looks forward to her future with him. He is confident he did the right thing.

Asking for her hand in marriage and seeking a better life for them both is a positive turn for Drake. He will not be alone anymore, and his children will now have a mother figure again.

In the small amount of time Drake has spent with Wren's family, he has gained respect for them. They have something that common folk generally do not have. Combined, they have confidence, wisdom, and strength. He knows Wren's demeanor comes from her family's faith and values. They are a very close-knit family. They firmly live out their convictions. Their commitment to the Father, the God of Heaven's army, overflows and reflects in their everyday walk. They intend to operate their day-to-day interactions from the overflow of the time they have spent communing with their God. They have a relationship where they talk to Him and gain guidance and empowerment like none else he has ever encountered. Their family gatherings and church connections have taught them the pertinence of complete surrender to God. They try to operate not out of fear or religious duty but out of love. They genuinely seem to want to live a life that pleases the Father. They know they are not perfect and are thankful for God's grace. But they also see that there is a right and a wrong. There are lies, and there are truths. Even though it gets complicated to navigate sometimes, a daily relationship keeps them on the right course. All believers must remain vigilant in the maintenance of their walk. Drake only grows more intrigued with her and her family. Wren often vocalized her family's origin in the Lord as the secret to her family's success! It is their conviction that whatever they put their hands to must be done well.

They are solution finders, and Drake can appreciate that. There is no denying Wren is a lovely woman that contains spiritual strength, compassion, and intelligence. He knows she will be an excellent asset to his present and future life, and having a partner to share things with again is good. He feels they complement each other well; where one is deficient, the other brings efficiency.

After having an extensive conversation, they decide to head to bed. They gather their glasses and bottle of champagne and take them to their wedding bed. Wren is most likely getting lightheaded from the drink and the emotional drain from the wedding festivities. Wren and Drake converse into the night until their talk diminishes to a peaceful quietness. Wren nestles into his arms, which makes her feel safe, secure, and loved. While there, she can see out the skylight of the heavens above them. Beams from the moon project down onto them. The enchantment of the stars and wonder before they sing to the things yet to be made known. What is beyond their world? She wonders. The scriptures reveal that the Father created the heavens. He made day and night and named the stars and positioned them in their domain. Wren takes a moment to silently thank the Father of Heaven for creating them.

She is delighted Drake chose this technological wonder to spend their wedding night. He is the love of her life, one that any young woman could hope for. A dream that produces a reality to the hope-birthed notion that all women can find their true love and build a life together. Her reality is proof! This wedding night exceeds all her expectations. She anxiously anticipates the surprise getaway he told her he had planned for them. He tells her to bring her identification papers and only pack a few lightweight outfits and personal items. He assures her that he will take care of everything else.

Breaking away from the silent stargazing activity, she returns her focus to him. Raising herself to look more intently at him, she looks into his gorgeous green eyes. They are the window of his soul. While admiring him, Wren sees adventure in their journey together. It would not be dull! He is a fascinating man, full of ideas and creativity. He understands the outdoors and loves incorporating it into his designs when creating an environment to live in. His appearance is in alignment with his charm and mystery. His six-foot-three frame, light brown wavy hair, subtle toned body, and humor suck you in. He dons one dimple that will appear when he smiles in a cocky way. His smile itself is a suitcase packed with mystery and charm. Of course, he captivates Wren. The first time she looked at him in the neighboring fields, he stirred the blood within her.

When Wren first meets Drake, he dons a three-day unshaven face and an unruly mess of hair. She loves how wavy his hair is. No matter how the wind blows it, the look works for him. She finds out, rather quickly, that he can melt her heart with merely a touch of his finger caressing her skin. Wren will abruptly lose all focus on anything but the sensation of that touch of affection he used so well. He loves tormenting her with that ability, catching her off guard. Anywhere with him, she wants to be near.

Realistically, she honestly does not know for sure where they are going to end up. She trusts him with mapping out of their future. Due to his line of work, confidentially is understandable. She is okay with starting anywhere and making their stamp on the world. Yet, that unknown part carries a bitter-sweet aspect to it. There is a measure of excitement and a fear of unknown possibilities. Nevertheless, because of her love for him and what they have together, she feels that she is able, with the help of her new husband, to cope with the uncertainties life will present to them.

Wren anticipates the following day. She hopes to wake before Drake and briskly run to her high place. She wants to be able to freshen up before he arises. She thinks she could make a surprise breakfast if she can get up early enough and allow him to sleep in. She hopes to make the first morning together another significant moment for them in their new role as husband and wife.

She has already experienced his doting on her on their honeymoon night, she earnestly wants to have the advantage of starting the first day honoring him. Her attention now turns to the present moment and the man beside her. Raising her hands to embrace his face, she kisses him. Sparks ignite. The moment is theirs, a connection between two people who love each other. They biblically solidify their commitment to one another. Wren is content and drifts off to sleep. She dreams of mysterious places where she and Drake could establish a life together. Unfamiliar faces and scenarios come and go before Wren falls into a deep sleep.

CHAPTER 15

A NEW DAY IS DAWNING

Before opening her eyes on the first morning of the marriage together, Wren takes a moment to reflect on her previous night. She smiles at the remembrance of it. He is so attentive, kind, and romantic. He is a very multi-talented person. From all she knows of him at this point, he is an Architect, Engineer, Naturalist, and researcher presently involved with a secret society that is working towards the betterment of procuring the Earth. He is a fantastic find. What man did she ever hear about going to such extremes for a woman they love? He takes her seriously and notes the minor details according to what she verbalizes to him. The décor, food, fireplace, and gifts show that he is a fantastic man. He said they could wait if she were too tired from the wedding festivities. She adored him for that. Wren, not wanting to wait, is even more adorable to Drake. He suddenly becomes uneasy and stammers when he attempts to reply. She put him off guard with her spunkiness.

She plans to spoil him. With that thought, she smiles and opens her eyes. She attempts to push back the covers and quietly get out of bed not to disturb Drake, yet as she stirs herself to rise, something is resisting her. While she is attempting to stretch, she feels restricted. She Opens her eyes and begins to look around. She realized that the morning calm she usually experienced and anticipated for her first day being married had turned awry.

Adrenaline floods in Wren's system. She has a flight or fight moment yet cannot act on it. How did this present situation transpire without her knowing? It rattled her. She closes her eyes and breathes in and out slowly. She wonders if she just had a bad dream, so she squeezes her eyes closed and purposely opens them with a strong intent of determination and alertness. She opens her eyes slowly and attempts to rise from her bed. She quickly discovers it is not a dream. She begins murmuring to herself, giving directions for her to keep calm. She does that to console herself when she gets anxious. It gives her the illusion of hearing her voice and that she is not alone and vulnerable. She provides rational problem-solving to sort out her situation so she does not feel isolated and vulnerable. Pulling herself together as much as feasible, she briefly assesses her surroundings; she discovers why she has resistance.

Wren has restraints put on her. She is secure in her seat, which seems to be a form that fits her body. Not having free range of movement, she is finding it hard to breathe, most likely due to the stress-induced anxiety of the moment. Her mind is swimming to stay above the water. The room shakes and seems to be swaying with rumbling sounds. She holds back her wanting to call out or scream because she does not want to alert the kidnappers. She tells herself, "Get ahold of yourself!" She has to try to make sense of things to figure out a plan of escape. First, she has to know with whom she is fighting.

The danger of her captors knowing she is awake is unsettling. All she can last recall is that she and Drake were in the woods in his module. They were alone, she thought. Creeps could easily have invaded their privacy! What did they plan to do with her? Where is her husband? She gasps as she takes notice of her environment. She is on a craft of some sort. It has a port window. She can see that it is dark outside. The port window could give more clarification as to where she is when morning comes. Wren swallows and realizes that morning is not coming. She sees what appear to be stars and cloudy mists glowing with spectacular colors. There are white, blue, pink, and yellow sparkling diamonds of light racing past them. These lights swarm about them as the craft is being catapulted through space. After a while, she finds comfort in looking at the views through the port window. She whispers, "Jewels of Heaven."

That is what her younger sister Cassidy always calls it. To Cassidy, the universe's celestial space is God's treasure that humankind cannot put a price on. Nor can human hands stuff any proceeds into their greedy pockets. It is not likely to be taken or concealed for selfish gain and is something for all to appreciate.

Wren comes back to thinking about the uncertainty of her situation. She drifts in and out of consciousness; each time she awakes, she tries to make sense of things. Her solving skills start by asking questions. Who might be behind this abduction? What purpose could anyone have to kidnap her? How could anyone get past Drake's security? Why would they want her? Finally, where is her husband? She is concerned for him. Is he in restraints like her? Is he in captivity somewhere nearby? Maybe the strange neighbors are behind this abduction. Those neighbors who want no contact with her family, whose property butts up against her family's property. These are the same neighbors that post no trespassing signs on the perimeter of their property. They are the ones standing between her and her High place. They post signs with the information that they are under construction and will incorporate more security measures.

The waters even have an image of an eye, indicating they are watching the postings. She assumes there will be security cameras. It makes sense now that her new neighbors are hiding something. She turns her thoughts on Drake. How sad it is that he is in this scenario with her. It's terrible to think he unknowingly entered a situation just by camping on her neighbor's property. She hopes he is all right. She feels vulnerable and angry that anyone thinks that anyone has the right to do this to anyone. In times in Wren's life, she often turns to what she has learned from the Word to bring wisdom and discernment. She recalls a sermon about how God loves so much that no power in the sky above or the earth below can separate His love from us. She assures herself that God is aware of where she is and knows how she is feeling. God knows how to provide a way to help her through this situation. Her hope is in God's proven faithfulness to those that are His. After all,

He created everything from darkness to light. He knows the number of hairs on her head. He knew her name while she was yet in the womb. There is nowhere anyone can hide from him. She senses a new strength building within her. She gains determination not to give up. She prays softly: "Father, you are the creator of Heaven and Earth; your love is so astounding to me that you gave me your Son Jesus, so I can now come before you with boldness! I ask that you send your angels to help free me from whatever this is. Can you send help as you did long ago when Peter was in the dungeon from his captivity? Father, I ask that you put me on the hearts of those who know me so they may intercede for me. Help me to know what to do and protect my loved ones and me from harm. Amen."

Before finding a way out of her current situation, she has to retrace her steps to gain a foundation to build an explanation. She is determined to find a way to escape and return home. It seems odd to think getting back home did not mean just going to the ranch anymore; now, saying I want to go home has a broader meaning. Now it means going back to Earth. She did not notice anyone nearby. She figures whoever they are; they will inevitably return. She resigns to her present circumstance for the moment. She fully surrenders her plight into God's hands. She must wait for Him to supply guidance and resources to meet her needs. Earth is where her life makes sense.

Wren dreams of her neighbors. She can see into their home. She is standing outside looking in without them knowing. It is as if she has x-ray viewing abilities. She can see right through the walls. There are people inside wearing similar apparel, and robots are serving them. They must be from outer space! She gasps and covers her mouth with her hands. She wants to know more, so she takes a deep breath and looks deeper into their living quarters. Maps post on their walls. Glowing lines crisscross each other, displaying the route destinations they travel. They are marking spots with a red pin flag. They may be essential locations. She pulls her attention back to the people again, watching them talk. She notices that they are getting into a heated debate of some sort. The disagreement becomes so intense that one of the others gets in between them, quarreling, and pushes them apart. The heated conversation is obviously due to something of significant proportion. She wonders what it could be. Could it have been about her? Then they all looked in her direction as if they knew she was there.

The next time Wren awakes, her head is throbbing, and she hears a man's voice. She is having difficulty processing his words. Her feelings flood with similar emotions of anger she had prior. Hold on! Her eyes are now looking like a deer dazed by the headlights. Even though she is groggy, she senses something familiar. It is a person talking to her. He is a male, and he is relaying scientific breakthrough information. He explains that she is not in danger and not to be afraid. He continues to talk to her about her present situation. He explains that she is transforming with elements of natural components added to technology, providing her with infinite boundaries. She will have the same appearance, form, and mind as her born human traits but with enhanced abilities. Her mind and body capabilities will become similar to those of a superhero. He calls his newly evolved creation a Hume-autic.

Putting tangible thoughts together at this point is challenging. He rattles on about scientific research blending natural resources with scientific innovations, eliminating most human frailness.

He continues to explain how he feels when he comes across her in the clearing. She captures his attention, and he is intrigued. When they develop a serious relationship, he knows she is the one for him. He explains past emotional pain. That pain was an experience of losing a precious person. He continues with the explanation that he does not want to lose another. Talking through it, he rallies a breakthrough for himself and Wren. He and his children would not have to experience another mother's loss. Wren's mind is spiraling; she is unclear about what it all means. He continues to explain. It is not accessible to all humankind yet. He knows she cannot comprehend yet everything he is telling her, but she needs to trust him and know she is in good hands.

Wham, it hits her like a loud wake-up call. Ok, she internally checks marks off one of her answers. The question of who her captor is presenting its unveiling. It is her new husband, Drake! How could anyone expect to remain calm, cool, and collected? Is he that out of touch with human emotions? She is not feeling so well and feels she needs to vomit. The room begins to spin, and she blacks out.

When Wren awakes, she notices that she is in another room. She is not seated in a chair anymore, but in a jelled bed, having multiple devices of technology surrounding her. She is lying in a slightly reclining position. She wakes this time, noticing a machine hovering over her midsection. She can see a new science at work from a monitor that hovers above her. She sees that she is wearing a lightweight iridescent gown. It feels quite comfortable. A monitoring droid that records her responses to the procedure recognizes her inquisitiveness and tells her that the apparel she is wearing keeps the core of her body temperature at comfortable level. It is neither cold nor hot. She can lift her arm and feel a cap covering her hair. She then looks at the monitor and observes what looks like her insides resisting a transformation. Her blood is in combat with intruders. Her heart, mind, soul, and now her blood is warring against the instruments of science. This science is the avenue that melds her into a new evolution.

Wren takes on the mode of unbelief. She feels helpless. She is being violated by not having been given a choice of being able to choose or not to choose this transformation. Looking at the monitors, mounted from the ceiling, she watches herself progress as if it is a movie and forgets it is her that this science is happening to. She can see inside her body a white smoke in the center of her form. Somehow, she knows it is the soul of her human existence. The smoke differs; it contains sparks of electricity and gold flecks. They intertwine like living glitter. She returns to the reality that her life has no value to this man. She witnesses her transformation and the merging of the natural with a science unimaginable. She feels like a science experiment and that she has replaced the white rat. She could not have ever imagined this advancement to be obtainable. To her, no matter how extraordinary it may be, it remains a fact that it is a violation of her rights!

He must have drugged her, dropping the substance into one of her many glasses of champagne. He is now using her like a lab rat. It is against her will! Did that not matter? Is there no value and honor for others to have a say and make their own choices and standards they chose to live? What about the life she has invested in on Earth? Will it ever matter again? She asks herself if her parents will recover from the loss. Will even she be able to recover from the loss?

Her earthly life's essence is now mingled with something that would make her a "Hume-au-tic." She is becoming a science-induced evolution. Anger fills her thoughts as she faces the betrayal of her husband. What is his intention regarding her? Is she just another science project? He has not mentioned that she could recollect that he is one of these transformations. Why would he not try his formula first on himself before others? Reasonably, is not that what mad scientists do? Take, for instance, Dr. Jekyll and Mr. Hyde. He began on himself! The thought of being on a science project is horrifying! How could he? She trusted him for the rest of her life!

Reflecting, she recalls hers and Drake's plan to forge ahead, like all newlyweds, and build a new life together. They have not even had a real honeymoon. Now it makes sense why he told her not to worry about what to pack. He consoled her by saying he had organizational skills and assured her everything would work out. He did not want her to know the exact location of their honeymoon until they were on their way. The training her uncle had imparted, the how-to of assessing strangers and their conduct, is ironic. Her investigation to free herself is a failure! She did not see this side of him at all! She is completely "bowled over." His charm, good looks, wit, and intelligence clouded the truth. He played it out well. She stews. She realizes he must have never loved her truly. How could he have, considering all that has taken place? She is a victim that willingly played into his hand like a whipped puppy. She made it easy for him.

Wren concludes she has been living in childhood fantasy, and true love must not be real. Believing she could find true love and start a life together and a family of their own is nothing but propaganda, pure nonsense now. Buying the wedding night apparel and being caught up in that little girl's dream of marriage, a house, children, and a white picket fence all seems so stupid! Now, she has to figure out how to get out of it. The big question remains whether her husband is the destroyer of her life or the key to a new and better way of life. That will be determined later.

CHAPTER 16

ADAPTING

Wren is one of many to experience the transformation into a Hume-au-tic. The Science Dome is a space station filled with them, and she has yet to have the pleasure of meeting them. Drake hopes that, given the opportunity, his wife will begin to comprehend the magnitude of the scientific breakthrough that Wren is now a part of and celebrate it. He hopes with enlightenment, she will come to appreciate the situation she is experiencing. She has become a space pioneer in a monumental spectrum of scientific advancements. She is an actual living product of the blueprint put in place for the future of humankind.

Drake is a significant part of this scientific breakthrough. He ponders on the thought of what unexpected and extraordinary turn of events has brought them together. Just the odds alone of him stumbling upon Wren are unfathomable. Drake was not looking to hook up with anyone at that point. But fate brings Drake and Wren together. What a treasure she is to him! However, his new bride and her family are the only individuals not given disclosure of Wren's circumstances to come. There was no opportunity to decide for herself or discuss with her family; which life she wanted to live.

He knows he took a risk and will have to hope for the best regarding the consequences of his actions. When they arrive at the Space Science Dome, he expects to have immediate repercussions for his unethical actions committed against Wren. The Dome's Procedures and protocol will mean the security officials will demand he is sent to his quarters and placed under house arrest. They will strip him of any privileges he had prior. He must participate in "a proceeding of conflict" with the Science Domes authorities.

Drake believes he did the right thing by her. It will raise the question of how healthy his state of mind is. He has faith in their love, that she will understand, and that because of that love, she willfully accepts her transition and join him and his children to live a long, satisfying life. His thoughts towards her transformation will most likely be, received wrong. He will appear a bit messed up in the head; for others to figure out why he risked everything. He understands how they might feel. Yet, he hopes she will be able to accept his actions once she can comprehend the depth of his thinking. Her ability to acclimate to the situation is what he hopes will happen.

Drake started the process of transformation on the night of their marriage. The Science team will have to finish the final process if they choose. The mind is delicate, and not all individuals handle the transformation similarly. Anyone going through the change must undergo several levels of testing with supervision and counseling. It is necessary to pass the tests before modifying any individual that can arrive at a complete Hume-au-tic stance. Drake hopes she will cooperate and be receptive to this abrupt change in her life. He hopes as a new couple, they will be able to pick up where they left off and live a long, happy life together.

Now on the Dome premises, Wren enjoys the momentary solitude made available by the science team. She finds sipping hot chocolate by the fireplace projected on the wall, and a soft throw blanketing her body is somewhat comforting. It gives her a sense of warmth and familiarity with the remembrances of her life on the ranch. She sometimes feels lost not having her family as her support while she transitions. She would have never imagined that someone would permanently remove her from her family, and she could not wrap her head around it. How can someone that says they love you to do this to you and your family? In committing to a relationship, she had been careful and strategic not to settle for the wrong guy.

Wren thought she was waiting for Mr. Right she was hoping for. Drake was the one she loved from the depths of her heart. He is the man she loves and chooses to commit to for life to raise their family. Together they are to change the world, simply living one day at a time. They will make it a better place. She is working through the betrayal that robbed her of her dreams. How did situations like this happen? She is contented to live on earth just the way it is. Her goals are to come to their fullness on Earth despite its problems. Exploring places and things on earth alone was enough to bring contentment. They dreamed of exploring the Earth's mountains, forestry, oceans, and valleys with her husband, children, friends, and family. She did not need to go to space to fill any desire for adventure to that degree. The family produced purpose and fullness in her. She does not want outer space life! She hoped to share her experience on the ranch with her children and how she grew up. She wants her children to have the support of family and community. She knows Drake holds a confidential job that requires her to separate from her family, but she did not think it would be a forever separation. She felt he would change careers in time, and they would relocate to her stomping ground.

If she can choose Space or remain on Earth, she will select Earth! It feels unfair and unethical to rob her of that choice! She wonders, though, now a part of the vast expanse of Space, if she can ever find her way to Earth again, where she feels most comfortable. All she knows now is that Wren has to face the reality that, given a choice or whether or not she likes the scenario, she has to come to terms with making a decision. She realizes she is moving forward in an unknown origin. The thing she has the most difficulty processing; is her husband's deception.

Wren believes she knows him well enough to accept his marriage proposal. She thinks she could trust him with her life. Yet she is obviously wrong because that same person takes her captive and routes her into Space. How could he think it would be all right to perform a life-altering procedure on her without her approval? That is pretty darn crazy. Maybe she did marry a mad scientist.

Drake is a stranger. Wren simply fell into a dilution with what he wanted her to see. Wren pieces together the crucial moments that give insight into her current situation. It is an odd twist that her sister, who is always fascinated with Space, remains on Earth, and Wren, who wants to be on Earth, is living in Space. Wren wishes she had paid more attention to Cassidy's hobby. With what little Cassidy was able to educate her sister about the cosmos, Wren will hold onto it. It is no longer a waste of time. Now, Wren sees her sister's impartations as a gift. Wren will put the shadows of her family in her heart. It is both beneficial and therapeutic to reflect on those pleasant memories.

Wren reflects on an old memory. She closes her eyes and thinks about her bedroom with the balcony. It was perfect for her sister to observe the heavens with her telescope. Three floors up made her room the highest point in the house. Cassidy could view the night sky with her telescope and discover more about what she calls the "Jewels of Heaven." Wren supports her sister even though it is not an activity she enjoys. Cassidy is her best friend. How could she not share in what made her happy? The sisters have a routine every Friday night while they live on the ranch. After dinner with the family, they head to town and hang out. They meet with friends at the coffee house for dessert and shop in the boutiques. When they return home, they grab snacks and hot drinks and head to Wren's balcony. Cassidy will pull the scope out of the closest and spend hours talking and viewing the stars. Eventually, Wren will go to bed and leave Cassidy observing the heavens into the early morning wrapped up in a quilt or sleeping bag. She tries to expose Wren to her knowledge of Heaven's domain as much as possible. Her teaching moments lead to pointing out different constellations and discussions about the mysteries of Space. It is nice that Wren's bed is just a few steps from the balcony doors of the observatory. It made it easy for Wren to retreat to the warmth and comfort of her bed when she felt tired. She was glad Cassidy came home in a safe place to observe the stars. When Cassidy was in college, she often associated with stargazers, made up of all types of strange characters that take a fancy to more things than just star gazing. Wren disapproved. Coming back on those Fridays kept their bond strong. Cassidy's informative hobby practiced Friday after Friday is now highly beneficial.

Wren knows the Dome authorities are watching her. She logically ascertained that they would observe and take notes on how well she adapts. It is great making it to the point where she could have the clearance to live in her private quarters, and not having constant staff present is a breath of fresh air. She is approved to live independently. She starts to focus on making a plan for her escape. She now lives outside the scientist's units and has 24-hour supervision. She is under observation, but they are mindful of her need to start acclimating to her new life on the Dome. They keep their distance, but she knows they are there.

Their monitoring is sometimes intrusive, but she understands they must operate within a safe protocol. While observing, if they thought she suspected they were there, the monitor quickly attempted to look like they were doing something else. It entertains her to watch them. They frequently used drones to pick up conversation or movements for her safety, and they could quickly expedite support if they needed to intervene on her behalf. The scientific team has to have a valid report of her stability before moving forward with her transformation.

It will be her choice if they give her an all-clear. She is not at total capacity at this point. They have to take every precaution with their new science. Opening up a larger expanse of her brain's ability means they have to grade her progress before agreeing that she would be able to handle it safely. The new brain's power will be far beyond her current capacity. Even though her privacy is limited, she is not hiding anything at this point to fret about their snooping. She will cooperate if it means she gets the personal free time that would help her start plans to escape.

When the authorities learn what Drake did, they enter immediate security mode. All prior scheduled transformations are on hold. Their full attention goes to Wren. Hindsight, they knew that Drake's grieving mode was functioning in denial. They concluded Drake's choice to remain in this mode was better for them. Continuing the science he and his mother worked so hard on together was his escape. They had worked side by side fervently with the conviction they were making advancements. The Dome officials remorsefully took accountability and admitted their failure to appropriately intervene in addressing his emotional health. They bypassed his emotional state for a higher level of scientific answers. They believed he could devise a solution in his driven form due to Corinne's death. They felt it would benefit the overall importance of continuing the research goal they were so near to attaining. They took advantage of his grief-driven work ethic because he was the probable one to find the missing equation of the science they needed. They never imagined that Drake would go to the extreme he did with Wren. His actions disclose his mental breakdown that affected his moral logic. He is not operating on all eight cylinders.

Drake is essential to obtaining the breakthrough they need to ensure the success of finding the missing link. They hold him in high regard and promote him to a high-ranking position in his line of work, despite his mental condition and processing his grief. This promotion gives him full access and the freedom to move and travel without restrictions. This freedom allowed him to pursue other projects aligned with his architectural engineering; they felt other work would help him find balance. After all, Drake always said that designing modules is a hobby. Yet now, due to the consequences of allowing him that freedom, they must unite and use all the resources at their fingertips to bring him back to good physical and mental health. They choose to isolate him and give him psychiatric care.

Concerning Wren's mental and physical health, they must navigate carefully for her and how it will affect Drake's healing. They must process Wren appropriately with careful preparation. Her ability to handle the moral betrayal is questionable. Before they could consider going further with her transformation, they had to be unanimous with the approval to move forward. It is their protocol to insist that their patients maintain their individuality. This mode of science is to enhance, not take away from anyone. It is a design that enhances humans' longevity, not a design that produces robots with no personality, values, or standards. They must have the ability to reason or operate with a moral code. If this science gets into the wrong hands, it will be a sad time for humanity. The current data would put humanity in imminent danger. It very well could be the demise of individuality.

The first approach to Wren's transformation is to allow short increments of expansion to her brain. It provides time for the natural function of her brain and body to assimilate the invasion of this science. She will need to score high on their graded scale before moving forward. Viewing recorded footage, she appears to have passed the tests that reflect her response to what Drake implemented on the craft. The true challenge, and revelation of how she will respond to her complete transformation having had a chip designed by Dr. Silverman already placed in her brain, will be after her full awaking. Before moving forward with her mental and physical enhancements, they must acquire data that rates her with high scores before moving in a positive direction. Wren is under observation while living independently yet secure living environment.

Drake also must obtain medical clearance before his release to a less secure lodging and have access to his children. Once he gets the all-clear, he will join the scientist team. Drake will take part in observing Wren's development. Soon he will have clearance to communicate with Wren under supervision. It is an intense experience for her, exposing herself to an abductor. It is a risky venture, seeking reconciliation. She may shut down towards him and forever choose not to have him in her life. Drake is hopeful; her response will flow in a more positive direction. He hopes she will allow him back in her circle. The reality Drake faces is that she may not forgive him. After all, he took her from her family, home, people, places, and things she held dear. His choice causes deep pain on many levels. Drake is aware of her hesitancy to see him face-to-face. He knows that somehow he must press into an acceptable resolution with Wren.

Wren is on the flip side. She knows she must get past the bazaar set of events that happened to her to proceed with gaining freedom. Wren knows that escaping means cooperating logically with the science team and Drake. Because of this conflict, regarding how severe it is, she knows she cannot allow herself to do what one would do in a normal conflict situation. This situation differs. She cannot respond impulsively, telling her instinctively to cut all ties with Drake and the team. She cannot seek revenge or retaliating measures because though seeking revenge may feel right, that would thwart her from finding some kind of regular back into her life, which she values more than anything else. She must discover balance concerning the situation's reality and devise a plan to take her back home. Wren knows Drake will be entering her personal life again. He is the only familiar person in the Dome she can relate to. Drake knows her story. He can bring closure and calm to her troubled waters. She has to reach a place where her physical and mental are in good standing.

The science team schedules a meeting with Drake and Wren. The schedule for them to meet is approved; for small increments. They need time to reintroduce themselves slowly, and the science team monitors closely in case of hostile reactions from Wren. Sincerely Wren does have hurtful questions to ask Drake. She wants to determine if he does love her. If so, then what is the motivation behind his betrayal? Are love and marriage just a ploy to get one more victim? The counselors did reveal their findings to her. They feel he indeed did have a mental collapse. She has some compassion but is perplexed at the gravity of his choices concerning her. She needs to know if it is true. Did he have a mental breakdown due to his love for her? Had he determined that he would not see another love slip away? Was he seeking to protect the one he loves with long life? Did he not tell her because he knew she would not understand and see it his way?

Wren saw no evidence of mental difficulty in Drake. Perhaps she wanted her dream of romance and marriage so badly that she walked blindly into his trap, ignoring any red flags. Flags like the secrecy stuff, the odd neighbors he was working with, and the oddity of how he got his module in the clearing and the techy watch. On and on, the flags jump into her mind's eye now that she can reflect and attempts to assemble the mysterious puzzle. If she finds everything true and he loves her, can she forgive him and adapt to this new life with him? She concluded that if there were any chance of their relationship working out, she must restructure her understanding of Drake and rebuild their relationship, even if it would mean they could only be friends.

Drake and Wren meet face to face for the first time since they landed on the Dome space station. The Doors slide open. Wren fidgets at the table where she is sitting with her counselor. Drake enters, accompanied by two guards, and Wren can sense his fear, humility, and more. He needs her forgiveness and acceptance. He sees the seat across from Wren and sits down. He gives a signal to the two guards to leave. They exit and stand outside the closed sliding doors. The counselor introduces them and tells them the rules they must play by. She leaves and takes her place in the monitoring room while Drake and Wren have alone time together. It has been at least a few months since they have seen each other. Wren and Drake expectantly grab each other's hands across the table. She cries and abruptly pulls her hands away. The monitoring team almost sent the guards in to stop their meeting. They stood guard but noticed that it looked like the two would settle down. Wren wipes her eyes and puts her hands over her face. Drake drops to the floor and sobs, telling her he regrets what he did to her. He continues to tell her he loves her. Wren is holding the sides of her head as if she cannot contain the intensity of his words. However, she listens and looks up and peers into his eyes. He says he did this to her selfishly because he could not bear to lose her. Lowering his gaze to the floor, he requests her forgiveness.

Wren gets up and moves over to him. She bends down while still wiping away the tears streaming down her cheeks. She lifts his chin and looks into his eyes again, seeing he is genuine.

"Please get up. I understand, and I have a briefing I read. I want to see you and see if we still have a relationship to build on."

Wren leaves him and begins to walk around. He sits at the table, rubbing his knees to relieve nervous energy. Wren begins to speak, putting her hands in her smock pockets. She is not looking at him for the most part. As she paces, she tells him:

"I have been working through different modes of grief.

I lost my dreams, my marriage, A life I expected to play out between us as man and wife. It is a life I knew, with family and community. But I expected to live and raise children. I don't know how long it might take to feel a sense of normal again."

Wren turns to him and stops.

"I do have you."

She wants to say love but just cannot at this time.

"You are my only normal here. I can do this if you will be honest with me from here on out."

Wren sits down in front of him at the table. Those in the other room watching let out a breath and relaxed, feeling they would not have to intervene. Wren likes her newfound strength, and the transformation has already initiated that enhancement. She could have brought harm to Drake if she had used those enhancements. Wren continues talking.

"It will get some getting used to, but I have spent time with others like me, and I see they are getting along fine."

She raises one eyebrow to make a point of importance.

"As fine as one can expect in this particular scenario. If I remain here in the Dome space station and choose to follow through with the complete transformation? I choose me."

Drake looks at her funny, trying to determine what that statement means. She sees that question in his expression, and she continues with it.

"I choose to do it with you alongside me! I do not know at what level that means regarding our relationship, but I would like to start over."

A solid reconciliation with Wren occurs after another

month of monitoring. A plan is drawn. Drake is on board with her. He has come up with a way she can get back to her family without the science dome interfering. Drake agrees with Wren that she should have the opportunity to return home. He is the one that paved the road to her great sadness. The afterthought of his conduct concerning Wren's relocation, and all that it involves, was a significant error on his part. He carries the heaviness of complications of that deed. He knows with certainty that it would be a crumbling wall between them if he did not try to correct his mistake. Drake comes up with a solution.

CHAPTER 17
TRUTH OR FICTION

As a father, he has to be creative and careful not to cause emotional trauma to his children. Drake knows his son Jesse learns well from stories and will approach his daughter Abigail at another time with a more casual presentation. Wren takes Abigail into the kitchen and engages her in a painting activity, giving Drake alone time with Jesse. She gets Abigal to bed shortly after and joins up with Jesse and Drake.

Drake divulges what is happening with Wren by using the method of storytelling. His son will initially think it is a fictional story, but Drake is confident he will connect the dots. Drake starts the story by telling Jesse how a man in the story wronged his new bride. He explains that though someone made a wrong decision that hurts someone, they can make it right again. He continues to explain that working through life's difficulties builds character and strength.

Drake is a good storyteller. His son Jesse seems to hang on to his every word. Drake makes any story come alive. It is family night, where the kids get to choose what they would like to do together. His son typically requests to choose his dad's stories over playing games. He feeds off every word his father speaks. It's as if his father's words are morsels Jesse is eager to grab onto and digest. After Wren puts Abigail to bed, she brings in some popcorn and drinks for the guys and returns to listen nearby while flipping through photo reels. Jesse loves her. Jesse noticed that when his father married Wren and brought her into their family, she had a sense of peace and grit about her. The story begins.

"Nerw#1, a Hume-au-tic, is the Bride, who appears to be operating in survival mode. To everyone else, her enactment will appear that she is rebelling against her husband and the Science Dome community. The illusion playing out is that she attempts to destroy her husband along with her. They decide a staged argument is the best way to make others believe what they as husband and Wife want them to believe. Nerw#1 trusts her husband's plan to free her from the boundaries set for all Hume-au-tics transformations completed on their SpaceStation. It is important to keep their change confidential and not permit interaction with their past life on Earth. It could expose the secret Spacestations location, which they could not risk."

His Dad stops and eats a few helpings of popcorn and offers more to Jesse, who plunges his hand into the bowl and moves closer to his dad. He is very intrigued by the tale and wants to hear more.

"Come on, Dad, keep going. I like this story!"

Drake smiles and looks up at Wren, who is dangling off the end of the couch; she is wondering, along with Jesse, what Drake might say next. She raises her eyebrows at him and nods for him to go on.

"It's important to note that this married couple has already lived together as husband and wife. Nerw#1 has already been a part of the family. Both husband and Nerw#1 hope the authorities and unexpected witnesses will conclude that she is deceased from the explosion they purposely set up as evidence. They are now in his lab. The explosion is recorded on the security footage. From the blast results, they will see Nerw#1's expulsion through the living membrane walls of the lab. It appears to cause her disintegration, and ashes fall to the floor of the area below. There should be no doubt about her demise. She was put on watch at the time due to her suspected difficulty transitioning from her human state to her new reality as a Hume-au-tic. Though she chooses to complete her transformation, she misses her Earth and the family left behind. They must conduct the enactment so that the authorities will have little or no concern that she may have survived. Even if they thought she might have a chance of survival, she would not last long due to her emotional state demonstrating no inner fight left to want to come back to her present existence. Jesse is shocked!

"Wow!" Drake smiles and continues.

DNA will be present in the ashes left behind. Nerw#1 is thought to be a total loss due to the intense heat resulting from the explosion. The mounted monitoring droid will be safe from the blast because it will have a sufficient cleared distance. It will accomplish all her husband determines it will. It was one of his personally designed droids, and he knew how to program it. It provides a recording that substantiates Nerw#1's emotional instability. The ranting and raving, the comments she yells at this husband are clear evidence of her intentions."

His son Jesse loves his dad. He understands the loss of his mother has been hard on his father. However, Jesse has not worked through the pain. He is having a hard time with feelings of abandonment by his parents. He is glad they have Javelin and now Wren, but they are no replacement for his mother or father. He recognizes that his father needs them to help. He does not want to confront his father at this point because he does not want to inflict any more pain his father might feel finding out how he is truly feeling. Jesse chooses to stuff his pain in a deep place. Yet, even though he has some unresolved animosity, he truly has reasonable admiration for his father's accomplishments and knowledge. He looks up to his father and hopes he will someday find his niche and make his dad proud.

Jesse likes his stepmother; she is incredible. Wren is so good to him and his sister. She loves them as if they were her own. Wren is genuine, tender, and intelligent. She contains all the qualities he would like to find in a wife someday. Wren would never flaunt her strengths. She loves the old fashion baseball and is the one that introduces him to the Three Stooges comedy show. Who would have thought stupidity, called slapstick, would be so enjoyable? They watch them together like clockwork every time it is on transmission. She pops a perfect batch of popcorn. His father approves. It goes with his father's impartation wishes that his children experience different things they do have access to on the Dome. Drake enjoys seeing Jesse and Wren bond. Jesse likes his dad's new interest in making food replicas of different periods. Jesse likes his dad's Coney dogs and French fries. These tender moments Drake gets to share with Wren and his children; are a highlight of his day.

Jesse notes how Wren makes their home enjoyable when his dad stays late in the lab. Considering how he feels about his dad marrying Wren, he believes his father genuinely seems to love her. The two are hardly ever apart. Jesse wonders how his father could fall in love with a Hume-au-tic. That may have something to do with why they have not had more children. His dad has always had many women pursue him, yet his father showed no interest in women after the passing of his mother. Yet, he brings Wren home. He notices how Wren acts when she is with his father. It is as if she gains strength being near him, yet, he can see that his father draws something from her too. He knows they are in love with each other. Even with all the women out there, he is proud that his dad remains faithful to Wren. To him, that says a lot. Jesse remembers Javelin commenting about the women coming after him. She said his dad is like honey water, and it draws the bees. It's true; wherever his dad is, women seem to flock. He carries a charisma and demeanor they seem to like. He knows Wren loves his father as well. She is patient, kind, and supportive of his work demands. She even gives him ideas for him to work on.

Jesse tunes back into his father's attention when he hears him clear of his throat. His father points to the beacon flashing on the mantle while he deliberately throws a pillow at him to get his attention.

"I see you zoned out on me for a minute. It is time to bring the festivities of the evening come to a close, Jesse. I will finish the story of Nerw#1 fleeing her entanglements."

In the first instance, you see Nerw#1 after the explosion. She is steadying herself on a craft prepared to take flight at the command of Sir Vince Knight. His young daughter is accompanying him. It appears to Nerw#1 that Sir Knight is hurrying to depart. Perhaps his motivation is similar to hers, and they, too, want to flee for freedom. She wonders if their story is as bizarre as hers.

Now, Nerw#1 is evolved and is equipped with enhanced abilities thanks to Her gifted husband's intervention. No other enhanced Hume-au-tic has this added innovation. It makes it possible for her to disguise herself. Her wardrobe mainly consists of intricate, designed white jumpsuits. They all are different but display a flare of edginess and elegance. The fabric of her wardrobe is her idea. Her husband is well-versed in technology and builds off her ideas. He makes it happen. It is important to note that the white fabric is similar to a blank slate. The technology incorporated into the material allows it to change colors and patterns. She likes to layer her outfits with colorful tunics and scarves. She also gives him the idea of designing boots that extend past her knees. They, too, contain the same capabilities as her advanced jumpsuits. Her completion, already a light creamy beige, makes it easy for the lights to project from her collar onto her face. Her husband makes the technology just for her use only. Access to this kind of technology provides her with camouflaging her outer appearance. She can blend into anything around her. Her escape back to earth is more promising. It would prove more advantageous to have this ability just in case the authorities doubted the deception of her planned demise. The dome authorities could search the craft she is on before taking off.

Nerw#1 slips onto the craft with no evidence of being seen. She chooses a shaded nook and takes a seat. She straps herself in and drapes a cloth over herself. She knows her dream of escape is still uncertain. The hope of her returning to earth and seeing her family again is still yet to happen. Even if she does get back to her family, she will not be coming back to them as she left. She will have to be careful not to expose the P.E.S. society. She has to stay hidden with a disguise, like the animated superhero Superman disguising himself as Clark Kent. She could not make known her advanced abilities. It would be risky for the science dome and the world as her family knows it. Only one more element to her escape is not yet known to her. Only her husband knows the extra element."

Drake takes an intermission and pours a tall, narrow glass of neon blue beverage. He starts drinking it when he sees his son jamming a handful of popcorn unmercifully into his mouth, and Drake aspirates his drink which causes him to spew it across the floor before him.

"Jesse, what in tarnation is that you are doing?" His son comes back with a witty remark.

"Dad, why did you spit all over the floor?"

Wren helps to clean up the mess on the floor and takes the near-empty bowl back to the kitchen.

"Your cheeks are bulging like a chipmunk." Wren fluffs his hair as she passes by.

After Drake's mess is taken care of, Jesse is instructed not to eat his popcorn in that manner again, and Drake proceeds with the story.

"You see, Nerw#1 never fully surrendered to her captivity. She held on to her dream and waited for the perfect timing to carry out her plan. She goes along with the transformation completion to become this superior version of humankind that operates on a higher level. Since her husband already got her started and she did like how it made her feel, she decides completing the transformation could only give her more advantages of finding a way to escape."

Drake pauses again and moves over to Wren in the kitchen to chat. Jesse watches as they enjoy razzing each other. He looks at Wren with admiration. She is an excellent addition to their family, Jesse determines. When she came, he got his father back. He believes she is why his dad smiles and enjoys life again. She is the reason he has a family again. Jesse wonders how his dad met Wren. Is she from the Space Dome or someone from his travels? All he knows is that his father said he met someone while on leave and fell in love. He told his kids he was bringing her back and assured them they would love her. The authorities told Javelin that Drake and his new bride were under quarantine for an undetermined time. It was a longer period than he usually had to endure before seeing his father. He speculates that it must have been someone from another place off the Dome.

Wren parts ways with Drake to clean up the painting activity. Jesse presses in to ask his dad some questions.

"What happened to her Dad? What happened to her family? Did she ever see them? Does anyone ever question where she came from?... Wren enters the room and moves over to Jesse. She glances up at Drake for his approval and gets his ok. She bends over to throw a hand of popcorn she took from the kitchen and tossed them in her mouth. Jesse and Drake watch her together. She changed into her white, specially designed jumpsuit. She is preparing to leave, but before she does, she touches Jesse's cheek and speaks softly into his ear.

"I am going to get to see them."

She tiptoes out the door and slips away into the shadows.

Jesse is stunned, with his mouth gaping wide open in awe. He looks over at his father and then toward the door and realizes that the Hume-au-tic his dad was talking about in the story is Wren.

"Oh my goodness! Nerw#1 Wren's name spelled backward!"

He begins jumping up and down while holding his head. He says repeatedly.

"What? What? What?" He runs to his father and grabs him by his shoulders, dad are you messing with me? Because if you are, it is not funny."

Jesse never understood how deep his father's despair played out. It was not until this story uncovered it. He knows he has been despondent, but only when Wren confesses her true identity does he finally realize that the woman in the story is who his father is saying is his dad's mysterious wife. Most likely, the reason his dad was unfair to Wren probably has to do with his father's grief and quarantine. He brings back a wife from one of his excursions! Jesse just goes numb. He cannot respond to the new information going through his brain. He sits silent.

There is a great conflict in Jesse's heart. His dad saw it on his face, and he realized it was a lot for Jesse to process.

"Sit down, Jesse. You look pale."

He gets Jesse a wet towel to place on his forehead. Jesse continues to breathe. One part of him is intrigued and in awe, wanting to ask more questions. The other part of him is in conflict and annoyed at withholding this information from him and Abigail. He knows his age is probably the issue of why they did not let him know. He knows he has to submit to their leadership as his parents, but this is a bit much for him. His trust in them is in question. His father and Wren kept it from them. Anger arises. He respectfully asks his father if he may be excused. He heads to his quarters to process things without his father looking on, fearing he psychologically harmed him by telling him about Wren. Does it mean Wren is gone now from their life? His heart sinks. Tears start falling, and he buries his face in his pillow. His dad knocks, but Jesse ignores him. Drake knows he must give him time to work through it. He is not sure it is a good time to let him know. But it is what it is. No turning back now.

CHAPTER 18

ACTING OUT

Drake reflects on the decision of his meddling with science to create an avenue of an indefinite measure. His beloved wife Corinne died. The grief he bore is beyond his scope of understanding. Diving into his work at the Techo lab is how he stumbled onto a new altering exhilarator that could affect the existence of humanity. Humans would become self-healing. When one human goes under transformation, they will have longevity, brighter minds, and more strength. They will never have to wait on an organ donor. It would mean no waiting lists for health care. If one had a chip inserted, no one would have to die. People would not need to be put on an Organ Donors list. All they need to do is find a Wellbeing Panel and schedule a healing appointment. Doing so now means he would not have to lose another wife.

Once he crossed over from the barrier of the perishable to the imperishable using his exhilarator component, his new wife would not cause separation or loneliness for him or his children. Drake considered things and reviewed the likely hood of survival in his head. He moved forward with the new formula between two options so that Wren would be better off with his interference than the vulnerable human state. Of course, some things could go wrong. With any perfectly worked-out plan, a glitch could ripple the outcome.

Drake named his new enhancement transformation a Hume-au-tic. It was evaluated and approved by the Cosmic Code Review Board. Many individuals have already gone through the process and are successfully living on the Space Dome Station. Most of the occupants of the space dome are Hume-au-tics and a few Dome Dwellers who choose not to transform.

Dr. Drake Silerman has proven his worth to the Procurement Scientist Society. He has been instrumental in finding the scientific solution for improving life. In addition, he has designed many breakthroughs using automated robotics in his mobile designs. On Earth, He founded a Techno lab Resource facility pursuing technological advances. He is honored for his designs. His units are unique in providing robotic assistants. He sold the company but continues to consult for them. He helps the Lab become the number one Universal lab. The Techno Lab gets the credit after he sells the company for any further development and alterations. However, it is evident to the public who the genius is behind it.

The Dome security was to see that during the escape falling out, Wren, fortunately, pushed Dr. Silverman out of the lab and locked the fire doors. That is what protected Drake from going down with Wren in her act of self-annihilation. They watch on the recorded cameras that she returns to the lab and starts pushing buttons. The next thing they see is an explosion, and they will assume that she projects through the membrane walls of the upper lab location as a result. Like a projectile, she flies through the walls and falls to the below ground. All the investigating authorities could find was ash. After it is confiscated and processed, it is evident that Wren's DNA is present.

The science team is sad to hear what happened to Wren and Drake. Wren is a beautiful soul, and they are remorseful. They write in their report that, tragically, she could not acclimate to her new life in the dome with Drake and the rest of the community. Drake now has another tragic loss to suffer. He will need extensive leave and emotional healing sessions scheduled. They will not abandon him nor ignore him this time. He is to have supervision and be ready to support him as necessary.

The Science Domes Newscast reports began announcing the sad occurrence regarding their esteemed Dr. Drake Silverman for losing his newlywed wife from a tragic accident. A memorial tape plays, expressing a mourning mode for Drake's loss, and plays throughout the Dome's media sources.

For Wren and Drake, it could not have gone any better. Wren did plummet down, but with a safety harness hidden amongst the exploding colors, the cameras did not see that. There are yellow, red, and orange colors that hide her exit into the ground maintenance tunnel. She waits there for a few days before returning to their home. She stays only briefly to say her goodbyes to her new family. She joins up with a pilot that flies her to a neighboring planet. There she hides out in a facility Drake frequented and designed. She was to stay there until the time Drake could meet her. Drake takes her to another neighboring planet to complete the last element for her escape. It is here on this planet; he has a secret lab. He created a time machine to take Wren back to the timeframe before she married him. She will look the same but still have her enhancements and all memories intact. Drake gives her a beacon device that will allow him to retrieve her when or if she is ready for him to be a part of her life.

CHAPTER 19

WREN'S RETURN

Wren awakes sweating and opens her eyes to find herself looking at the ceiling. Wren comes to her senses and realizes she is not where she went to sleep the previous night. She returned to a time machine that Drake secretly designed. It is astounding that her husband had the genius to find the science of time travel. A time she could go back to before their marriage. She escaped from the Dome authorities, but it was a bittersweet experience. She did still love Drake and his children. Now Wren is back on Earth with her family.

"It worked. Drake did it!"

Wren erupts from her bed to see if she looks like an average human. She immediately runs to the mirror in the bathroom and tugs on her skin. Dashing back into her bedroom, she runs to her sister's room. Upon entering, Wren rips back the blanket that covers her sleeping sister's head and jumps on the bed straddling her legs on both sides of her sister. She grabs one of her bed pillows and begins pounding her sister with a pillow; while jumping up and down. Wren yells.

"You're here. You're here!" Cassidy deflecting the blows now with her arms, shouts at Wren.

"Are you crazy?"

Cassidy shouts as she naturally defends herself, deflecting her face with her arms. She giggles after Wren stops and realizes she is a victim of another one of Wren's weird moments. Wren jumps down from the bed and kisses her sister's cheek. She runs out of her room and down the stairs and searches for all she once thought she would never get a chance to see again. The greatness of her separation is why Wren is displaying intense interactions. She wakes up everyone in the house. Bounding to the birdcage, she shouts.

"Are you there, Jasper?"

Wren yanks off the cover from the top of the cage and startles the family bird named Jasper. He responds to her rudeness with a squawk. When Jasper sees it is Wren, he jumps to the edge of the perch to get a closer look at her. She squeals with delight at his presence and continues to the next pet.

"Chester, she calls, here kitty-kitty."

Chester wakes up slowly, yawning and stretching before he jumps off the couch. Wren watches Chester stretch, arching his back sequentially to the spreading of claws before he heads her way. He slithers past, touching her bare leg with his soft fur. Wren stops and closes her eyes to savor the moment. He moves out through the cat door. She recalls the cat door being a particular project with Cassidy. They installed the door all by themselves, under the supervision of gramps. She runs to the window seat and plops down. Sitting with one leg tucked under and the other stretching down to the floor, She pulls up the blinds and watches her cat disappear into the early morning mist. Wren suspects he is in search of an early morning snack. One he might bring back as a present.

"I hope not." She says to herself, smirking.

A smile radiates on Wren's face as she reflects on her morning already. She drops the blind back onto the window sill and heads to the couch. She is not alone; her family is now standing in the living room with her. Wren begins breathing erratic in the presence of her disgruntled morning family. Her grandmother quickly strolls over to her, sitting on the window seat, and puts her arms around her.

"Missy, what is going on? You have everyone up and alarmed at your behavior this morning. Did you have a bad dream?"

Not giving Wren a chance to respond, her parents quickly chime in with their parental support mode. Her mother takes the opposite side of where her grandmother sits and grabs Wren's hand. Her Mother and father nod in agreement with her grandmother's concern. Her father is now walking toward her. He grabs a chair from the kitchen and sits on it backward, leaning his arms on the back while his legs straddle the seat. Facing her Father looks over her face to get a reading of what he thinks might be going on with her weird display that morning. He responds.

"Well, let's see, Wren may have second thoughts about

getting married. Her situation is probably coming to fruition of the bitter-sweet reality that happens when one marries."

Wren is feeling uncomfortable and repositions herself on the seat. Her mom lets go of her hand and pats her leg. Her mother gently takes hold of Wren's chin with her hand and looks into her daughter's eyes.

"Yes, It is quite a life change. You know, getting married and making an immediate move to another country, you will be leaving all you have ever known. She will be leaving the security of her family that she knows to live in another unknown military location."

"How do you feel about this entire spoof your father is projecting, Wren? Is your father

correct?" Wren takes a moment and looks at them. She adores them, but what a perfect way to handle all this. She stands up and replies.

"Yes, you are right! Last evening, I had a horrible nightmare of being separated from you." Cassidy chimes in.

"Hello? Just last night, you were ready to go with him boldly where ever he goes, you will go thing!"

Gramps interrupts her sister's ranting by holding up his hand to her.

"For Wren's sake, let us consider that a lot has transpired. She is in turbulent waters. Allow her to have a moment." Gramps looks at Grams and nods.

"I'm hungry, ma. Let's see what we can rustle up for breakfast."

Her Grandparents head to the Kitchen. They start getting coffee brewing and ovens warming up. Ingredients, bowls, and utensils are brought out and put on the counter to prepare homemade biscuits, eggs, bacon, and fried apples. Before you know it, all sorts of welcoming smells Wren took for granted permeate the air. Cassidy sets the family table that her grandpa designed. He built it using three-planked boards cut from one of their trees on the ranch, and it is a piece of art. She puts placemats, napkins, condiments, dishes, and silverware out. Today, she places a lit candle in the center of the table for ambiance as if it is a celebration. Her parents head to the porch for an intimate conversation on the Swing. Wren goes upstairs to get freshened up and change out of her shorts and tee shirt she slept in. She knows her parents are continuing the discussion regarding her bazaar behavior.

Before joining them, Wren sits in her comfy chair and reflects on her situation before she was shanghaied into space. She recalls her family's counsel at that time, taking place on their ranch porch. They are spending time together sipping from their cups of hot beverages. Wren snuggles in her favorite quilt while sitting on the porch steps. She is warm and cozy with her big wooly socks and thermal leggings. In the cool of the evening, she is good to go. She loves those relaxing nights watching the sun go down with her family. They frequently settle on the porch in the evening, with some relaxing on the swing, others in the rocking chairs, and others choosing other seating.

Wren reflects on what her family said. She listens to the wisdom that her family imparted regarding the wedding. Then, she thought she had a firm understanding of what she wanted to do. She believed she could handle separating from her family and friends and living on the ranch. However, to be fair, she did not know Drake was taking her away forever and she would never see them again. All that she is aware of is that she must accept the course laid before her. It means she would accept to leave with her new husband to an undisclosed military base location and not see her family for a long while.

Her fiancé not being present during this family moment is a thing he decided was good. It does give her time to process with her family. Before heading home that day after spending time with them at their pig roast, he did share with her that he wanted her to be sure. That is something to consider. He told her he loved her, but she had to understand that there would be no turning back once she committed to the move. Now to some degree, she considers Drake to be telling a partial truth. However, it still is deceptive. He tells her he does not want her to suffer because of his military orders. He wants and hopes she will choose him, but she must understand that she will be isolated from those she knows, which will most likely be challenging. He tells her that marrying him will mean she must agree to his assignment's peculiar circumstance and importance. She is often left alone to fend for herself and cannot fly home or call her family.

Returning to the family interactions on the front porch, she recalls her uncle Spence moving over and giving her a side-way hug.

"I will miss you, nugget!"

His nickname he gave her when she was young. Aunt Lacy interjects.

"Yes, sweetheart, you go where ever your love is. That is what married couples do. However, you have to be certain you can handle that. I must say, joining your family on the ranch after losing your uncle has been my lifesaver. We need family."

Wren thinks about how she responded to their wisdom then and how she would respond differently now. She had a view of what it would be like to be without them, and she did not like it. She will do things differently the second time around, and there are no rose-colored lenses she is looking through now.

Grandma hollers.

"Breakfast is ready. Come to the table."They all gather around the table.

Wren comes downstairs and joins the family at the table. The family starts passing around the food and pauses only to pray and thank their Heavenly Father for his provision and resources. After the meal is near being finished, Wren interrupts their silence.

"You know, after a good night's sleep. I have reconsidered what was discussed with me earlier, and I have decided to wait. I truly do not want to rush into anything, and I have decided to wait until he returns from his duty and revisit the marriage."

With that comment, the family all clamors to her. Mom responds,

"Oh, angel, we only want you happy. If you truly love this man and know he loves you, you are strong enough to do this! I know you will be fine. If marrying him will make you happy, we are all in for you."

Her father comments.

"You could marry him and stay here while he is on duty. Your choice not to marry him right now is also fine, and you can wait just as you said and see how things pan out. I will not deny as a Father, I would prefer that you remain to hear so you will not be alone or vulnerable while he is off on assignment. With the downtime. You can continue teaching, and we would not have to be without you for so long."

Her mother chimes in.

"Amen to that!"

Wren finishes off her glass of milk and sets it down. She wipes her mouth, feeling all eyes are on her. She anticipates how to respond. She stretches her arms out past both sides of her placemat. She is going to tell them her final decision. She sits up and announces her decision.

"So be it! The wedding is off until further notice. Drake will understand because he knows I need my family."

Her father directs the family to celebrate her decision and close this conversation. They finish their meal and chat about trivial things at the ranch, and Grandma cuts through the chatter.

"Well, you all did a good job cleaning up the goods; now, who will help me with the dishes?"

"I will."

Cassidy and Wren both volunteer. Later in the evening, when the family disperses all to their own spaces, Wren curls up, putting her chin on the back of the couch. She is looking out the big picture window at the sky. She now thinks about what she left behind in the home, secretly hovering above the earth. Wren knows her mother is present, and Wren talks to her.

"I am happy that we have neighbors that are branching out. Even though the Waters are strange, if it were not for their new business, I may not have ever met Drake."

"That is a thought," her mother says.

Wren's mother slips beside her on the couch and wraps her arms around her daughter. She leans against her daughter's head, looking out the window together.

"Yes, it is nice to have neighbors to chat with over the fence."

Both chuckle at her comment. Chatting over the fence means talking to the critters in the fields between the two properties. The menagerie of donkeys, horses, and goats brings her joy. Nevertheless, her mother's thoughts turn to Wren. She is sensitive to her daughter's recent fear of the unknown. Her father, who is listening to them from the kitchen, interjects.

"Yeah, there is still so much space out here that a spaceship could come down, and no one would even know it."

Wren is startled at his comment. Cassidy comes down the stairs to see when her sis is coming up,

"That's right, Dad," said Cassidy.

"One could be conversing with some spaceman and unaware of it. The spaceman can purposely put on a front about being a vacationer passing through for a short time, and Drake could be one for all we know."

Wren threw a couch pillow at her.

"Well, Cassidy," Wren retorts.

"You always liked the idea of space interaction. Maybe you should consider making more human-to-spacemen connections than your star-gazing telescope. I am sure you would like cosmic company!"

"Why, if I were not married already, I might consider pursuing radio conversation!" Wren

gets honest with Cassidy and the family.

"That sounds mighty bold, Cass, but despite someone being near or far, it benefits us to weigh out an unknown individual who may dwell amongst us briefly. We don't know what they could be hiding. With all kidding aside about aliens walking among us, logically, how much do we know about Drake? We truly only have known him a few short months. I want to make sure I get to know him better. I will wait a bit before jumping into a marriage commitment."

Grandfather comes into the kitchen to get a glass of water. He hears her explanation of her choice he shouts out.

"That is good to hear, Honey Bear. You are using wisdom." Wren responds with fondness.

"Thank you, Grandpa. It is always comforting to know I am always your Honey Bear."

CHAPTER 20

JESSE'S HOPE

It is time for Jesse to go by a mature form of his given name. He wants to go by Jess now. It is during this time he starts thinking about what his niche is. Jess approaches his father with the idea of starting him on a course of becoming an Aero-flight Cadet, and Drake believes it is a promising avenue for him to pursue. His father signs him up for Cadet School. Drake likes that Jess will train on operating and repairing the module Drake designed. After Jess takes lessons on the dangers and mechanical operations, he will be cautious in navigating the module and learn how to read the maps programmed into the flight units and operate the robotic support crew.

Jess is ecstatic about it! Yet, Jess has something else on his mind. He wants to see where his father has been going when he takes leave alone. Jess looks closer at the schedules to see if the time frames his dad leaves are taking him to Miona and that it appears to be a preferred destination. He continues to read his father's log ledgers and confirms that he takes the same Banyan module each time he travels to Miona. For as long as Jess can remember, his father routinely took leave for excursions to gather resources to places where he could harvest naturally grown species of plants that he could use to advance research. This time it was different. When his mother passed, his father increased his trips apart from them. Jess did not like it, but he knew his father left them in good hands by choosing Javelin to oversee them in his absence. He knew his father loved him, but he missed him terribly during those times. Sometimes he hated the job that his father had that took him away so often. Yet, having Javelin as their caretaker was a comfort and eased his loss of having his father there. She loved them, and they loved her back. His sister and Jess bonded with her because she seemed to be there, feeling more like an aunt than their mother's best friend.

Jess noted that his father also went to the planet Gustus a lot. Jess thought it odd because Gustus is considered a hostile planet. Not only were the natural inhabitants and environment unpleasant, but it is suspected outlaws hid out there. He finds no one else on the outgoing flight logs that purposely journey there but his father.

"Eureka, Jess shouts. I got something!"

He reflects on his father being the number one techno lab developer. He is an architect-engineer that designed modules that are more than living quarters. His father did that for a while before he directed all his energy into finding the missing link for the Science team's schedule.

"I wonder if my dad built something or is working on something on Gustus? Something he does not want the P.E.S. to know about?"

His Dad and Grandmother always tended to work like that. They prefer to work alone and off-grid, so no one would interfere or thwart their work.

Jess got close to his teacher during one of his routine training courses on navigating Banyan crafts. He was like a surrogate father figure. His teacher took a liking to Jess and taught him things about managing the computer-generated mapping program installed in the Banyan craft. He even taught him how to maintain and fly it. In exchange, Jess helped with odd jobs and taught him how to play electronic games. Jess got quite good at maneuvering the Banyan module by the end of his training course. His trainer advanced to master video games. His teacher loved it so much that he equipped one of the Banyan vessels with gaming capabilities where they could view the games from the ship's window. He installed a special screen that pulled down, allowing it to receive the transmission from the small handheld device. It made a huge gaming screen.

Jess arrives back at his family dwelling before anyone else. Sitting down in his cove of their living quarters, he decides to take this time to see if he can find more information about Wren and his dad. Using the Com-pu-port, Jess chuckles to himself because he realizes that, finally, the use of the cove is being used for more than entertainment and socializing. The cove is now a coveted spot where he gathers information to find answers to questions he is searching out about Wren and his Father. Access to the Science Dome's library of information is one of his prime resources. He starts today by requesting information on Wren's past. Com-pu-port blinks back.

"None present."

It denies access, so he approaches it from a different angle. Jess asks some pressing questions again.

"Com-pu-port, who has access to Wren McCarthy's information besides Dr. Drake Silverman?"

"That information is classified," Com-pu-port blinks back.

"Ok, Com-pu-port, what flights were scheduled to take off from the Space Dome after the period of Drake and Wren's quarantine?"

It blinks back a list of scheduled flights, and the listings stream down the screen.

"Woo hoo! Got it!"

Jess looks intently over the names on the list and sees one with a Sir Vincent Knight. That is the name he remembers his father used in the story. He looks up his public info and discovers he is a craft Direct IV flight commander. He left for planet Miona.

"I know that craft. Dad took it out frequently."

His dad's scientific clearance allows him to take off whenever he desires. He has permission to get free time to explore and gather more resources and time to refresh. The Domes officials have complete confidence in his ability to keep confidentiality.

"I remember that. Dad scheduled a flight out soon after Wren's departure to Miona to jog over to Gustus. It is a small, secluded planet, barely recognizable as a co-inhabited planet., and it's not even on the Cohort of Planet Inhabitation Association list."

Further, Intel helps Jess to conclude that Flight Commander Sir Vincent Knight has a daughter. He has a daughter that is Jess's age, and her name is Kelsey.

"Now we are getting somewhere, he says. I will see if I can get some information from her."

Jess rises early to get a chance to talk to his father over breakfast and before he leaves for his lab.

"Dad?"

"Yes, Jess."

"Do you vacation to other planets other than Gustus? I looked over the flight journals, and it says you are going there from Miona."

"Really! I am impressed. How detective of you? What clued you to do that?"

"When I went to Cadet mapping school, I became friends with my flight trainer. He said he knows you. He told me he is the one that makes ready your craft before you head out to run on one of your leave excursions. He said you went to Gustus frequently."

"Yes, Jess, I do."

Drake rubs his head as he used to when he was younger.

"I like the seclusion there. You know I need places to gather new specimens for my research and, simultaneously, choose a place to relax and give my overworked mind a break."

"Yeah, now that I am older, can I go with you next time?"

"Sure, we have been unable to do that since Wren joined us."

Drake rises, throwing down his napkin and grabbing his lab coat off the hook.

"I need to head out, Jess. See you there later?"

"Sure, Dad, I will head over in a bit."

When Jess decides to visit his dad at the lab, he finds his dad preoccupied. Jess gathers he is thinking about Wren. He can see his father is struggling with his task, making adjustments on the telescope. Jess attempts to get his father's attention. His dad is always in some zone. It is difficult for his dad to be interrupted. When Drake is in that "caught up in the moment mode," it is common for him to get lost in his thoughts and shut everything around him. Sometimes it gets aggravating for Jess. Jess brushes it off and chooses not to take offense because he knows his dad has difficulty stopping the wheels from turning in his mind. Drake can be triggered immediately and zone out into his thought process. Jess has learned how to bring him back from his reclusive composure. Drake's genius is odd sometimes for others to understand, but he is hard-working. He supports his father's need to have scheduled breaks. It is something his mom recommended for his mental health. It helps him stop the gerbil in the wheel and calm his thoughts.

Drake finally looks up. He is pleasantly surprised to see Jess standing below him.

"Hi, Son, what are you up to? I expected you earlier, Jess. You usually like spending time here when I am on sight."

Drake flips the lens down and takes off his goggles. He steps off the platform to give Jess his full attention, and Jess tells him he has been studying planets. This activity, Jess liked, got Drake's curiosity up, and Jess has not appeared to be interested in that subject.

"Well," Jess says.

"I was watching some old transmissions and learned that in some of the documentaries, there is some hypothesis that there are probably other planets like Earth in our solar system. It seems to be accurate on where these suspected planets are located, but they are limited in giving proof. Then I discovered in our Dome library that the P.E.S. knows these places and has actual flight names and routes to get there."

"What a way to go, Jess, merging your knowledge, asking questions, pursuing answers; good Job!" Drake rubs the sweat off his forehead with a hanky from his pocket.

"So, what have you concluded so far?"

"Well, you know how certain factions hid on different planets in the Star Wars movies so that Darth Vader and his master did not know their whereabouts?"

With a cunning look in his eyes, he watches his dad squirm. Jess looks up at his father. It is amusing to Drake to see his son operate in detective mode.

"Yes," Drake says.

He suspects his son will try to pry some information out of him; regarding Wren. At that moment, he goes into deep thought. He knows now is a perfect time to tell Jess about how Wren got into their life. However, he felt it was a learning moment to get Jess to take his investigation further. He wants him to search for answers instead of handing them to him. After all, that is what scientists are all about. Jess is likely going to follow in his footsteps. The element of hunger for information is vital. The act of finding answers, those common-minded individuals would not even take the time to step out of the box and probe, is a very promising mile marker to what his son is becoming. He is becoming an independent thinker. Parents long for this season. As a parent, he has to tread lightly, guiding Jess. He has to allow Jess room to spread his wings so he will develop into a healthy, functioning young adult. It works best without Jess knowing it. Parents frequently use this method to bring their children to a self-reliant point. It is gratifying and healthy that his son falls right into step in that process.

"Dad, Dad, you are lost in your head again."

Drake comes out of his thoughts and turns to Jess. Embarrassed now, Drake responds.

"Oh, sorry for that. Are you heading out? I know you want to do more digging to find out how Wren got here and how she left. How about we schedule a lunch at three-ish and review your findings?"

"That will be great, Dad! I do have some leads I want to investigate."

Drake laughs with him.

"Yes, you do that, son; just do not do anything I would not do."

Jess responds.

"Yeah, Dad, which does not leave me much left that you have not already done."

Jess loves it when he can razz his dad.

"Well said, come here, he hugs Jess and sends him off.

"Now get going so I can get my work done before 3:00."

"On it, Dad."

Jess exits the lab. He heads to the places he feels might be most conducive to his search.

Drake returns to the collimation of his telescope while Jesse heads back to continue his search. He chooses to sit outside his Dad's lab first, where he commonly crashes to play his electronic games. He ponders about the following action he prefers to take.

"I did not get very far with my dad, but I did clear a path I can return to later."

He returns to their quarters and asks Com-pu-port a few more questions.

"Com-pu-port?"

"Yes, young Jesse, how may I help you?"

"Where is Wren Silverman presently? Is she in a reasonable range of my location?"

"No, young Jesse, she is out of reasonable range. Would you like to know anything else?"

"No, Com-pu-port, except for one protocol thing. Will you stop referring to me as young Jesse? I would like for you to address me as Jess, please."

"Understood, making that acceptable change now."

Jess decides to go to the unlimited information lead. A source that does not have limited access. Does he wonder what Commander Sir Vincent Knight's daughter looks like? At 3:00, he meets with his father.

"Dad, will Nerw#1 ever come back? I mean, Wren?"

Jesse has already learned that Nerw1 is Wren spelled backward. Drake walks behind him and ruffles his hair.

"Jess, I miss her as well. I am hoping we will see her again. She has to choose us for herself this time. I learned a tough lesson that no one should ever impose a life-altering situation upon another without proper allowance for them to process and choose for themselves. You never know how a free-willed individual chooses to walk. That is the beauty of it because when they choose you, it is a celebration! In the creator's realm, all things are possible. Look around. Dreams are made into a reality."

Drake continues.

"There will continue to be advancements and things discovered that will change how we perceive things. Your mother and Wren have taught me that God is more than a scientist who created the universe. We must not forget God is the Alpha, the ultimate one. He is in the business of supporting us to expand and grow. He is the Greatest Artist, scientist, and lover of all time. He is the tree, and we are the branches. He provides the resources we are to grow and be fruitful. He is the father, and we are his children. Any good parent wants their children to mature into their own found beauty. I know that's what I want for you."

Drake and Jess finish eating and clear away their dishes.

"Hey, Dad, you think we can take a flight now? Sis is at camp this week with Javelin and her girls, which gives us the liberty to have some guy time together."

Drake chuckles.

"I will see what I can do to make that happen."

Drake pats him on the back.

"For now, why don't you get that ball off the shelf and see if we can knock the dust off it; in the Sports Arena."

"Cool, Dad! You're awesome!"

That's what a parent longs to hear. Drake is happy where he is with Jess.

As Jesse runs to get the ball, Drake looks at his Compu-port. He pulls up Wren's pictures and maps showing her route in the time machine she took to return to Earth. Drake sinks back and reflects on his spiritual journey since meeting Wren.

He rehearses the dance of how they met. He is thankful they both have come to the same belief; regarding who the Creator is to them. Wren displays, in her actions, a realness to her faith. She reveals a personal relationship with her God. Drake, though believing God before meeting her, was then operating in the frame of thinking that God was a science-minded God. His relationship is now on target. He finds her faith both refreshing and liberating. It is what stirred him back into a closer relationship with the lord. He now understands that the relationship God wants is for him to not only know about Him but be intimate with the Father. To know his heart and character, and for God not to be just his God, but his Savior, Creator, and Friend. He now knows how to communicate with his God.

Through Wren's influence regarding the "Father of life," Drake is grateful for their meeting. Most importantly, he is mindful he has reached a relevant restoration of who he is because of her. Due to her influence, his heart aligns with God's heart. Peering out the port view window of his living quarters, Drake relays a message through the Waters to Wren. He reads aloud his letter,

"We miss you terribly. Sometime soon, I hope you contact us, Wren. Jess and Abigail continue to ask about you. I am watching and waiting. I will handle things differently if you decide to give us another chance. I can promise you that!"

THE END

LETTER FROM THE AUTHOR

Creativity is an inherited trait of Father God. It is He who formed all of creation. God is the Creator we should revere. He alone is righteous, holy, and authentic. It is not so incredible to behold that He transcends time because He created it. God is the time machine, and he knows our beginning, middle, and end that life is bestowed on us. He can enter our life any moment He wants. Time travel does not escape the imagination to become possible.

I acknowledge the potency of what this fictional story presents as the answer to this world's dilemma. There is a bigger picture to grasp, however. There are gray areas that humankind will have to navigate through. The issue of increased population, neglect in caring for our world, and the science that forces us to face the question of how far we should allow ourselves to go, considering our future existence and what each of us can do to bring morally acceptable solutions. I propose that whatever way we seek a solution, go to the Father first. He will have the ultimate answers because He alone has the eyes to see the expanse of time. He alone sees the true heart of man. He alone has the best resources to solve your dilemma.

If you want to reconnect to the Father's heart? If you hunger to find purpose and meaning? Ask Him how you can do that. Reconcile with Him. Listen. Align it to the Holy Scriptures and see your life unfold to new possibilities.

May God Bless and keep you in your life's journey. May His face shine upon you!

Blessings,
Patty

ABOUT THE AUTHOR

Patty was born and raised in Ohio. Graduated with a Bachelor's Degree from Asbury College in Wilmore, Ky. concentrating in Christian Education, and received her Master's Education Degree from Antioch McGregor in Yellowsprings, OH. with a focus on Special Education. She resides in Tipp City, OH, as a devoted housewife, grandmother, and retired Pastor's wife. She loves gardening, painting, writing, and worship. She leads a Women in Pursuit Bible study and teaches a Prophetic class for her church. She treasures her family and friends and strives to love them well.

STUDY QUESTIONS

(Corresponding with each chapter)

1. What factors contribute to Wren's feelings of humiliation and embarrassment in her encounter with Drake? How does she try to recover her dignity?
2. How does Wren's special place on the mountaintop contribute to her sense of solitude and tranquility?
3. How does Drake's encounter with Wren challenge his perception of finding love again and the possibility of a future relationship?
4. What are the three personality types speculated by Drake and his father, and how do they describe each type?
5. What determines the quality of life for those who choose the natural function over enhancements?
6. How does Drake's perception of Heaven influence his feelings about his wife's passing?
7. What are the key skills and knowledge that Drake teaches Jesse and Abigail during their hiking excursions on Gustus?
8. What is the significance of "The High Place" for Wren, and how does it provide her with a sense of privacy and connection to nature and God?
9. How does Wren's encounter with Drake impact her emotions and actions?
10. How did Drake and Wren resolve their initial misunderstandings and agree to go on a date?

11. Why does Drake believe his snooping is justified, and how does it relate to his understanding of people?
12. How does Drake's decision to remove his watch reflect his concerns about revealing his true identity and technology?
13. How does Wren's interaction with the festival vendors and her reluctance to accept accolades demonstrate her humility and appreciation for the community?
14. Why does Wren decide to purchase the expensive gown? What does it symbolize to her, and how does it relate to her future plans?
15. How does Wren's faith in God influence her mindset and actions in her current situation?
16. How does Wren's past relationship with her family, particularly her sister Cassidy, influence her current thoughts and feelings about being in space?
17. How does Jesse feel about his father's marriage to Wren? How does he perceive their relationship and what qualities does he admire in Wren?
18. How does Drake's plan unfold after Wren's supposed demise? What measures do they take to ensure her escape and disguise her survival from the authorities?
19. How does Wren react to her newfound ability to travel back in time? Describe her initial actions and interactions with her family members.
20. How does Drake convey his feelings for Wren and his desire for her return?

Index

A

anxious, anxiety 4, 146, 154, 157, 232

B

believe, belief xi, 30, 49, 70, 93, 130, 135, 194, 213, 220, 256, 295

C

career 85, 161, 165, 193, 194

D

dream, dreams 49, 61, 65, 66, 73, 189, 219, 227, 232, 240, 251, 261, 262, 271

E

eternal, eternity 70, 92

F

forgive 148, 249, 251

G

grace 38, 89, 226

H

hope 7, 20, 51, 65, 75, 79, 85, 89, 93, 95, 148, 150, 165, 167, 173, 185, 190, 193, 196, 212, 219, 223, 227, 234, 242, 257, 261, 271, 289

I

initial 191, 294, 295

J

Jesus 39, 93, 235

K

knowledge 56, 57, 61, 68, 111, 245, 258, 285, 294

L

law 108, 137
love 108, 137

M

message 71, 155, 158, 199, 289

N

nice 16, 75, 81, 108, 154, 162, 181, 187, 189, 191, 202, 246, 277

O

open x, 8, 25, 28, 31, 35, 49, 75, 93, 110, 130, 134, 138, 144, 165, 174, 180, 181, 217, 251, 263

P

passion 35, 59, 85, 86, 90, 102, 188

Q

quarrel 20

R

revelation 18, 54, 249

S

save xi, 185, 192, 219

T

test 113
truth xi, 39, 70, 71, 116, 121, 129, 174, 178, 240, 274

U

understanding ii, 29, 93, 100, 109, 127, 251, 265, 273, 295

V

vision 65, 113, 179, 189

W

won, win, winning 30, 209, 212, 213

Y

yield 135

Z

zone 8, 14, 46, 110, 171, 206, 284

www.ingramcontent.com/pod-product-compliance
Lightning Source LLC
Chambersburg PA
CBHW060548310726
48982CB00008B/1048/J

* 9 7 8 1 0 8 8 2 2 6 7 6 6 *